"Courting lessons?" Rhett couldn't contain the skepticism in his voice even as his heart sank at Isabelle's suggestion.

Nothing proved a woman's disinterest more than her trying to foist him off on one of her friends. It didn't make a lick of sense in this instance, though, because Isabelle was interested. He'd seen it in her eyes during that first tug of attraction on the hotel porch. Why, then, was she so eager to pass him off to someone else?

A blush rose in her cheeks. "We, um, don't have to call it anything official like that. I'll just try to help you overcome whatever it is that makes you nervous."

He shrugged. "There's no point in accepting your offer. The lessons wouldn't work, anyway."

"You don't know that."

Oh, but he did. Ellie had tried to help him and failed. Lawson's advice hadn't worked, either. The Bachelor List had been wrong. God seemed to have turned a deaf ear to his prayers for this area of his life. Then again, perhaps the problem was that he'd been depending too much on other people. Maybe he ought to see if there wasn't something he could do to help himself. Something like courting lessons, perhaps?

Noelle Marchand is a native Houstonian living out her childhood dream of being a writer. She graduated summa cum laude from Houston Baptist University in 2012, earning a bachelor's degree in mass communications and speech communications. She loves exploring new books and new cities. When she's not scribbling out her latest manuscript, you may find her pursuing one of her other passions—music, dance, history and classic movies.

Books by Noelle Marchand

Love Inspired Historical

Bachelor List Matches

The Texan's Inherited Family
The Texan's Courtship Lessons

Unlawfully Wedded Bride
The Runaway Bride
A Texas-Made Match

Visit the Author Profile page at Harlequin.com.

NOELLE MARCHAND

The Texan's Courtship Lessons

⬡ **HARLEQUIN**® LOVE INSPIRED® HISTORICAL

Recycling programs
for this product may
not exist in your area.

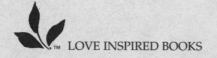 LOVE INSPIRED BOOKS

ISBN-13: 978-0-373-28323-1

The Texan's Courtship Lessons

www.Harlequin.com

Printed in U.S.A.

Trust in the Lord with all your heart; do not depend on your own understanding. Seek His will in all you do, and He will show you which path to take.

—*Proverbs* 3:5–6

This book is dedicated to my editor, Elizabeth Mazer.

Chapter One

December 31, 1888
Peppin, Texas

He'd found her.

Every false start, every mistake, all of the embarrassment of his previous failed attempts at courting and years of waiting faded away in that moment because he *knew* this was the woman his heart had been hoping for. It didn't matter that she, like everyone else at the masquerade ball, was wearing a mask and he didn't know her name or have any other clue concerning her identity. He was going to marry her... Probably. Maybe. If he didn't mess things up like he usually did.

Rhett Granger kept his gaze riveted on the woman he was certain was his future wife as he crossed the crowded hotel ballroom toward her. She wore an emerald sheath dress belted at the waist with a braided golden rope. Heavy gold jewelry draped around her neck and delicate wrists while a low crown encircled straight black hair that looked to be a wig. Cleopatra,

Queen of the Nile, had more than her fair share of admirers hovering around, hanging on her every word. He'd be able to dispatch them with ease if he was half the swashbuckling buccaneer his tricornered hat, black leather pants and gray poet shirt portrayed him to be. He wasn't, but he still managed to cross the room.

The closer he got, the more something about the woman seemed unerringly familiar. Then again, something about everyone at Peppin's New Year's Eve Ball seemed familiar. That was probably because Rhett had met most of the folks who lived in this town at some point during the two and a half years since he'd moved here. He probably already knew or had at the very least met "Cleopatra" at some point before. Perhaps that meant there was a reason they weren't already a couple.

His courage faltered slightly along with his steps. Then, she glanced up and caught him staring at her. Her eyes widened before her thick, dark lashes lowered demurely. The soft light from the gas chandelier hovering above the dance floor did nothing to hide the slight blush that appeared just below her gold mask. No way was he turning back now.

He swallowed hard, squared his shoulders and continued on. He lingered near the outskirts of her circle of admirers to observe her. She was putting on a good show, but he could tell she was uncomfortable with all of the attention. The tension was there in her smile. Eyes that should have sparkled looked dull with disinterest. Her slim fingers hovered near her temple before coming to rest behind her neck as though a headache was starting. Her gaze gradually lifted back to his, revealing her deep green eyes. She tilted her head as

though to ask a silent question. Was he there to join
the fray or free her from it? Her rosy lips lifted in a
hesitant smile that said she hoped it was the latter.

His heart began to pound in his chest. He opened
his mouth to ask her to dance so that they could fall in
love and get married. No words came out. He clamped
his lips shut. He swallowed. He tried again. Not even
so much as a grunt. Fine. Not a problem. Or at least,
not an unusual one. He was accustomed to finding
himself tongue-tied around beautiful women. This
time it wouldn't stop him. He didn't need words to
ask her to dance.

He unclenched his suddenly moist fist in preparation to offer his hand, already envisioning her taking
it and him leading her onto the dance floor. Instead,
another man brushed past him to stand in the middle of
the circle. He was dressed as a roman warrior though
he'd opted to wear pants under the kilt-looking part of
the outfit. The Roman removed his helmet and gave a
deep bow before Cleopatra. "Milady, may I have this
dance?"

She glanced at Rhett then back to the Roman before speaking in an accent that sounded like a strange
mixture of a Southern belle and an English lady. "And
you are?"

"Mark Antony."

Her mouth fell open. Pursing her lips closed, she
narrowed her eyes in what seemed to be suspicion.
That didn't stop her from placing her hand in Antony's
and allowing him to lead her to the dance floor. The
small gathering of her suitors disappeared like bees
around a wilted bloom, leaving only Rhett to stare
after the woman in disappointment. Why wasn't he

surprised that another man had swept in and taken the woman of his dreams while he stood around like a bumbling idiot? Oh, that was right. It had happened before—several times.

The last time had been the most embarrassing because he hadn't bothered to hide his interest in Amy Bradley from the town. He hadn't felt the need to. After all, they'd been paired on the infamous Bachelor List—a list of matches created by Ellie Williams, the town's most successful matchmaker. What could go wrong?

Him. He'd gone wrong precisely as he always did anytime a relationship took a turn toward romance. Not that he could call what had happened with Amy a "romance" even if it was the closest he'd ever gotten to one. All they'd shared were a few drawn-out glances and several laborious chats after church on Sunday. Still, it had been enough to give him hope.

That hope had been most decidedly and publicly destroyed when Amy eloped with a not-so-former suitor more than two months ago. Did that mean that Rhett had lost his only chance at love? He'd rather think that just this once Ellie had been wrong, and Amy wasn't the woman he was supposed to end up with.

That meant his true love might still be out there. He wanted to find her, but what would happen if he did? The same thing that had happened with Cleopatra— nothing. Absolutely nothing.

A heavy sigh filtered through his lips as Cleopatra and Mark Antony floated past him in a waltz. Why wouldn't God take away whatever stupid affliction he had that changed him from an intelligent, personable and confident man into an ineloquent, dull-witted, insecure boy at the first sign of romance in a relationship? Perhaps he was destined to be alone for the rest of his life and this was merely God's way of showing him that. In that case, the kindest thing he could do for himself would be to stop getting his hopes up about something that would never happen.

He bowed his head. *God, show me what You want me to do. Send me a sign or—*

Rhett jerked as something bounced off his chest and landed on the floor near his boot. He knelt to examine it more closely. An arrow? It was. Though, it had been made in miniature out of papier-mâché.

He glanced up to find a woman grinning down at him. She was dressed in a pink dress that flowed and draped like those of ancient Greece. A small set of wings peeked out from behind her shoulders and she carried an equally small bow to go with her arrows. Was she…? Cupid. She was Cupid, which meant…

He stood and crossed his arms. "Ellie Williams, who gave you a weapon?"

The blonde glanced around as if looking for someone, then vanished into the crowd. She returned with her husband of two months in tow. "Lawson gave me a weapon and showed me how to use it."

"I don't know what I was thinking." The small shake of Lawson's head was exaggerated by the huge hat, which, along with his costume, designated him as one of the three musketeers. Rhett was pretty sure that meant Lawson's brothers-in-law were the other two.

Lawson winked at Ellie. "She's already dangerous enough without it."

Rhett glanced away, feeling decidedly uncomfortable as Ellie sent her husband a look that was warmer than Texas in the spring. Once they were finished staring into each other's eyes, Rhett presented Ellie with the arrow. "I believe this is yours."

"You can keep it, Rhett. I have plenty of them left. Look, it says 'Happy New Year' on the shaft."

He handed it back to her anyway. "Thanks, but—Wait. How do you know who I am? I thought my costume disguised me pretty well."

Lawson nodded. "It does. Ellie, how did you know it was Rhett?"

"I have my ways."

Her cryptic answer didn't fool him. "You saw me, didn't you? You saw me try to ask that woman to dance."

Lawson frowned. "What woman?"

"Cleopatra," Ellie answered, then winced. "I mean, what woman?"

"What happened, Rhett?"

"Same old, same old," he said. The couple had witnessed his limitations when it came to communicating with the opposite sex on numerous occasions. "Who is she, though, when she isn't Cleopatra?"

Ellie shrugged. "What makes you think I would know? Midnight isn't too far away. Stick around for the unmasking and find out for yourself."

"Actually, I think I'm going to head home." He hadn't decided on that until he said it, yet he knew that was probably the best idea he'd had all evening. They both protested, but Rhett knew it was the right decision. There was no point in sticking around. He'd probably only find some way to make a fool of himself again. It would be far wiser for him to go home.

Of course, he'd be alone on New Year's Eve. But how was that different than any other day?

He pushed away the loneliness and disappointment that threatened him. It was going to be a new year. Perhaps it was time to put old dreams aside and move on.

Tonight, she was a woman of intrigue, sophistication and mystery—Cleopatra, Queen of the Nile.

At least, she would let herself pretend to be that until the stroke of midnight when the masks would come off, and she'd turn into a pumpkin. Or, more accurately, she'd go back to being practical, boring and uninspiring Isabelle Bradley. There were only fifteen minutes left before that would happen. That mean meant the only person who knew her true identity, besides the four male boarders who'd escorted her from her family's boardinghouse, was Marc Antony.

He smiled down at her. "You look beautiful, Isabelle."

She feigned disinterest. "What makes you think my name is Isabelle?"

"Because you're the only one who ordered a wig like that from my family's mercantile."

Her dance partner was Chris Johansen, then. She'd suspected as much. She didn't even bother to hold back her frustrated huff. She'd gone through a lot of trouble to disguise herself from her older sister's former suitors. Apparently, her efforts hadn't worked. "Sophia promised she wouldn't tell anyone that I'd ordered the wig."

"Don't worry. My little sister refused to answer a single one of my questions about who it was for. I figured it out on my own by looking at your account records."

Why he'd go through all of that trouble was beyond her. She simply couldn't get used to the tenacity or attentions of Chris and her other so-called suitors. They'd never paid her any mind before her sister's elopement. She could hardly take them seriously now when, despite their best efforts to prove otherwise, it was obvious they were only seeking a replacement for Amy. Isabelle aspired to few things in life, but allowing herself to become a faded tintype in the eyes of a man who should cherish her for herself was not one of them. She'd try to make that clear by avoiding the men altogether. They didn't seem to be getting the message. Perhaps she ought to try being a bit more assertive. Starting with "Mark Antony."

Isabelle pinned him with an accusatory stare as he whirled her around the crowded dance floor in a waltz. "Well, all I have to say is you've got a lot of nerve, Chris Johansen, dressing to match me. What exactly are you trying to achieve by doing this? Because the only message I'm getting is that you're a cheater."

He rolled his eyes. "I didn't know what else to do. I've been trying to get your attention for weeks. You won't stay still long enough to listen."

No, she hadn't, but perhaps he'd leave her alone if she let him say his peace. After a long-suffering sigh, she nodded. "All right, I'm listening now. What is it you want to say?"

"You and I have been friends a long time, haven't we?"

"Uh-huh." She found refuge from his too-intense eyes by scanning the crowd of onlookers. It wasn't until her gaze landed on the tall, powerfully built pirate who'd approached her earlier that she realized she'd been looking for him all along. He stood at the edge of the dance floor talking to a couple. They must have been saying their goodbyes for he shook the man's hand and received a quick hug from the lady. He turned. For one intense moment, their eyes caught and held across the distance. But then the steps of the waltz spun her around and she lost sight of him.

"Isabelle, did you hear me?"

She forced herself to refocus on her partner. "Hmm?"

"I was trying to ask you—" He froze, which was probably a good thing since he looked downright exasperated.

It was only when he turned slightly away from her that she saw the man at his heels. Dressed in a costume fit for a drawing room in Regency England, he gave a shallow bow. "May I cut in?"

Chris scowled. "No."

The gentleman stroked the curves of his immaculately shaped auburn mustache as he affected a very poor English accent. "Mr. Johansen, it is common courtesy to yield in such occasions."

Chris's eyes narrowed. "How do you know who I am?"

"As an artist always knows his own work, a barber recognizes every haircut he gives."

As Chris slid his fingers through his blond hair, Isabelle barely withheld a groan of recognition. She should have recognized Amy's childhood sweetheart the second she saw his mustache. "John Merriweather."

"Miss Isabelle, I presume." He bowed again. "May I have this dance?"

Chris kept hold of her hand. "Now, see here, John. You'll just have to wait—"

"Absolutely, you may cut in, Mr. Merriweather." She glanced between two men—one dejected, the other gloating. Lifting Chris's hand, she placed it squarely in John's. "It might look a little strange, but you gentlemen enjoy yourselves."

She lingered only long enough to watch their mouths drop open as they jerked their hands back and glared at each other. Their protests rang in her ears as she left them on the dance floor. Fearing one or both might attempt to follow her—once they were done arguing with each other—she slipped out a side door into the hotel's garden. A cold wind set her teeth chattering and hastened her down the path leading to the wide back porch. She reached for the door to reenter the hotel, but hesitated. Stepping farther into the shadows of the porch, she considered her options.

If she went back into the ballroom, she'd likely spend the rest of the night trying to avoid Amy's spurned suitors. Her only other option was to leave the masquerade altogether. She grimaced at the thought of returning home early on a night free from her parents' suspicious and watchful gazes. As much as she loved them, their overprotectiveness of her and her fifteen-year-old sister, Violet, had become stifling.

In the aftermath of Amy's elopement with a former boarder at the family's boardinghouse, her parents had become fixated on not letting that situation repeat itself. They'd even gone so far as to say they'd sell Bradley Boardinghouse if one more thing went wrong. Isabelle had laughed the first time they'd said it, thinking they were joking. They weren't. However, all they'd done so far was talk about the possibility of selling. She was certain that with a little time they'd regain their love for the boardinghouse and no longer be tempted to consider anything as drastic as that. In the meantime, she'd simply have to make sure nothing else went wrong.

The sound of the door opening startled her from her reverie just as a man stepped out onto the porch. It wasn't merely any man, though. It was the pirate she'd noticed inside. A coat covered most of his costume now, but he still wore the unmistakable tricornered hat. He paused to remove it. His mask came off next. A soft gasp filled her lungs as the golden light of a nearby lantern illuminated his handsome features. Shock eased his name from her lips with a mix of amusement and exasperation. "Rhett Granger."

He spun toward her. His eyes widened as she stepped from the shadows. "It's you. What— Why are you out here? In the cold porch. On the cold. In the porch. I mean…" He shook his head and gave up.

Tilting her head, she stared at him in confusion. Land sakes! What had happened to him all of a sudden? She hadn't heard him stumble around with his words like that since he'd been sweet on Amy.

From what she'd seen, Rhett had been left truly brokenhearted by Amy's elopement. Isabelle had gotten to know him relatively well in the few months since her best friend, Helen, had married his best friend, Quinn. Before then, she'd only really thought of him as one of Amy's admirers. Now she knew for certain that he was as honest, trustworthy and honorable as his reputation said he was. He was also about ten times as exasperating—usually.

Tonight, his amber eyes showed a vulnerability she'd never seen before. It prompted her to offer a gentle smile. "It was getting a little crowded in there. What about you? Where are you going?"

He shrugged his broad shoulders. "Home. I'm not really in a party."

He didn't seem to notice his mistake this time, and she didn't have the heart to point it out. Stepping forward, she grabbed the lapels of his coat and rattled them lightly in an attempt to shake him to his senses. "But it's New Year's Eve!"

"Yeah, I'm aware of that." He softened the statement with a teasing grin. She felt his chest swell against the coat as he took a deep breath, which made her realize she was still holding on to his coat. She immediately released it. Before she could step back, he'd taken off the coat and wrapped it around her shoulders. "You must be freezing."

"I didn't realize how much until now." She snuggled into the coat's warmth. "Thank you."

He slipped his hands into the pockets of his black leather pants and tipped his head toward the door. "You should go inside where it's warm."

"I'd rather not."

"Then will you at least allow me to walk you home?"

Suddenly realizing she still had her mask on, she lifted her chin. "Do you know where I live?"

She was really asking if he knew her true identity. He seemed to understand that because he stepped even closer. He lifted her chin to survey her more closely. She watched his gaze trail from the tip of her nose over her cheeks. It rested upon her lips for an interminably long time before dropping to her chin and returning to her eyes. It only seemed fair that she take the same liberties. The dark shadow of a two-day-old beard covered his square jaw, stopping right below his perfectly sculpted nose and cheekbones. His eyebrows were two thick slashes over his dark lashes. As she watched, the color of his amber eyes deepened.

Encircling his strong wrist with her hand, she tugged lightly. He released his hold. She stepped back and struggled to gather her thoughts. What had they been talking about? Oh, yes.

"Well? Do you know where I live?"

Rhett could do nothing but stare into the face of Isabelle Bradley. Had she felt it, too? There had been some kind of tug between them. He'd felt in that moment as though he could have done something crazy— like kiss her.

He'd noticed little things like the myriad shades of green that made up her eyes and how they shifted like when the sun hit the waters of a slow-moving creek. Her lashes were so dark brown they almost would have looked black if not for the hint of gold that shone in the lantern light. Her lips were pink and bow-shaped. He couldn't help wondering if they were as soft as they looked. Startled by that thought since he had no business thinking it, he gave his head a little shake.

This was Isabelle Bradley. The woman had made no secret of the fact that she found him exasperating. In truth, that was no surprise because he'd tried his hardest to be exasperating. Something about her had always gotten under his skin. She made him uneasy— not in a way most women did that so often resulted in his stuttering and stammering. It was more akin to when he was at the forge waiting for something to reach the right temperature. That anticipation, that sense of knowing was the same. He merely hadn't realized it until now.

"Rhett?" The impatience in her tone made him realize she was still waiting for an answer.

Of course he knew where she lived. A person couldn't be in town more than a few minutes before hearing about Bradley Boardinghouse. It was one of the best and most reputable places to stay in Peppin. The only reason he wasn't living there was because the man who'd sold him the smithy had offered him a cabin as a package deal. However, that didn't mean he was going to let Isabelle know that he was onto her. He figured if Isabelle had wanted him to know who she was beneath her mask, she would have already told him. He didn't see any harm in playing along with her. "Sure, but Egypt is pretty far away. Don't you think we'd better start walking?"

The triumph in her smile told him he'd made the right choice. "Actually, I have a better idea. I don't want to go back to the party and neither do you. So let's don't. Let's go on an adventure instead."

If he'd had any doubts to her identity, they would have been put to rest then and there. He only knew two women who'd suggest something like that. One was inside dressed like Cupid and attacking people with arrows. The other was standing before him on the porch with pure mischief in her smile. He lifted a brow. "Is that right? And what makes you think I'd go anywhere with you? If I remember my history lessons correctly, men who hang around Cleopatra for too long end up dead."

She gave a delightful little laugh. "Oh, and associating with a pirate isn't dangerous?"

"I prefer *buccaneer*, but you make a valid point." He took her hand and pushed back the sleeve of his coat to reveal the set of bracelets draped around her wrist. He trailed a finger across the most expensive-looking one. It was gold with a set of emeralds. Realizing the clasp was slightly open, he eased it closed. "Perhaps you should reconsider giving a command like that when you wear treasure such as this."

"There's nothing to reconsider." She affected a haughty tone to fit her character. "I'm not a woman whose decisions or opinions can be easily swayed by danger...or men."

"An admirable quality in a queen to be sure. However, there is one *small* problem." He leaned closer and lowered his voice to confide, "I'm not a man who'll accept a command without question."

"And what *is* your question?"

He broke from her gaze for only an instant before whispering, "Where are we going?"

That won him a smile. "If I told you that, it would take away part of the adventure. I can tell you a few things. It's somewhere not far from here. Few people know about it. We will be able to view the fireworks undisturbed. How does that sound?"

Scandalous. Yet, it was hard to say no to that hopeful look in her eyes while she was all but swallowed in his coat. She was adorable and beautiful all at once. Furthermore, romance was in the air and he wasn't panicking. He had no idea why that was the case, but he knew one thing. He wasn't going to leave her side until he found out.

Chapter Two

Sometimes... Well... *Rarely*, Isabelle had an idea so brilliant she surprised even herself. As she stepped from the fire escape to the roof of the hotel with Rhett right behind her, she knew this was one of those times. Rhett didn't seem quite as convinced. He frowned at the flat expanse that slanted only slightly toward the back of the building. "Are you sure this roof is safe?"

"Certainly. It was inspected only a few weeks ago. It's in tip-top shape."

He glanced at her curiously. "You know that for a fact? How?"

"I just do." Her father was a silent partner at the hotel in addition to being the owner of Peppin's best boardinghouse, but there was no reason to mention that and give a hint to her identity yet. "It sure is dark up here. I guess we should have picked up a lantern or a candle when we stopped to get my coat."

He shook his head. "We wouldn't want to chance a fire."

"True." The soft glow from the gardens below drew her toward the back edge of the roof. Suddenly, the cold wind changed direction with a mighty swirl that made her stretch out her arms and close her eyes. "Have you ever wondered what it would be like to fly? Imagine. The ground racing by beneath you. Nothing holding you up but air. It must be so freeing."

"Yeah, we won't be trying that tonight." He caught her arm and guided her away from the edge.

"Am I worrying you, Rhett?"

"Not at all." His nodding head belied his statement.

She laughed. "Well, if I can't fly, how am I supposed to have my adventure?"

He thought for a moment then grinned. "I've never danced on a rooftop, have you?"

"Danced on a… No, I can't say I have, but there's no music." Realizing she could still hear the faint strains of a reel from the ballroom, she amended, "Leastwise, none loud enough to be useful."

He pulled his harmonica from his pocket, which she was pretty sure was its permanent residence. "I thought you'd never ask."

"I didn't."

He ignored her. "Stay on this side of the roof if you want to avoid breaking your neck. How about a waltz—Chopin, Number Seven?"

"Is that a rhetorical question?"

It was. She shook her head when he began playing almost before she'd even finished talking. Her protests fled after his first few notes. They were soulful, smooth, lilting. Her lashes drifted closed without her permission as the passion he infused into each note enveloped her like a warm embrace. Before she knew it, the last note was fading into the night. She opened her eyes to find Rhett watching her with a bemused half smile tugging at his lips. "You didn't dance."

"That was... You...didn't, either. Play it again, Rhett."

This time she couldn't break away from his riveting gaze as he started over from the beginning. She swayed in time with the music then smiled when he mirrored her movements so that it felt as if they were dancing together without even touching. The sway became a waltz. Isabelle spun, her skirt swirling out around her. Rhett brushed past her. Suddenly, they were waltzing around each other, nearly colliding at times but never touching, held only by each other's gaze until Rhett drew out the last note long enough to give a deep, courtly bow. She responded in character with a regal curtsy.

A gust of wind swirled past her with enough force to urge her a step closer to Rhett, yet she hardly felt the cold as she responded to the warmth of his smile with one of her own. The faint sounds filtering up from the party below turned into a full-blown commotion. She forced herself to speak, though her words came out rather low and breathless. "I suppose it must be midnight."

"Must be." He tilted his head and lifted a brow. "There's a small matter of tradition, you know."

"Tradition?" She watched the focus of his amber eyes shift toward her lips. Realization spread through at the speed of her racing heart and instant blush. "Oh, I suppose there is. However, under the circumstances..."

He eased close enough that she had to tilt her head back slightly to look at him. She had a feeling she should step back, but the message didn't quite make it to her feet, which stayed resolutely put. The moon drifted from behind a cloud to highlight the strong angle of his jaw and she got a little distracted. She'd been saying something. "What I mean is, I don't think it's necessary..."

A distant whine filled the air before a pop of sound and color filled the night sky. The fireworks were starting. She should point that out. My, but he was taking his time, wasn't he? If he really was going to kiss her, why didn't he do it instead of hovering a breath away and making her all sorts of confused? Her lashes fluttered closed of their own accord. His first kiss was featherlight and unsatisfyingly brief. Just as disappointment set in, he kissed her again. This time, pressing one hand against her back to draw her closer and tilting her chin upward. She leaned into him.

Light flashed against her closed eyes while a boom rattled the building beneath her feet. She assumed it was a side effect of the kiss until Rhett pulled her down to kneel on the roof beside him. Dazed, she stared up at the black sky as balls of colored fire rained toward them, out of control and dangerously close. She screamed as sizzling green light whizzed past her, then she covered her ears as the explosions continued. "What is happening?"

"The fireworks. They're misfiring. We need to get off this roof. Now."

He practically carried her to the fire escape. She tried to keep up with him as they began their descent but her skirt billowed in the wind, making it hard for her to see each step. Rhett offered her a guiding hand.

She shook her head. "Go on ahead. You'll make it down faster without me. I'll be right behind you."

He shook his head. "I'm not leaving you, Isabelle."

"You're part of the fire brigade. Someone may need help. Go!"

He hesitated only long enough to nod before taking off down the stairs.

Rhett hated to leave Isabelle behind, but she was right. He was a volunteer firefighter and, by the look he'd gleaned while they were on the roof, something had already caught fire from the initial explosion. Whatever it was looked to be close to his own cabin, which meant it was in a residential area. Someone could be trapped or hurt. Still, as he neared the bottom of the steep, winding staircase, he couldn't help glancing upward to make sure that Isabelle was managing all right. She looked to be making a steady, if somewhat cautious, progress down the stairs.

Missing the next step completely, Rhett stepped into nothingness. He pitched forward, tripped down the next couple of steps and grasped the railing in time to keep from tumbling the rest of the way face-first. His panting breaths filled his ears along with the thundering of his racing heart. Pausing only an instant longer to regain his equilibrium, he marched back up the stairs to Isabelle. He ignored her startled look as he grasped her hand to help her navigate the last flight of stairs. "I almost broke my neck rushing down. There's no way I'm letting you do the same."

Her eyes widened. "Oh, Rhett, did you hurt yourself?"

"I don't think so." A twinge of pain in his right

ankle belied his statement, but he ignored it as they finally made it safely to the ground. He didn't bother to release her hand as he led her toward the back garden gate. "Come on. I know a shortcut."

They cut through the alley to the next street, where they merged with the stream of people rushing toward the fire. The whistling and popping of fireworks had faded away, leaving only shouts and confused murmurs to fill the night air. The pain in his ankle continued to build until it slowed his steps enough for Isabelle to notice. She latched on to his arm with her free hand as they wound through the crowd. "You're limping."

"I'm fine." That wasn't entirely true, but at the moment he didn't care. They were getting close to the corner where he lived. Too close. He ignored Jeff Bridger, the local deputy, who was trying to keep everyone back, and pushed to the very front of the crowd. His stomach dropped all the way to boots then rose to his throat. He swallowed hard even as a groan filled his chest.

Isabelle's voice seemed to come from a great distance. "Is it your leg?"

"No, that's my house."

He heard Isabelle's gasp as she took in the sight for herself. Meanwhile, he could do nothing but stare at the bright orange flames that engulfed the entire front half of the structure. Plumes of smoke drifted upward to mingle with the night sky. Fanned by a gusting wind, the fire sent sparks spiraling toward the house next-door to his. The sight was enough to set him in motion. He stepped forward to speak with the deputy. "Jeff, have my neighbors been accounted for?"

"Yes, and they said you were at the masquerade." Jeff must not have attended for he was dressed in his normal cowboy garb complete with a badge on his chest. "The sheriff was looking for you, though. I reckon he wanted to make sure you were safe."

Suddenly, a musketeer and a man in a Renaissance costume broke free of the crowd. Deputy Bridger called out a warning to anyone who might try to follow them. Ignoring it completely, Rhett went after them, drawn by the urgency in their gestures. They stopped to speak to another musketeer who'd been dousing a pile of leftover fireworks. Rhett could only maintain his running stride for a few seconds before the pain in his ankle forced his steps to slow to a walk. That gave him time to recognize the voice of his best friend, Quinn Tucker, despite the man's Renaissance costume. "There's no time to argue. I'm going in."

"I'm the sheriff of this town," Sean O'Brien declared. "It's my responsibility to keep everyone safe. *I'm* going, and that's final."

Rhett finally made it to the outskirts of their small circle. "How can y'all be arguing at a time like this? No one should be going anywhere until we put that fire out."

The three men turned to stare at him with shock and relief plainly written across their faces. Quinn stepped forward to pull him into a bear hug. Rhett thumped him on his back more in an effort to knock some sense into him than anything. Having had enough of the display, Rhett stepped away only to have Lawson, the third man from the argument, slap him on the shoulder. "We were arguing about who would have the privilege of saving your hide."

"My hide is fine, but I do appreciate your concern."

Sean blew out a heavy breath of relief then nodded beneath his jaunty wide-brimmed hat. "We were afraid you might be trapped inside the house since you'd told Lawson and Ellie that you were going home early."

"Oh." Rhett glanced back in search of Isabelle, but she'd been swallowed by the crowd. "I meant to, but I got a little distracted."

"Good thing, too." Quinn crossed his arms and nodded toward the fire. They all turned to follow Quinn's gaze in time to see the front of the house collapse in on itself. Rhett braced himself for the wave of despair that was sure to hit. Instead, he only felt the numbness of shock. That was probably for the best. Right now, his focus needed to be on others. "Was anyone else hurt?"

"My pa would know." Lawson scanned the crowd, presumably for his adoptive father, Doc Williams. "I'm sure he's here somewhere. I think I'll scout around to see if I can find him or someone who might need him."

"My house is a lost cause. Our focus should be on keeping the fire from spreading."

Sean nodded, already backing away. "I'll get some men to help me soak down the houses beside yours."

Rhett glanced around for some way to be of use. "Come on, Quinn. Even if we can't save the house, we need to keep the fire under control. Let's join the bucket brigade."

Quinn stopped him after only a handful of steps. "You're limping. Why didn't you say you were hurt?"

"I twisted my ankle on the way down the fire escape. That's all."

"Fire escape?"

"Yeah, I was on the roof with…"

Suddenly realizing the facts might sound a little less than respectable, he decided to stop talking. Apparently, the decision came a second too late for the confusion in his friend's gaze had turned to speculation. "With a distraction? A *female* distraction perhaps?"

"I didn't say that."

Quinn lifted a brow. "Want to tell me what's going on?"

How could he when he hadn't even had time to sort through it himself? He shifted his focus back to the fire. "There isn't the time for that, Quinn. We need to find some way to help out."

"What you need to do is sit down. I'll find Doc. Meanwhile, you should resign yourself to staying with me and Helen for a while."

"Staying with…?" He blinked, realizing he had no place to sleep tonight. "Y'all don't have to do that. I can stay at the hotel."

"For how long?"

"I don't know. But I can't stay at your place long-term, anyway. Y'all are practically newlyweds. Besides, I've got a business to run in town. I need to be close to it."

Quinn gave him a doubtful look. "Depending on what Doc says, you may not be running anything for a while. Now, will you go sit down?"

"No. I told you I'll be fine." Rhett did his best to minimize his limp as he walked to the bucket brigade. He didn't want to sit down until the fire was under control, and he knew no one else's house was in danger. He might be starting the New Year with nothing more than a pirate costume and a harmonica, but that didn't mean anyone else should have to lose their home.

Knowing he'd be too slow to do much good at the front of the line, where men raced back and forth to the fire, he stood near the back and helped pass buckets down the line. It wasn't something that took a lot of thought, so his mind strayed back to those few minutes when he was alone on the hotel roof with Isabelle. It had been beyond perfect. He hadn't stammered or stuttered once as far as he could remember. He'd kissed her, though. He remembered that—vividly.

Had his prayers finally been answered, then? Had God taken away his impediment around women? What other explanation could there be for what had happened with Isabelle?

He couldn't think of one. Of course, he wasn't exactly of a mind-set to try too hard at it, either. With so much turning to ash around him, how could he not fan the few embers of hope still burning in his heart?

As soon as Rhett left her, Isabelle took off in the opposite direction. He might not realize it yet, but he was going to need someplace to stay. She knew exactly who could help him with that. She stumbled into that very man as she rounded the corner toward Main Street. "Pa."

"Isabelle!" Her father pulled her into a tight hug then stepped back to look at her. "Are you all right? What was that sound?"

"I'm fine." She told him about the fireworks exploding before explaining that Rhett's house was on fire. "Surely, there's something we can do to help him now that he has nowhere to go."

For the first time since Amy's elopement, she saw her father's eyes fill with a mix of determination and purpose regarding the boardinghouse. "Of course we can. We have a vacant room. He'll stay with us rent-free for a while."

"Thank you, Pa. I knew you'd feel that way. The only problem is that he hurt his ankle in the rush to get to the fire. I'm not sure he'll be able to make it up the stairs right now."

"He can stay in my study until he's healed a bit." He gave her arm a gentle squeeze. "Go on home, sweetheart. Help your ma set up one of the extra mattresses in that room. I'll see what I can do to help at the fire."

She rushed home to do exactly that. When her younger sister offered to help their mother set things up for Rhett, Isabelle found herself returning to the fire. The scene was far less chaotic than when she'd left it. The volunteer fire brigade seemed to have everything under control, though they still battled to put the fire completely out. Bystanders, mainly women, watched in groups. Most still wore their costumes from the masquerade, but had taken off their masks. That helped her spot Helen and Quinn near the front of the crowd.

"I was wondering where you were," Helen said as she gave Isabelle a quick hug. "Quinn and I have been trying to figure out what we can do for Rhett."

Quinn grimaced. "More like, what he'll let us do."

"Where is he?"

Quinn nodded toward the fire. "He's somewhere out there battling the fire even though I know he's in pain. He says he twisted his ankle coming down a—"

Isabelle hushed him as she glanced around, half expecting to find her father standing behind her with a scowl on his face. Thankfully, he was nowhere in sight. He might be a little more reluctant to extend their family's hospitality if he guessed she'd been on the hotel roof with Rhett. Her father had taken her up there before, and he'd never said that she *couldn't* go up with anyone else. He'd only said she shouldn't go alone. Of course, there was also the not-so-little matter of the midnight kiss she'd shared with Rhett. "I wouldn't spread that around if I were you. It might get someone in trouble."

Helen's mouth fell open then curved into a smile. "It was you, wasn't it? You're the distraction Rhett told Quinn about."

"He doesn't know it was…" Her voice faded at the memory of Rhett's words after the explosion. *I'm not leaving you, Isabelle.* Her mouth fell open. He'd known who she was. For how long, though? Since before the kiss? Surely not or he wouldn't have instigated it in the first place. Quinn's voice pulled her from her thoughts. She glanced up at him, not liking the thoughtful, speculative look in his eyes one iota. "Isabelle, maybe you'd have more success in convincing him to sit down and let Doc take a look at his ankle."

"I doubt it, but I'll try."

He wasn't in the bucket brigade anymore, but one of the other men was kind enough to point her in the right direction. She was glad to find Rhett off his ankle even if it was only because he had to kneel to work the handle of one of the town's outdoor water pumps. He didn't seem to hear her call his name as he determinedly filled buckets for the other men. She placed a hand on his shoulder only for him to shrug it off without looking. "For the last time, Quinn—"

"Rhett."

He glanced up. His eyes widened then filled with warmth. He released the handle of the pump. Someone else immediately took his place as he struggled to his feet. His ankle gave way as soon as he put weight on it. Isabelle quickly slipped an arm around his waist to brace him. "You need to let Doc look at your ankle. Let's find you someplace to rest then I'll go get him."

His lips pressed together in a grim line, but he agreed with a single nod. She guided him toward an out-of-the-way spot nearby. He put his arm around her shoulder, but barely put any weight on her as he limped toward the raised wooden sidewalk nearby. He gave one final hop then turned to sit down. Catching her hand before she could leave, he tugged it gently. "Wait. Sit with me for a minute."

A protest rose to her lips. Then she looked into his eyes. She saw the intensity there. She realized he wasn't trying to put off being seen by the doctor. He wanted to talk about their kiss. What was there to say? It had been a simple New Year's Eve kiss between friends. Nothing more, nothing less.

Then why were her cheeks burning? Why was her heart fluttering? Why was panic seeping through her body? She pushed away those emotions with a lift of her chin as she lowered her gaze from his to their joined hands. His grasp was gentle, easily breakable. Yet, it held her like a butterfly caught in a net. "Rhett, we don't have to talk about this."

"I think we should."

She glanced around to make sure no one was within listening distance before sitting beside him on the sidewalk. "It was merely a kiss. A simple mistake prompted by a silly tradition. I don't expect anything more to happen between us. You don't have to worry about that."

"You don't *expect* anything more or you don't *want* anything more?"

"Is there a difference?"

"Yes. A big one. I didn't expect to kiss you tonight. That doesn't mean I didn't want to or wouldn't want to again."

Her mouth fell open. "Rhett Granger, I'm surprised at you. If you think—"

"Well, good. I'm surprised at myself, too. You saw me with Amy. I was constantly tripping over myself, saying all the wrong things, outright panicking. I'm always like that when things turn romantic, but that hasn't happened tonight with you." His amber gaze captured hers, his bemusement obvious. "Not even before the kiss. Not even now. I was hoping that meant something."

She stared at him as disappointment battled for dominance with whatever strange emotion made her heart flutter. She'd intended to write the kiss off as a mistake, hoping it didn't mean exactly what he was saying it did—Rhett was no different that her sister's other suitors, or her parents, or the town. He saw her as nothing more than a substitute for the woman he'd loved and lost to another man. Only this was even worse because he seemed to particularly appreciate the fact that he didn't find her as attractive as he had Amy. What other explanation could there be for why he didn't get as nervous around her as he did with someone he was actually attracted to?

He shrugged and ran his fingers through his hair as some of his boldness faded into a bashful smile.

"Besides that, I thought tonight was pretty special—before the explosion."

Her heart softened at his words. She didn't want to admit it, but there was no denying it. "It *was* special."

Unfortunately, that didn't change anything. As flattering as his interest was and as sincere as he seemed to be in comparison to her sister's other former suitors, she would still never be Amy—the one he truly wanted. She wasn't even the mysterious Cleopatra he'd approached in the ballroom last night. She was simply boring, ordinary Isabelle. Once she figured that out, he was bound to be disappointed. She'd save them both a world of trouble by putting a stop to this right here and now.

Yet, how could she while looking straight into the hope in his eyes? Besides that, he was still in the midst of losing his home. It didn't seem fair or kind to rebuff him right now. If only there was a way to help him find the relationship he was seeking—one that didn't involve her. She froze as a sudden flash of insight showed her a perfect way to help him and distract him from any ideas he might have about her.

Chapter Three

"Courting lessons?" Rhett couldn't contain the skepticism in his voice even as his heart sank in his chest at Isabelle's suggestion. He knew from past experience that nothing proved a woman's disinterest more than her trying to foist him off on one of her friends. It didn't make a lick of sense in this instance, though, because Isabelle was interested. He'd seen it in her eyes during that first tug of attraction on the hotel porch.

Furthermore, she could say all she wanted about their kiss meaning nothing. That didn't mean they hadn't *felt* something. He knew for sure that he had and, if her response in that moment was any indication, she had, too. Why, then, was she so eager to pass him off to someone else?

He searched her face for some clue. Perhaps his question was written across his expression, for a blush rose in her cheeks. Her lashes lowered to guard her eyes. "We, um, don't have to call it anything official like that. I'll just try to help you overcome whatever it is that makes you nervous."

"Why?"

Her gaze shot to his. "Why what?"

"Why do you want to help me?"

Her mouth opened then closed. "It's the right thing to do."

He narrowed his eyes, sensing there was more to it than that. He couldn't quite put his finger on what it was, so he guessed. "Are you sure it isn't because my house is burning down and I twisted my ankle?"

"I'm sure." A hint of a smile curved her lips at his doubtful look. "Well, that isn't *entirely* the reason."

"What's the rest of it?"

"None of your business."

She was definitely up to something. For some reason, he didn't think it was entirely altruistic. He shrugged. "Well, it doesn't matter. There's no point in accepting your offer. The lessons wouldn't work, anyway."

"You don't know that."

Oh, but he did. Ellie had tried to help him and failed. Lawson's advice hadn't worked, either. The Bachelor List had been wrong. God seemed to have turned a deaf ear to his prayers for this area of his life. Then again, perhaps the problem was that he'd been depending too much on other people. Maybe he ought to see if there wasn't something he could do to help himself. Something like courting lessons perhaps?

He sent her a sideways glance. "How would you be helping exactly?"

Her eyes went blank for a second. She blinked then smiled brightly. "Just leave that to me."

"You have no idea, do you?"

"I have a few ideas." She lifted her chin. "I need time to develop them."

"Right," he drawled.

She lifted a brow. "So you'll do it?"

"How about you let me know what you come up with, and I'll think about it?" That way he'd have an out in case he'd already tried whatever she came up with. There was no use repeating something that had already failed.

"Wonderful!" A delighted smile blossomed upon her lips before it eased into one of compassion. "I'm so sorry, by the way, about your house."

"Thank you. I appreciate that you stopped me from going home early. More than my ankle might have been hurt if you hadn't."

Her eyes widened. "I hadn't even thought about that. Oh, that reminds me. I was supposed to get Doc. Don't move an inch, Rhett Granger. I'll be right back."

She kept her promise of returning quickly with the doctor. Quinn and Helen followed after them, along with a tall, bookish-looking gentleman with spectacles whom Rhett recognized as Isabelle's father, Thomas Bradley. Everyone seemed to want to speak at once. Eventually, they all deferred to Doc Williams. "If his ankle is as swollen as I think it will be, we won't be able to get that boot back on. It would be far better to have him settled wherever he'll be staying while I examine him."

Mr. Bradley nodded. "To the boardinghouse, then."

"The boardinghouse?" Rhett glanced at the concerned faces around him in confusion.

Isabelle nodded. "We're offering you a room at our boardinghouse. Isn't that right, Pa?"

"It certainly is. Your first week with us will be free given tonight's unfortunate circumstances. After that, you are welcome to stay on as a renter should you choose to do so."

Helen's empathetic gaze met Rhett's and she nodded. "It would be a good alternative since you don't want to live with me and Quinn. I felt right at home during my stay at the boardinghouse when I first came to Peppin. The Bradleys are wonderful people. I'm sure they'll look out for you while you heal."

"I definitely appreciate the offer." He wavered about whether to insist on paying for all the time he'd spend there. Deciding he didn't want to take the chance of offending the Bradleys by rejecting their kindness, he gave them a grateful nod. "What's more, I'd be happy to accept."

Quinn and Helen left to fetch Rhett some necessities. Isabelle led the way to the boardinghouse while Rhett followed with Doc and Mr. Bradley bracing him on either side. Rhett was ensconced in Mr. Bradley's study by the time Quinn and Helen met up with them. They deposited the toiletries and other items gifted to Rhett by Johansen's Mercantile before Doc shooed them out as he had the Bradleys. Rhett held back a groan as Doc carefully pulled the boot off.

After a thorough examination, Doc shook his head. "Well, Rhett, it doesn't look like anything is broken. My diagnosis is that you have a severe sprain, which was probably made worse by your continued exercise on it during the fire. I'm going to leave a mild pain reliever with you. I'm sure my wife knows of a few natural remedies that will help you recover. I'll send her by tomorrow."

Doc's tone turned as stern as his look. "The most important element of your recovery is rest. I want you to stay off your feet as often as you can for the next forty-eight hours. After that, you'll need to use crutches for at least two weeks. You must allow the ankle to heal properly. Otherwise, you'll be far more likely to sprain it again in the near future. Now, let's get it wrapped and elevated."

Rhett was silent as he let the doctor work. Inside, he felt far less compliant. He could manage two days away from work since one of those days would be a holiday anyway, but two *weeks*? How could he possibly keep the smithy closed that long? Yet what else could he do? How likely was it that he'd be able to walk back and forth between the forge and the anvil on crutches while handling metal hot enough to be malleable?

He shook his head. He'd have to take it one day at a time. Perhaps he'd recover more quickly if he was diligent in following the doctor's orders and implementing whatever natural remedies Mrs. Williams offered. A few minutes later, he patiently listened to Helen's admonishments to do exactly that. Quinn said his farewells and ushered his wife out of the room after urging Rhett not to worry. Mrs. Bradley bustled in to ask if he needed anything. She left a bell for him to ring if he changed his mind. Mr. Bradley gave him an old set of crutches he'd found in the attic and directions to the water closet should a trip be necessary. Finally, everyone went to bed and he was left alone with his thoughts.

They should have centered on the fire, his living situation, replacing his belongings, figuring out his work predicament or any number of things. Instead, his mind was filled with thoughts of one person—

Isabelle. He punched his pillow and shifted around in a vain attempt to get comfortable. Why did he always do this to himself? Why did he always get his hopes up when he knew it never worked out? He'd truly thought this time was different. Not solely because he wasn't nervous around her, but because she was something special.

Why hadn't he realized that before? Perhaps he hadn't been looking. He'd focused his attention on her sister because it had been easier to engage her interest—at least from afar. Isabelle was more of a challenge to get to know simply because she wasn't quite as bold around men as her sister had been.

However, his relationship with Quinn and Helen had allowed him to spend more time with Isabelle. He'd found himself enjoying that time more and more.

She was interesting and witty. She didn't mind his teasing and could give back exactly as much as he gave out. Yet, she seemed to have a sensible head on her shoulders—sensible enough to want to avoid a relationship with him. That was what she was doing, wasn't it?

He assumed so. Although, he technically hadn't asked to court her. She also hadn't actually refused him. She could have easily made it clear that she would never have any feelings for him beyond friendship despite the kiss they'd shared. Instead, she'd simply changed the subject to finding him a different sweetheart—while holding his hand.

The more he thought about their conversation, the less sense it made. The more he thought about her, the less he wanted to give up on the idea of seeing where a romance with her could lead. Of course, he would never ignore the fact that she hadn't agreed to a courtship. However, courting wasn't the only way to get to know someone. They were living in the same house now. Surely, that would give them a chance to get to know each other better. Perhaps, after a while, she might be more open to the possibility of a courtship with him.

It seemed unlikely at this point. However, he'd do all he could to make it as difficult as possible for her to try to hand him off to someone else—even if that meant only being her friend for a while. He could be content with that. He could only hope he was right about actually having a chance with Isabelle one day.

If not, he was setting himself up for disappointment like never before.

Rhett had been right. Isabelle had no idea how to help him overcome his fear of women. She'd never call his problem that to his face. Essentially, that was what it was, though. She wished she'd been able to think of something other than courtship lessons to distract him from his interest in her. Taking responsibility for the success or failure of someone else's love life was a lot to handle when she'd never even had one of her own.

"Is something bothering you, sweetheart?" Concern and amusement filled the Virginia drawl her mother hadn't been able to shake after twenty-five years of living in Texas. "You're awfully quiet this morning. Besides, if you rub that dish any harder, you'll make a hole right through it."

"Oh." She glanced down at the serving plate she was drying off, then poured the scrambled eggs onto it. "It will just be extra shiny this morning, I suppose."

Her mother's searching blue eyes met hers. "You can talk to me about anything. You know that, don't you?"

She knew her parents *wanted* her to feel that she'd be able to talk to them about anything. However, she couldn't help feeling as though confiding in them would be dangerous. For instance, did they really want to know that she'd kissed a man on a rooftop last night? The same man, by the way, who was now occupying her father's study? Absolutely, they would want to know that. What would it get them once they knew? A bunch of worry and anger, that was all. Rhett would end up on the street. Isabelle would end up in Virginia.

"Isabelle?"

Her gaze refocused on Beatrice's. Thankfully, her father provided a timely distraction by entering the kitchen without his spectacles and with his vest unbuttoned. "I was getting dressed when I thought I heard Violet crying in her room. I asked her what was wrong through the door. She said something about her hair looking horrid and her dress being dumb. All I know is she's going to be late for her book-club party, and I'm going to be late for my meeting at the hotel if she doesn't come out of her room soon."

Isabelle frowned then glanced at her mother. "Ma, you know I'm no good with hair. Amy always did mine for special occasions. Violet's been so excited about wearing it up for the first time. I'd hate to bungle it."

"Oh, dear." Beatrice wiped her hands on her apron then removed it entirely and placed it on the hook beside the door. "I'd better go see what I can do. Thomas, you need to finish getting dressed so you'll be ready to go when she is. Isabelle…"

Isabelle followed her mother's gaze toward the breakfast they'd prepared. "I can handle this."

Her mother gave her a grateful smile on the way out the door. Already buttoning his vest, her father followed Beatrice out. Isabelle was left to pull in a deep breath and figure out what was left to be done to get breakfast on the buffet for the boarders who should be wandering downstairs within the next few minutes. She'd just placed the last biscuit in a serving bowl when a knock sounded on the kitchen door that led to the dining room. She turned in time to see two of the boarders enter. "What are y'all doing in here?"

Hank Abernathy, a clerk at the hotel, grinned unashamedly. "We saw Mrs. Bradley go into the family wing of the house and thought you might need help carrying food into the dining room."

"I'm surprised at you boys." She crossed her arms and lifted a brow. "Y'all know the rules. Absolutely no boarders allowed in my ma's kitchen."

Peter Engel, who worked in the telegraph office, blushed bright red. He lowered his gaze to the floor as though wishing it would swallow him whole. Unable to let him suffer for long, Isabelle allowed a smile to warm her voice. "Now, take this food and get out."

Peter's head shot up. Hank chuckled as he stepped forward to take the serving plate filled with eggs and bacon along with a bowl of fruit. She gave Peter the pancakes and biscuits before following behind the men with the steaming carafe of coffee. Wesley Brice entered the room from the hallway as they placed the food on the large oak sideboard buffet. "What's all this?"

She gave him a cheery smile but the Texas and Pacific Railway worker was too busy frowning at the other boarders to notice. "It's breakfast."

"I meant the rule breaking."

Hank rolled his eyes. "Good morning to you, too, Wes."

"Mrs. Bradley was busy," Peter said, standing frozen with a serving spoon of fruit hovering above his plate. "Isabelle needed help."

"She kicked us out of the kitchen right quick, too. She just sent the food with us on our way out."

"Yes, but I forgot a few things. I'll be right back." Isabelle returned to the dining room a few moments later with butter, syrup, cream and sugar.

Wes poured exactly the right amount of cream and sugar into a cup of coffee before giving it to her. He then handed the cream to Hank and the sugar to Peter since they were already sitting down. Returning both items to the sideboard, he met Isabelle's gaze with concern. "Where did you disappear to last night?"

A sudden vision filled her mind of Rhett's amber gaze catching hers as they whirled around each other on a rooftop beneath a million stars. She shook it away and glanced back at Wes. Mindful that the other boarders were listening, she stalled to gather her thoughts. "What do you mean?"

"One second you were dancing with Mark Antony. The next, you were gone."

"Oh. Well, Mark turned out to be Chris." She paused to blow on the steam from her coffee as Wes grimaced, Peter lifted a brow and Hank shook his head in sympathy. The boarders always seemed to be around when her sister's suitors decided to try to pay her court. It was downright embarrassing having an

audience for those types of things. "Then, John Merriweather decided to cut in. Chris wouldn't have it. They
started arguing, so I left them on the dance floor."

Hank toasted her with his coffee cup. "Good for
you. I see why you would've wanted to make yourself
scarce after that. You should have come to one of us,
though. We would have been glad to dance with you."

"Too glad, maybe," Wes muttered as he threw a
meaningful glance toward Hank and began to fill a
plate with food.

Gabriel Noland must have heard the conversation
out in the hall for he sent Isabelle a sympathetic glance
as he entered the room. "I'm surprised Isabelle got
to dance at all with you three standing around like
guard dogs."

Isabelle seized the opportunity to change the subject to something that might ease the odd tension filling the room. "And what were *you* doing all evening,
Gabe?"

"I thought you might want to see." He handed her
the sketch pad that had been tucked beneath his arm.
"The latest ones are near the back. I stayed up almost
all night finishing them."

Sitting in the nearest chair, she set her coffee on
the table and wiped her hands on a napkin before flipping to the back of the book. Images from the previous night filled each page in startling detail since
each could have only lasted a few moments at most.
She was aware of Gabe taking the seat beside her,
but didn't bother to look up. The boarders had moved
on to talking about the fire and Rhett coming to stay
with them. She figured as long as she looked busy,

no one would ask her any more questions that she'd rather not answer.

She froze as she recognized the tableau playing out before her on a page of the sketch pad. It featured her caught in the throes of indecision. Her hand was in the grasp of Mark Antony, who bowed over it with old-world elegance. Meanwhile, her gaze and attention were consumed by the pirate behind him. There was a shared longing on their faces that surely couldn't have been there last night. Isabelle almost jumped at the sound of her father's voice. "Are those your sketches from last night, Gabe?"

She casually turned back to a much less incriminating sketch of someone else as her father stepped up behind her. She lifted her gaze to Gabe's, suddenly aware he'd been watching her reaction. Gabe smiled. "Yes, I think I'll get several good paintings from my efforts last night."

Her eyes widened then narrowed into warning slits. "In that case, why don't I put this somewhere safe for you? We wouldn't want it to get stained by being around all this food."

"I'll sit on it. How's that?"

She had the distinct urge to pop him over the head with it. Gabe had no idea how blessed he was that her mother entered the room to distract her father with the news that Violet was ready to go. Beatrice decided to take a breakfast tray to Rhett. Isabelle would have volunteered to do it in her stead, but didn't have the nerve to suggest it in front of Gabe. The boarders lingered over breakfast since none of them had to rush to work on a holiday. However, once the plates were taken to the kitchen, they all slipped away to their various amusements outside the house.

With the dishes washed, Beatrice pulled out her baking supplies. "Poor Rhett must be bored to tears in the study by now. Why don't you play a game of spades with him or something? Be sure to leave the door open. I'll join y'all in a little while. I want to whip up some plum pudding and a bit of wassail in case we get any callers."

"All right, Ma. Let me know if you change your mind about wanting my help in here." Isabelle removed her apron and gathered a deck of cards from the parlor. She was right about to knock on the study door when the front door opened and Violet walked into the foyer. Isabelle changed course to greet her. "Violet, how was your literary circle's New Year's Breakfast?"

"Positively exquisite." The fifteen-year-old's blue eyes danced as she removed her hat and scarf. "We've decided we're going to have one every year."

"And how did your hair turn out?"

Violet spun to show off the elaborate chignon. "What do you think of it?"

Isabelle winked. "Gorgeous, darling."

"I'm almost glad Ma and Pa said I can only wear it up for special occasions. All these pins digging into my brain..." She gave a little shudder before shrugging out of a familiar navy coat.

Isabelle frowned. "I thought you were going to wear your new coat? It's so much nicer than this old one. It was Amy's first, you know—"

"Oh!" Eyes wide, Violet turned to stare at the floor by the front desk. *"Oh!"*

"What?"

Violet dropped to her knees by the coatrack. Her hands swept back and forth across the floor as she crawled toward the front desk. Isabelle watched mutely then glanced around to make sure that no one else was around to see her little sister's strange behavior. "Violet?"

"Isabelle!"

Holding back a laugh, Isabelle knelt beside the desk. "What *are* you doing?"

"Did you find it?" Violet crawled from beneath the desk to search her eyes. "Did you find Ma's bracelet— the one she lent you to wear to the masquerade?"

"Ma's bracelet?" Isabelle glanced down at her bare wrist, remembering seeing Rhett push back the extra length of his coat sleeve to reveal the bracelet. She recalled the soft imprint of it upon her skin as he smoothed closed the clasp that had eased open without her realizing it. She couldn't remember anything about it after that. She slowly shook her head. "I haven't seen it since last night."

Violet groaned. "Isabelle, I've done something terrible. Truly, I have. I *was* going to wear my new coat this morning, but Pa said it was too thin since it's really only supposed to be a raincoat. He said I'd catch cold and made me come back inside to change. I didn't want to go all the way to my room for my other coat, so I took yours."

"What's wrong with that?"

"The bracelet was caught inside your sleeve. It fell out when I put your coat on. It slid across the floor and lodged halfway under the desk. I was in such a rush that I didn't stop to pick it up. I just…left it there thinking no one would see it. I planned to get it as soon as I came back. Now it's gone."

A cold, sinking feeling settled in Isabelle's stomach. "No, it has to be here somewhere."

They searched every inch of space in the foyer but found no trace of the bracelet. Isabelle caught her sister's hands to still their wringing. "Calm down, Vi. We need to think this through."

"There's nothing to think through. Bracelets don't disappear. Someone must have taken it. It had to be one of the boarders."

Isabelle shook her head. "We don't know that for sure."

"Well, I don't have it. Neither do you. Pa left the house before I did. He hasn't returned yet, so he couldn't have taken it. Rhett can hardly walk. What about Ma? Have you been with her the whole time?"

"No. She brought Rhett his breakfast and retrieved the tray. Perhaps she found it."

"Then wouldn't she have mentioned it?"

Isabelle frowned. "Probably, but we should check her jewelry box to be certain."

"And if it isn't there?"

"Maybe whoever took it will return it. Meanwhile, we can't let our parents find out about this. Or anyone else for that matter."

Rhett's voice filled the hallway. "Why is that exactly?"

Gasping, Isabelle whirled to find him balancing against the doorpost of the study with curiosity wrinkling his brow. She glanced back to exchange a panicked look with her sister. Violet recovered first. With a quick glance toward the kitchen, she caught Isabelle's arm and towed her across the hall toward Rhett so they could speak more quietly. "Because if our parents find out there's a thief in the boardinghouse, we might as well kiss Peppin goodbye."

Concern filled Rhett's eyes as he turned to Isabelle for confirmation. "You'd have to leave town?"

She nodded. "After Amy's elopement, they said if anything else goes wrong, they're going to sell the boardinghouse and move us back to Virginia, where they're originally from."

"Well, we can't have that." He frowned. "We need to figure out who took the bracelet and find a way to get it back."

Violet wrinkled her nose. "How are we going to do that?"

"First off, y'all had better check your ma's jewelry box like you said. The other thing we need to do is to keep a close watch for anyone behaving oddly or guiltily. Y'all would be better judges than me on that since I don't know the other boarders well. Let's see how all of that works out, and we'll go from there."

Isabelle nodded, then blinked, unsure of how "we" suddenly included him. She wouldn't complain, though. Having him on their side was far better than letting him tell their parents about the missing bracelet the first chance he got. She could only hope that the three of them would be able to curtail this problem before it became a situation requiring her parents' attention. The last thing she wanted to do was, as Violet had put it, kiss the boardinghouse and Peppin goodbye.

Of its own accord, her gaze drifted to Rhett's smile. She shook her head to keep her thoughts from straying where they didn't need to go. He caught her gaze and his eyes seemed to darken. She swallowed hard. She'd get the bracelet back, find Rhett someone else to court and her life would go back to normal. End of story.

Chapter Four

Rhett hadn't intended to eavesdrop on Isabelle and Violet's conversation. It had simply been nigh on impossible not to since it had taken place only yards from the study door. Of course, once he'd realized what he was listening to, he hadn't exactly tried not to hear it. He didn't like the idea of the Bradley girls dealing with a possible thief by themselves, which was why he'd inserted himself into the situation. That and the fact that, prior to overhearing them, he'd been staring at the ceiling for thirty minutes after giving up on his attempts to read one of the few books he'd been able to reach. Being an invalid was duller than he'd ever imagined. He needed a project to keep his mind occupied.

Isabelle had checked her mother's jewelry box, but the bracelet was still nowhere to be found. Knowing there was nothing else they could do to search for it at the moment, she and Violet stayed around to play a few card games with him. Eventually Mrs. Bradley brought his lunch and took her daughters with her when she left. Only a few minutes later, Isabelle returned to announce that he had a visitor. "It's the sheriff. He's waiting in the parlor. I thought you might be lying down and figured you'd want to sit in the chair with your leg propped up while you talked with him, like you did for our card games."

"I'd appreciate that."

After helping him get situated, she straightened the bed then sent him a pointed look on the way out. "I'll go get him so y'all can talk about your business."

He grinned, easily catching her subtle warning not to mention the thief. "My business, meaning not yours?"

"Exactly." She smiled.

She was out the door before he had a chance to respond. Sean entered only a moment later, with a pair of freshly hewn crutches in his hand. "I come bearing gifts. Made them myself. Although, I see you've already got a pair."

Rhett glanced at the set already leaning against a nearby wall. "They worked great in a pinch but they're a bit too short for me."

"I pegged you at about six-two and fashioned these accordingly. Want to try them out?"

"Sure thing." He rose from the chair, where he sat with his leg propped up. Setting the new crutches in position, he moved back and forth across the room. "These are perfect, Sean. Thank you."

"Glad I could help." Sean waited until Rhett sat down, then took the chair opposite him. "I wanted to let you know what I've learned about what happened last night. It seems that a couple of teenagers weren't satisfied with the fireworks display the town had planned, so they stockpiled enough for one of their own. They'd planned to set them off farther outside of town. However, the load fell out of the wagon right at the corner near your house. No one is sure how a spark hit one of the fuses, but it set off the whole lot."

"I hope no one got hurt."

"A minor burn here or there is all. It could have been a lot worse. As it is, the boys have been scared out of their wits more than anything."

"I can imagine. It was scary enough as far away as I was. What's going to happen to them now?"

"Setting off fireworks within the town limits is a misdemeanor, so ultimately that will be for the judge to decide. Do you think you're going to press charges?"

Rhett grimaced. "They're so young. I'd hate to do it."

"I know. Unfortunately, their age doesn't change what happened. People could have been seriously injured or even killed. Your house was destroyed. Several others were damaged. If you don't bring charges, someone else probably will."

"Yes, but those wouldn't be as bad."

"True. It's up to you. Judge Hendricks is a fair man—kind, wise and has a knack for coming up with the right solution."

"I'm sure he is, but I'm probably going to forego any legal proceedings. I had insurance on the house, so I ought to be all right without adding to whatever those kids will have to face from everyone else."

Sean nodded. "Meanwhile, you have an army of volunteers working to clear the debris off your lot. Anything salvageable will be placed in boxes for you to look through later. Once that's done, better prepare yourself for some visitors. I'm sure you'll have a lot of folks dropping by to check on you."

Though he was embarrassed at the thought of all the attention he'd be getting, Rhett couldn't help but appreciate the way the town was rallying around him. "I appreciate everything you've done, what the others are doing now and all of the support I've gotten. Please, let everyone know that."

"You're our neighbor and our friend. It's the least we could do. Actually, there's one more thing. The town got together and… Well, here."

Rhett took one look at the money inside the envelope Sean handed him and shook his head. "I appreciate this, but it isn't necessary."

Sean held up his hands when Rhett tried to hand it back. "Don't give it back too quickly. You might not be able to work for a while. It might come in handy."

"I'll be fine." Rhett frowned. "Tell you what. Why don't we start a fund to buy a new fire wagon for the town with this money? That way the whole town would benefit."

"You're really going to refuse to take it?" At Rhett's nod, Sean finally accepted the envelope. "Then I think your idea is a good one. This amount isn't quite enough, but it's a good start."

"Maybe we can find some way to raise the rest of the money. We ought to do it soon, while the subject is on everyone's minds. I'd suggest a benefit dance, but the town recently had a masquerade ball."

"I think the church has the corner on the box socials, although it's probably too cold for one anyway."

"Yeah, the event would have to be inside." His hand strayed toward his pocket, where his harmonica was safely tucked away. "We have a lot of talented singers and musicians in this area. Do you think folks would pay to see them perform?"

Sean grinned. "I do—especially if you were playing. I reckon we could draw a lot of people that way. With folks knowing what you went through, it would set their minds at ease to see that you're all right. That'll be particularly true once they find out you didn't take any of their money."

"I know I could rope Quinn into playing his banjo. Chris has his fiddle. In fact, I'm pretty sure everyone in his family plays some kind of instrument or another."

"My wife is quite a hand at the piano," Sean added.

"That's a fact," Rhett agreed, having heard Lorelei play nearly every Sunday at church. "I'd be happy to recruit talent, but managing the actual program isn't exactly the kind of thing I'd be good at."

Sean grimaced. "Me, neither."

"Then who's going to plan all of this?"

Sean leaned back in his chair and crossed his arms. "Well, now, that's a good question."

"It seems like the kind of thing that needs a woman's touch, doesn't it? I'd hate to impose on anyone. It might be a lot of work."

Sean nodded. "Ellie's good at planning things. I'll ask her. If she can't do it, she might be able to point me in the direction of someone who can. I'll send them your way to talk about the performers."

"That sounds good." Rhett moved to stand when Sean did, then smiled ruefully and settled back in his chair. "I'd see you out but…"

Sean grinned. "Don't worry about it. Take care of yourself. Let me know if you need anything. I mean it, Rhett."

"I will. Hey, before you go, you said the volunteers were putting anything salvageable in boxes for me. How much have they found?"

Sean winced. "What I should have said was *if* they find anything, they'll put it in a box for you."

"Meaning?"

"We haven't found anything worth saving yet."

Rhett sighed. That was disappointing, but pretty much what he'd expected. "I have a feeling I'm going to be starting over from scratch."

"Perhaps. That doesn't entirely have to be a bad thing, though. It's a new start in a new year—a blank slate. You can make whatever you want out of it."

"That's exactly what I've been thinking."

"Good." Sean straightened to leave then hesitated. "Be encouraged, Rhett. God is going to bring something good out of this for you and your future. That's who He is and how He works."

Rhett nodded. Reading his Bible, growing up in church, watching the lives of other believers had given Rhett plenty of evidence that God had good plans for His people. Trouble was, in Rhett's experience, God sure seemed to take His time when it came to working those plans out in his life. Rhett was tired of waiting for things to change and sick of depending on others to make it happen. If life was a blank page, then it was time for him to take the pen in his own hands and do a little writing. Whether that or even God would help still remained to be seen.

The bell on the front desk rang frequently to announce Rhett's steady stream of visitors after the sheriff left. Isabelle didn't mind because it gave her an excuse to watch the door. In truth, she was waiting for the boarders to return in the hopes that one of them would hand her the bracelet along with a reasonable explanation for having it. Gabe was the first to return. He absently tossed his coat onto the rack, muttered a quick hello and rushed up the stairs, already flipping through his sketchbook. She listened to his door ease shut and knew she probably wouldn't see him again until supper a few hours from now. There was nothing strange about that.

She glanced up when the front door opened again and was relieved to see Ellie and Lawson Williams enter. As the town's unofficial matchmaker, Ellie was exactly the person Isabelle should ask about the courting lessons she'd promised Rhett. She greeted the couple with a quick hug. "I'm sure you're here to see Rhett. He's right through that door and ready for visitors. Ellie, would you mind if I borrow you for a few moments before you leave? I need a bit of advice."

"Well, now I'm too curious to wait. Why don't we talk now?"

Remembering that Rhett had been able to hear her entire conversation with Violet earlier, Isabelle glanced toward the study. "All right, but let's not do it here. The walls have ears."

Ellie followed her gaze. "I'm guessing those ears belong to Rhett."

Lawson grinned. "Why don't y'all go for a quick walk? I'll visit with Rhett."

"Thanks, Lawson." Isabelle quickly bundled up in her coat, hat and gloves before she and Ellie walked down the porch steps out onto Main Street.

Ellie slipped her hands into her pockets as she sent Isabelle a concerned look. "Is everything all right?"

She'd meant to keep the conversation light, but her response somehow came out a bit drawn-out and shaky. "Yes."

Ellie frowned. "Isabelle, what is going on?"

Isabelle pressed her lips together. *Don't say it. Don't say it.*

"Isabelle?"

"I kissed Rhett."

Ellie stopped in her tracks in the middle of Main Street. "Wait. What?"

Isabelle closed one eye and winced before tugging her friend across the street to the courtyard. "I did. I kissed him. Well, actually, he kissed me. Or we kissed each other. I don't know. It just sort of happened because it was New Year's Eve. Then the world exploded. And I can't believe I'm telling you this."

Ellie shook her head and waved her hands in random circular motions. "Whoa. Slow down. My mind needs to catch up with your words. You and Rhett kissed on New Year's Eve. That's…" Ellie nodded then grinned. "That's wonderful. Hurray!"

Isabelle glared at her. "No! Not wonderful. Not hurray. This is bad."

"It is?"

"Yes!"

"Why?"

"There are so many reasons." Isabelle shook her head as she led the way down a path strewn with dead brown leaves. "First of all, I don't go around kissing men willy-nilly. That is not the kind of girl I am. Second, I had on a mask, so I thought he didn't know who

I was, but he did. He knew the whole time. Third, he's living in the boardinghouse now, and it was my idea to have him there. Finally, if my parents find out any of this, they will not be happy at all. In fact, they will probably throw him out."

Ellie grimaced. "Oh. Well, the only thing that really sounds like a problem is the part about your parents. The rest seems pretty romantic to me."

Panic surged through her. "No romance. Absolutely not. This would be the worst possible time for one with everything so up in the air."

"What is up in the air?"

"Nothing. Never mind." Her parents were trying to keep their doubts about the fate of the boardinghouse in the family circle until a decision had officially been reached. "Most important, I refuse to even consider a man who was in love with my sister just a matter of months ago."

"Hmm." Ellie started walking again, albeit very slowly. "What does Rhett have to say about all of this?"

"He…" She could almost see the confusion and disappointment on Rhett's face as she offered the courting lessons in response to his overtures toward…what exactly? She hadn't let him finish. His words had started to sound too similar to what she'd been hearing from John and Chris, so she'd cut him off almost instinctively. "It doesn't matter. I've made my decision."

"I see." Ellie's knowing gaze said she probably saw far too much, at that.

"The reason I'm telling you this is because I need your help. Rhett's a good man. He deserves to find someone." She bit her lip. "What I mean is surely there is some other girl we can send his way…"

"Distract him?"

"Yes!" Seeing the disapproving frown that earned her, she amended, "No. Ellie, you're a matchmaker. Surely, you had someone in mind for him when you made the Bachelor List. I mean that's what the list does, right? It pairs the town's eligible bachelors with the women you think would be a perfect match for each of them."

"Yes, that is what it does."

"So?"

Ellie stared at her for a moment before shaking her head. "I'm no longer in possession of the Bachelor List. Quinn has it and refuses to give it back. He told me some nonsense about it belonging to the bachelors. He's going to pass it along to someone else eventually, I suppose."

"Well, we don't need it. You created it, so you know everything that's on it. Who did you match Rhett with?"

"That is a private matter between Rhett and me... and Lawson. Lawson knows."

Isabelle lifted a brow. "And Quinn and whoever else happens to get their hands on that list."

Ellie placed a calming hand on her arm. "Isabelle, I care for you dearly. You are one of my closest friends. However, I'm getting more than a little tired of being questioned about that list. My policy is not to discuss its contents with anyone. I'm afraid that includes you."

"All right." She pulled in a deep breath. "I understand. I won't bother you about it again."

"Good."

Her mind scrambled to find some way around this

new obstacle. "I'm all for letting Rhett choose his own woman anyway. At least, as long as it isn't me."

Ellie rolled her eyes. "Honestly, Isabelle."

"I *am* being honest. The real problem here, and the one I need your advice on, has nothing to do with the list. In a moment of desperation, I offered to help Rhett overcome his trouble with women."

"Did you, now?"

Ignoring her friend's smirk, Isabelle nodded. "Yes, I did. Unfortunately, I have no idea how to do that."

Ellie sighed. "Well, I hate to tell you this, but I already tried to help Rhett. I didn't end up making it any better. In fact, I'm afraid I might have even made it worse."

"Oh."

"Hold on. Don't give up on me yet. Let me think about it for a minute." Ellie bit her lip and stayed in deep contemplation as they passed the steps of the courthouse. It was only when they turned back toward the boardinghouse that the matchmaker spoke again. "Perhaps Lawson and I skipped a step when Rhett asked us for advice. We gave him tips on how to communicate better. I think the problem is he never gets that far. He just panics."

Isabelle narrowed her eyes and bit her lip. "So we need him not to panic."

Ellie nodded. "Figuring out why he does it and where that fear comes from might help him get over it."

"How do I do that?"

"Get him to talk about it. Listen. Support and encourage him as he faces it." Ellie shrugged. "That's my best advice."

Thinking over the list of duties Ellie had prescribed for her, Isabelle nodded. "I can do that."

Ellie gave her a knowing look. "And you really want me to believe you're doing all of this solely to distract him."

"Well, I'm also doing it to help him, so my motivation isn't *entirely* selfish…only partially." Isabelle opened the boardinghouse door then leaned back against it to allow Ellie to enter first.

Instead of walking inside, her friend lingered. "Right. All I have to say is… Never mind."

Isabelle narrowed her eyes at her friend. "What? Go on, tell me."

That was all the encouragement needed to prompt a grin on Ellie's face which was followed by a quick wink. "That must have been some kiss."

Isabelle leaned back against the open door and stared after her friend, who soon disappeared into the study. "Honestly, Ellie, of all the nerve…"

"Amy!" a man's voice called.

Her heart jumped into her throat as she glanced around in search of her sister. Instead, she saw John Merriweather walking up the path to the front porch with a box of candy in hand. She glanced around one more time to make sure she hadn't missed anyone, then released the door to meet John at the porch steps. She frowned at him in confusion. "Did you call me Amy?"

"Did I?" He smoothed his flawlessly shaped mustache. "That was her favorite color, you know."

She followed his gaze to her blouse—Amy's blouse, to be exact. It was one of the many hand-me-downs she'd received over the years. "Yes, I know."

"How is Amy, by the way?"

She stared at the man, feeling appalled. At least Chris and Rhett managed to call her by the right name. It was past time to put an end to John's childish she-nanigans. Pulling in a deep breath, it came out in a bit of a huff. "Married. Amy is still most definitely married. I expect she'll stay that way."

"Yes, of course. I only meant…" He trailed off as though he wasn't entirely sure what he'd meant and in spite of herself, she couldn't help feeling sorry for him.

"John." She touched his arm to pull his dejected gaze from the ground. She tried to keep her tone kind yet firm. "I know that you were sweet on her in school, but that was a long time ago. She kept meaning to tell you it was over. She just never could turn down that particular kind of candy. At least, that's what she told me. I need you to trust me on this. She moved on. Perhaps it's time for you do the same."

A slow grin spread across his face. "I am so glad to hear you say that, Isabelle. I'd started to think I wasn't making any progress with you, but now I know that isn't true. I'll go straight in to talk to your father."

Eyes widening, she instinctively cut him off as he made a beeline for the front door. "Wait. My father isn't here right now. Besides, I didn't mean you should move on with me. My feelings for you are platonic—strictly platonic."

"Oh…" For someone who'd been all fired up to set their courtship in motion, he seemed unfazed by her rejection. "All right. If you don't mind, I'll keep the candy."

"By all means."

He tipped his hat and turned on his heel. She waited until he was a ways down the block before she rolled her eyes and shook her head. As frustrating as their exchange had been, it had still gone far more smoothly than she'd anticipated. Hopefully, he wouldn't be back. That left Chris and Rhett. She hardly saw Chris because he stayed so busy helping with his family's mercantile. She'd find some way to deal with him later if he persisted in pursuing her. For now, her focus needed to be on Rhett. Or, rather, on finding someone else for him.

Despite Ellie's comments, she would not fall into the trap of thinking about that kiss. It wouldn't be happening again. The best thing she could do for Rhett and herself was to get started on those courting lessons—as soon as possible.

Chapter Five

Rhett waited with bated breath as Doc surveyed his ankle the following afternoon. The man gave a satisfied nod before rewrapping it. "Rhett, this looks much better. I can tell you've been following my orders, because the swelling has gone down considerably. You can move about the house on your crutches freely now."

"Thank you. Much of the credit for my condition goes to the Bradleys. They've taken excellent care of me over the past day and a half." Rhett glanced over Doc's shoulder to where Mrs. Bradley stood by the desk and gave her a grateful smile.

The woman had been particularly diligent in making sure he'd had everything he'd needed to be comfortable in the makeshift bedroom the study provided. She hadn't budged one bit when he'd tried to convince her it would be all right for him to join the other boarders for supper last night or breakfast this morning. He'd dearly wanted to look each man in the eye for any sign they might have betrayed the trust of Isabelle's family. Instead, he'd had to be content with the Bradley girls' description of a normal boardinghouse supper where everyone had behaved as they usually did. The investigation for the missing bracelet wasn't getting off to a very auspicious start.

Violet was determined to find out who'd seized upon her mistake of leaving the bracelet lying on the floor. Isabelle still seemed to be hoping this was all some kind of misunderstanding. Rhett simply wanted to find some way to be useful. He'd found that if he leaned to the left in his bed a bit, he could catch a glimpse of his blacksmith shop through the trees in the courtyard. The sight of it closed up was near torture since most of the other businesses in town had reopened after the holiday. He still wasn't sure when he'd be able to open his doors again. Perhaps he'd have a better understanding of that once he was used to walking on his crutches.

For now, he'd be glad for the chance at a change of scenery. As grateful as he was that he'd been allowed to sleep in the study, he was determined to return the full use of it to Mr. Bradley. Rhett had hardly seen the man since moving in and couldn't help suspecting it was because he'd commandeered the man's workspace as a bedroom. "Doc, is there a way to use the crutches to go up and down the stairs?"

"There certainly is."

Mrs. Bradley's eyes widened. "Rhett, I know we said you'd move upstairs eventually, but we don't want you to do anything dangerous."

Doc handed Rhett his crutches. "It's actually quite safe once you get the hang of it."

At the base of the stairs, Doc showed him how to plant his crutches on the ground then push off them to place his uninjured foot on the next step. Rhett went up the entire staircase that way. Once he reached the top, he found a long hall lined with doors. Violet exited one to his right then froze when she caught sight of him. Her eyes widened as she glanced toward the stairs and placed a finger in front of her lips.

All right, then. Rhett tried not to visibly react to her warning as he turned to look down the stairs. "Doc, how do I get down from here?"

In the corner of his eye, he saw Violet frantically shake her head at him. She needn't have feared because Doc only mounted the bottom few steps. "It's the same process, but in reverse. Plant your crutches on the next step then set your foot down. Be careful not to swing out."

Rhett did as the doctor said and soon reached the bottom. He thanked Doc Williams for his help. After the man took his leave, Rhett turned to Mrs. Bradley. "I'd like to practice that a few times."

"Go right ahead." She glanced up at the ceiling. "Isabelle thought you might be ready to move upstairs, so she's preparing a room for you. It's the second door on the right. I'd better check on Violet. She's keeping an eye on supper for me. It should be ready soon. We'd be happy to have you join us at the table."

"Thank you. I'll do that." He started up the steps while Mrs. Bradley turned to go across the hall to the kitchen. He forced himself not to rush as he moved up the stairs. Once he reached the second floor, he motioned Violet over. "Your ma is looking for you in the kitchen. You'd better get down there. Where's Isabelle?"

She pointed to the room she'd been standing outside

of then rushed down the stairs. Rhett swung himself
down the hall past the room Isabelle was supposed to
be preparing for him and pushed open the door Violet had indicated. Isabelle was peering into a box as
she sat in the middle of the room with a full bottle of
whisky in one hand and a bottle of gin in the other.
She set them aside and glanced up, clearly expecting
to see Violet for her green eyes widened upon meeting his. "Rhett, what are you doing here? What did
you do with my lookout?"

"I sent her downstairs because your ma was looking for her. A better question is what are *you* doing
in *here*?"

"I'm searching for the bracelet, of course." She
nudged a few things around in the box. "All the boarders are at work except for Gabe. He works in his room,
but he's so focused that he hardly notices anything."

"You do know it's getting close to supper, don't
you? The other boarders will be back any minute."

"That's all right. I'm done here." Giving the box
one more cursory look, she replaced the bottles before sliding it under the bed. "I may not have found
the bracelet, but this stash of liquor doesn't speak well
for Hank's integrity. He knows it's against the rules
to have it here."

Rhett tensed when he heard the sound of the front
door opening followed by male voices. "Isabelle,
someone's here."

She jumped up from the floor. "Head toward the
stairs."

He backed up and nearly stumbled over his crutches
in his haste. Righting himself, his crutches clacked a
quick rhythm on the hardwood floor as Isabelle closed

Hank's door and locked it. The voices grew louder. A fleeting touch of Isabelle's hand on his back was the only warning he received before she slid to a stop in front of him. He channeled his forward momentum into a hop. She braced her hands against his chest to keep him from mowing her down. Footsteps sounded on the stairs. He planted his crutches on the ground and had just stopped swaying when a man reached the top of the stairs.

Isabelle released him and reached for the doorknob. "Rhett, this will be your room. Oh, hello, Hank."

"Isabelle." A man with gunmetal-gray eyes and light brown hair grinned at her before extending a hand to Rhett. "I've seen you around town, but I don't think we've officially met. You must be Rhett Granger."

Rhett shook his hand. "I am. And you're Hank."

"Yep. Hank Abernathy. It's a pity about the fire." The man glanced down to the spot where Isabelle's hands hand been an instant ago. He lifted an eyebrow and his smile turned a bit sly. "Glad to see you're doing all right."

"Thank you."

The stiffness of Rhett's response didn't seem to bother Hank. The man tipped an imaginary hat. "See y'all at supper."

Rhett waited until the door closed behind Hank to meet Isabelle's gaze. As one, they sagged in relief. He lowered his head and whispered, "I don't like him."

"Oh, he's not so bad," she whispered back, then grimaced. "At least, I don't *think* he is. The liquor smuggling does give me pause."

Rhett heard the footsteps on the stairs and suddenly realized how close they were standing. He straightened. Isabelle stepped back. They were both a second too late. Although he hadn't exchanged more than a few passing pleasantries with the man walking toward them, Peppin was small enough for Rhett to know his name was Wesley Brice and he worked at the T&P Railway in some capacity. Isabelle greeted him. He nodded in return, but pinned Rhett with a steely glare before entering a room down the hall.

Tilting her head, Isabelle bit her lip. "I have an idea. How about I go downstairs before we get into any *more* trouble?"

He grinned. "Sounds good."

She tilted her head toward the door they were standing beside. "Your room is unlocked. Go ahead and look around if you like. I'll see you downstairs for supper."

"Thank you for getting my room ready."

"You're welcome." She gave a little wave then hurried down the stairs.

He stepped inside the room that would be his for the undetermined future and found it matched the homey elegance that filled the rest of the boardinghouse. The warm green color of the walls contrasted nicely with the oak floor. A bed stood against the wall on his right, covered in a cream quilt that had some sort of star pattern traced out in a darker green. A chest of drawers stood by the wall nearest the hall. It was flanked by a washstand. A writing desk sat beneath the window that faced Main Street.

Realizing he was a bit winded from using the crutches, he fumbled to pull the chair from beneath the desk then sat on it. A knock sounded on the partially open door. Wesley Brice entered the room before Rhett could even bid him to enter. Rhett shook his head in confusion at the man's glare. "Is there a problem?"

"There might be if you have designs on Isabelle."

"Excuse me?"

Wesley sighed and stepped farther into the room. "Look, normally I try to stay out of other people's affairs, but I saw what the Bradley family went through after Amy eloped. They were frantic and hurt. Nothing has been quite the same since. They don't trust their boarders anymore and for good reason. It's going to take some time for us to earn their trust back. We can't do that if you come in here and start breaking the most important rule by sneaking around with Isabelle."

"I'm not sneaking around with Isabelle. We were merely talking." At the man's doubtful look, Rhett added, "Very quietly. Listen, why don't you sit down and tell me what rule you're talking about?"

Wesley sat on the edge of Rhett's bed. "It's spelled out in the nonfraternization clause in the rental agreement you signed."

"Well, that explains why I'm confused. I haven't seen a rental agreement let alone signed one. For the moment, I'm a guest, not a boarder. I'm supposed to decide if I'm going to stay here or not by the end of the week. What does the clause say?"

"Well, I don't remember the exact wording. The gist of it is that flirting or getting too friendly with the Bradley girls can be grounds for eviction."

Rhett frowned. "Is that legal?"

Wesley shrugged. "It's Mr. Bradley's house. I guess he can make the rules."

"Flirting I can understand, but what qualifies as being too friendly?"

"I don't want to find out. Rule of thumb? Better safe than sorry, so keep your distance. I do know one thing, though. You should be glad that I'm the one who saw y'all in hallway a moment ago and not her parents." Wes combed his fingers through his hair and sighed. "I'm sorry if I was rude to you. I guess I get a little overprotective when it comes to this family. They're nice people. I don't want to see them hurt again."

Rhett nodded. "I understand, and I appreciate the warning."

Wesley finally offered a smile along with a handshake. "In that case, I guess this is a little late, but welcome to Bradley Boardinghouse. I'm Wesley Brice. Most folks call me Wes."

"Thanks. I'm Rhett Granger." He shook the man's hand as a bell rang through the house.

"That means supper is ready." Wes eyed the crutches. "Are you joining us downstairs?"

"Yeah, but you go ahead. It might take me a while to get there."

Rhett waited until Wes left before releasing a sigh. The news about the nonfraternization clause certainly complicated things. It also made Rhett feel incredibly guilty. While the interaction Wes saw had been innocent, Rhett couldn't deny that he had designs on Isabelle. They were honorable, probably somewhat foolish and ill-fated designs—but designs nonetheless. He understood the reasoning behind Mr. and Mrs. Bradley's rule and had every intention of following it as long as he stayed at the boardinghouse. That meant if he was truly planning to court Isabelle then he needed to find someplace else to live before he began. Until then, it might be wise to do as Wes had suggested by keeping his distance.

Isabelle rang the triangle bell again as Wes and Hank descended the stairs and entered the dining room together. The front door opened then slammed shut behind Peter, who hurriedly draped his coat and hat on the coatrack. She called a greeting to him. He smiled then ducked his head. Her father emerged from the family wing of the boardinghouse. He gave her a quick hug since it was the first he'd seen her since he'd returned from the hotel, then followed Peter into the dining room. Isabelle moved to the foot of the stairs. She was still missing two.

Gabe finally breezed past her muttering something about how meals always came at the most inopportune times. She put the triangle aside and was about to check on Rhett when he appeared at the top of the stairs with his crutches in tow. She frowned up at him. "You aren't really going to go down the stairs on those, are you?"

"Sure am. They're how I got up here in the first place." He placed his crutches on the first step and lowered himself down.

She rushed up to the step that was only two below his. "Did Doc approve this?"

"And your mother." He repeated the process.

"Well, I don't like it one bit." She narrowed her eyes at him. "Are you laughing at me?"

"I would never."

She tilted her head to capture his gaze. As she'd suspected, his amber eyes sparkled with laughter. "This isn't funny. You hurt yourself by running down stairs to begin with."

"I'd hardly call this running." He tried to place his crutches on the next step, but she hadn't moved back yet. "Isabelle, if you don't stop hovering, I'm going to break both our necks."

She backed away, but stayed close enough to steady him if need be. She let out a sigh of relief when he finally reached the ground floor. He eyed her as he paused to catch his breath. "Please, tell me you don't plan to do that every time."

"Next time I won't look. Come on. Supper is getting cold. Find a seat and I'll fix a plate for you."

As usual, there were multiple conversations happening rather loudly as Isabelle stepped into the dining room with Rhett trailing behind her. She pulled out a chair for him and took his crutches as he sat. Her father appeared at her side to relieve her of them. "Rhett, I'm glad you could join us this evening. I hear you've been able to make your way upstairs."

"Yes, sir. The study is all yours again. I just need to move a few of my things out of there."

"No hurry. It's good to see you up and moving around." Thomas left to store the crutches out of the way.

Violet stepped up to hand Rhett a glass of lemonade. She caught Isabelle's gaze and lifted an inquiring brow. Realizing Violet wanted to know if they'd found the bracelet, Isabelle shook her head. Violet gave a single disappointed nod. Isabelle quickly filled a plate for Rhett and placed it on the table in front of him. He glanced up with a smile. "Thank you."

Gabe slid into the chair at his other side. "Did you say something to me?"

Rhett turned to look at the man. "No. I was thanking Isabelle for the plate. I don't think I've met you before."

"I don't think you have, either." The man flashed an easy grin. "My name is Gabriel Noland. Most everyone calls me Gabe. You have an interesting face."

"I— What?" Rhett sent her a confused look.

Isabelle bit the insides of her cheeks to keep from laughing. She was about to remind Gabe not to start conversations like that when she caught sight of his dinner roll. She placed a hand on his shoulder. "You didn't wash your hands."

"How would you know?" He followed her gaze to the black fingerprints on the bread. "It's charcoal. It's perfectly harmless."

"You know the rules. Go wash up. Hurry, now." She waited until Gabe heaved a tortured sigh and walked off mumbling to himself before she left to prepare her own plate. By the time she sat down in the empty chair beside Rhett, Gabe had returned and was campaigning for Rhett to sit for a sketching. The ringing of a spoon against a glass brought everyone to attention. Mr. Bradley cleared his throat. Everyone bowed their heads.

As they prayed, Isabelle couldn't help sneaking a glance at the boarders. How could one of them have stolen from her family? She hated suspecting any of them. Part of the reason she'd hoped to find the bracelet in one of their rooms was so she could clear the others of suspicion. Unfortunately, there had been no trace of it. She needed to face the fact that she'd probably never find it. Whoever had taken it had likely sold it or sent it away somewhere by now. How much longer did she have before her parents asked about the bracelet?

That question haunted her all the way through supper and the parlor games afterward. It was only when she found herself alone in the study with Violet that she allowed herself to vocalize it. Violet frowned as they stripped down the temporary bed that Rhett had been using. "I don't know. I suppose they've forgotten about it after everything that happened with the fire and Rhett staying here. I overheard Pa saying there's been some trouble at the hotel between him and his partner. I'm sure they're preoccupied by that, as well. I'm more concerned about what we're going to tell them when they finally do ask about it."

Isabelle shook her head. "I guess I'll say I lost it. That's the truth, after all. I just didn't realize it until you found it and it got stolen."

"That's probably for the best."

She took the sheets Violet handed her and dumped them into the small laundry basket she'd brought for that purpose. She scanned the room to make sure everything had been set to rights. Rhett's belongings had already been moved upstairs, so the only trace he'd been there was the mattress in the middle of the floor. Her father had told them that he'd move it later. Isabelle set the basket on her hip in preparation to leave and managed to knock a few things off the desk in the process.

She set the basket on the floor as Violet hurried to help her gather the loose business papers. Isabelle reached for one of the folded newspapers then froze. She finally picked it up for a closer look and felt her heart sink in her chest. "Violet, look. This is a Virginia newspaper."

Violet leaned closer. "Those are job listings!"

"None of the ones circled have anything to do with boardinghouses, either."

"Let me see that."

Isabelle surrendered it to her then immediately regretted doing so when the girl left the room. Isabelle hurried after her sister. "What are you doing?"

"I'm going to ask our parents a few questions." Violet walked down the main hall toward the kitchen, where their parents often sat and talked at the end of the day.

Isabelle caught her arm. "I'm not sure that starting more conflict is a good idea."

"Don't you want to know what's going on?"

"We already do. Violet, we can fight this, but not by fighting them."

"Then how?"

"I don't know, but let's put the paper back. If you want to ask about it, do so when we're not upset."

Violet handed the paper to her. "Here. Take it, then. I'm going to go to my room and…and write very angry things in my journal."

Isabelle couldn't help but smile at that as her sister stormed away. Alone in the hall, she sighed. Ever since Amy's elopement, life for her family and their boardinghouse seemed to be getting increasingly complicated. Now this…

She looked at the newspaper again and realized it was several weeks old. Perhaps her parents had already abandoned the idea. Or maybe her father had already applied for these positions and was waiting to hear back from his potential employers.

She shook her head. She couldn't even think about that. The boardinghouse was too important—not only to her family, but to her future. Obviously, she wasn't the kind of girl to draw genuine interest from men. Since she didn't want to settle for less than that, marriage was highly unlikely for her. She was counting on the boardinghouse to be her means of income and security for the future.

It still could be. As far as her parents knew, "one more thing" hadn't happened yet. They wouldn't find out that it had, either. She just had to make sure nothing *else* happened. Of course, she hadn't done a very good job of stopping anything from happening so far. Despite that, she wouldn't concede defeat on the boardinghouse until her whole family and everything they owned were settled in Virginia.

She had a lot of fight left in her yet. That was good, because it looked as if she was going to need it.

Chapter Six

Rhett's plan to keep his distance from Isabelle had lasted about as long as it had taken him to reach the stairs last night before supper. Today, he was determined to do better. He managed to make it almost to dinnertime before he found himself alone with her in the parlor. Sitting in the window seat, he stared across Main Street at a familiar building. "You know, the great thing about this house is that I can see my smithy from practically every window."

She left the towels she was folding on the nearby settee to peer out the window beside him. "Are you sure that's a good thing? You don't exactly sound happy. You sound more..."

"What?"

She searched his face. "Desperate."

"I guess I am. I've even been trying to convince myself that I can handle my tools and my crutches at the same time."

"Don't. You know better than anyone how dangerous your work can be." She shook her head before returning to the pile of laundry. "I've burned myself a couple of times while cooking and that was from metal that was completely solid. I can't imagine handling metal hot enough that you can shape it while trying to balance on crutches. As far as I've heard, most of your customers are helping with the cleanup of your house. I'm sure they'll understand that you need to take some time off."

He sighed. "I know. It's just hard to sit here and not be able to work or begin to put my life back into some semblance of order."

"Surely there are other ways you can do that without risking further injury."

"Maybe." He thought about it for a minute then nodded. "There are a few practical things. For instance, I need to take care of some business at the bank. I should survey the damage on my property at some point. I also ought to pick up a few things from the mercantile. And I promised the sheriff I'd help recruit some talent for the benefit I told you about."

"All of those things will definitely help you move forward. We can do them today if you want." She paused then gave him a rueful smile. "I didn't mean to invite myself along, but I'd be happy to help you if you'd like."

He might have refused her offer, but he'd been on crutches long enough to know how challenging it could be to do simple things for himself. "That would be great. Are you sure you wouldn't mind? What about your parents? I'd hate to take you away from your duties."

"Of course I don't mind. I'm sure my parents won't, either. I just need to finish folding this pile and put it away, then we can leave."

"Here. I can help you with that." He took the ends

of the sheet she offered him. Each fold brought her closer to him. He lowered his voice even though her mother was in the kitchen and her father was across the hall in the study. "By the way, I think we can take Wes off of our list of suspects."

"We can? Why?"

Wes seemed too loyal to her family to betray them by stealing—unless he'd said that to throw Rhett off the scent. Then again, there was no reason anyone would suspect Rhett knew anything about the stolen bracelet. Nor did Wes have to warn Rhett about the nonfraternization clause. But Rhett couldn't exactly explain all of that to Isabelle. "Trust me."

She gave him a curious look along with another sheet to help her fold. "All right, but what about the others? Did any of them raise your suspicions last night?"

"Honestly? It was kind of hard to tell. They all came across as a little…" He searched for a diplomatic way to put it.

A hint of a smile touched her lips. "A little what?"

"Strange."

She laughed. "They all seemed perfectly normal to me, so that doesn't help."

"No, it certainly doesn't." He rubbed a hand over his face. "What are you going to do if we don't find the bracelet?"

She set the sheet aside and folded a fluffy white towel. "Honestly? I'm not really expecting to find it anymore. It's been too long. Whoever had it has probably sold it by now."

"To whom? This town didn't have any pawnshops the last I'd heard. The sheriff keeps a pretty tight rein on everything else."

"I don't know." With everything folded, she stacked it back in the laundry basket. "Maybe they gave it to someone or mailed it somewhere."

"Then perhaps there's a chance we can get it back."

Her green eyes met his. Shaking her head, a slight smile curved her lips. "Why won't you let me give up on this?"

He leaned forward. "Isabelle, if someone thinks they got away with it this time, then there's no guarantee it won't happen again."

"I hadn't thought of that."

"I'm not sure how long I'll be living here. However, I'd rather you face the thief while I'm here than when it's just you and Violet on your own—especially since you don't want to tell your parents."

"All right. We'll try to find out who did it, even if we don't end up finding the bracelet." She abandoned the basket to sit beside him in the window seat. "Searching the rooms didn't help."

"You didn't search Gabe's."

She rolled her eyes. "He's hardly ever leaves his room, so I'm not likely to, either."

"Looking for suspicious behavior didn't work." He frowned. "What else can we do?"

They shared a moment of thoughtful silence before Isabelle suddenly straightened. "Motive. We need to find a motive."

"But it was probably a crime of opportunity."

She shrugged. "Even so, there had to be a reason for someone to take it rather than return it."

"That's true. My first guess would be money. My second would be to use it as a gift for a woman since it's jewelry."

"None of the boarders are courting anyone as far as I know, and I'm pretty sure I would know because they're with me all the time. Let's focus on who might need money."

He smiled. "Besides everyone and anyone?"

"Right." She groaned. "How are we ever going to figure this out?"

"Let's try to cross people off the list of suspects. We already eliminated one."

She lifted a brow. "For reasons you won't disclose."

"Exactly." He grinned. "So who should we focus on next?"

"What about Gabe? He's an artist. Paint supplies are pretty expensive. He might have been running short. On the bright side, he thinks your face is interesting and offered to sketch you. That means you have a reason to seek him out. You can talk to him and try to figure out how he's doing."

"Perfect."

"Your sarcasm is duly noted. But, since I'm going along with you on finding the thief, I think it's only fair of you to get started on your courting lessons right away."

Rhett wasn't at all sure how finding the thief was suddenly *his* idea when Isabelle and Violet were the ones who'd come up with it. He also didn't remember officially agreeing to the courting lessons. Still, there was a hint of desperation in her voice that was utterly intriguing. He wouldn't mind spending time with her even if she was preparing to foist him on some poor unsuspecting friend of hers. Deciding not to be insulted by her downright eagerness to do so, he finally gave in.

* * *

Isabelle couldn't believe how little of a fight Rhett had put up about the courting lessons. She'd prepared herself to do some major convincing, but hadn't had to. It was encouraging to see someone so eager to better themselves. It was also a relief to know he was putting that little matter of their kiss behind him to focus on finding another woman.

She sorted the linen onto its appropriate shelves before hurrying out the closet door. At least, she tried to hurry out the door. It refused to budge. The problem wasn't a new one, and she knew exactly what to do. She turned to the right, then knocked on the wall loudly and repeatedly. She heard a hinge creak in the next room. She automatically stepped back as the door was shoved open from the outside. By the time she stepped into the hallway, it was empty. "Thanks, Gabe. I'll try to remember to tell my pa to fix that."

There was no response, but then she hadn't expected one. She dropped by the kitchen long enough to let her mother know she was going to help Rhett with a few errands and wouldn't be eating dinner at home. They stopped by the bank first then headed to Maddie's Café. As soon as Rhett entered the café, he was approached by Judge Hendricks, Mr. and Mrs. Greene, and several others who expressed their concern for him and commiserated about the loss of his house.

Isabelle gave Rhett a few moments to respond to each of them before shooing them all away as kindly as possible. She had no doubt he must be tired from all the walking and probably wanted nothing more than to sit down at the nearest table. The grateful smile he gave her when he finally sat down told her she was right. She leaned his crutches against the wall then grabbed two menus from a nearby table. "Do you need one?"

He shook his head. "I'm pretty sure I have it memorized."

"I've never been here for dinner before." She glanced around at the café. Its pine tables gleamed in the sunlight that streamed through the large front window. The cheery bell over the door chimed every few moments to announce the arrival or departure of a customer. "If I come here, it's to visit with friends, so I normally order a slice of pie and some coffee."

He nodded toward her menu. "Take your time. I'm in no rush."

As she perused the menu, a strange awareness seeped through her. Something about being in the café felt odd to her. It wasn't because she was ordering dinner, either. She'd never been here with a man before. At least, not while sharing a meal together. Alone. Of course, they weren't really alone. They were surrounded by a room full of chaperones. Still, it felt rather scandalous.

She stole a glance at Rhett. He seemed unaffected as he browsed the menu despite his earlier claims about having it memorized. An errant wave of dark hair fell over his brow, which furrowed slightly in concentration while he worried his bottom lip. The door opened, allowing a shaft of light to trace its way across the angles of his stubble-laden jaw. He must have felt her gaze on him, for his amber eyes lifted to capture hers. He lifted a questioning brow and smiled. "Know what you want?"

She rubbed the nape of her neck as she edged out

a nervous smile in return. "Perhaps this dinner was a bad idea. We don't want to give anyone the wrong impression."

"Nonsense." He leaned forward and lowered his voice. "You promised me courting lessons. That's why you're here. You can't back out on me, Teach."

"Well, we don't have to do them right now."

"Why not? We're already here. We'll get to them as soon as we order." He waved at Maddie, who immediately began to wind her way through the tables toward them.

Isabelle frantically glanced down to survey her menu. "I'm not ready yet."

"Sorry. When in doubt, go for the special. Isn't that right, Maddie?"

"Absolutely." The pert brunette grinned as she set two glasses of water on the table for them. "Today, it's chicken potpie."

Isabelle handed Maddie her menu. "I'll take it."

"So will I." Rhett offered Maddie his menu while adding two sides and two drinks to their order. "Before you go, Maddie, have you heard anything about anyone willing to sell or rent a place in town?"

She set the menus on her hip. "My husband is willing to do either with the place he lived in before we were married. Should I tell Jeff you might be interested?"

He nodded. "Sure. Tell Deputy Bridger I'd like to view the property. Meanwhile, if anyone asks, I'm willing to sell the lot my house was on."

Isabelle could hardly wait until Maddie left to ask, "You really aren't planning to stay at the boardinghouse?"

He shook his head as he traced a pattern in the condensation on his water glass. "Not for the long haul."

"Why not? Don't you like it there?"

"Of course I do. The room is great. Your family is wonderful. The boarders seem…"

She rolled her eyes. "I know. You told me. A little strange."

He chuckled. "Yeah. It's just that I'm used to having a place of my own."

"Well, that's…"

"Disappointing?"

Strangely enough, that was exactly the word she'd been searching for. She had no reason to be disappointed, though, so she amended, "Understandable. I suppose. How long are you planning to stay with us?"

"I don't know. It depends on how long it takes me to find another place and what kind of agreement your father and I work out."

She nodded, but knew better than to delve into the business side of the boardinghouse. Her father had made it clear that subject was off-limits to his daughters. She would hardly know what a rental agreement looked like let alone what the normal terms were. "I take it from your conversation with Maddie that you aren't interested in rebuilding your old place."

"Starting from scratch would take too long." He waited for Maddie to deliver their food then said grace before continuing. "If a man is serious about getting married, he ought to have a house for his wife to live in. Don't you agree?"

She barely held back a frown. He sure seemed to be putting a lot of faith in her efforts to help him, considering he hadn't even liked the idea to begin with.

Knowing better than to look a gift horse in the mouth, she nodded. "I suppose so."

"How about we get started, then?"

"All right. Why don't you tell me when and how your problem began? That way, we'll have a better idea of how to fix it."

"That's a good idea, but I'm afraid it won't be that easy."

"Of course not," she mumbled as she took her first bite of chicken potpie.

"What's that?" When she shook her head, he continued, "I've tried to pinpoint the moment it started a hundred times. I never can because I've always been shy in that respect. I thought I'd outgrow it, but it seems to get worse as I get older."

That wasn't very helpful. It also made Ellie's advice pretty much unusable. Apparently, she was on her own in this. She frowned and tried a new tactic. "All right. Take me through what happens. You see a girl you might be interested in. What are your first thoughts and actions and so forth?"

"My first thought…" He stopped eating to stare out the window unseeingly. "It would probably be along the lines of *this could be my future wife*."

She nearly dropped her fork. "Wait. Is this before you've even met her?"

"Usually." A slow smile tilted his lips in response to her disbelieving look. Tilting his head, he shrugged. "What? I'm not ashamed to admit it. Love happens quickly in my family. My parents got married after knowing each other two weeks. My grandfather knew my grandmother was the one for him the moment he laid eyes on her. He just *knew*. And he was right."

"Rhett, if that happens *every* time you see someone you like, how can it be real?"

"It doesn't happen every time. And even when it does happen, I'm never completely sure. I think *maybe* she's the one. That 'knowing' thing only happened once."

"Really? What happened to that girl?"

He took a sip of coffee then shrugged. "Let's just say she didn't agree."

Amy. It must have been Amy. Poor man. Her elopement really broke his heart. No wonder he was so quick to latch on to me. She lowered her gaze to her plate and tried to figure how to get their conversation back on track. "Let's keep going. After that thought, what comes next?"

"Either I panic and avoid her, or approach her then panic and make a fool of myself."

She nodded, having witnessed it herself when he'd been sweet on Amy. "It seems to me that it all hinges on the idea that you are interacting or are about to interact with the future Mrs. Granger. You're putting extra pressure on yourself."

"The future Mrs. Granger. I like that." He grinned. "I reckon you might have a point, at that. So what do I do?"

"Stop thinking of each woman as your future mate. Women are merely people. Even if you know from the start that you're interested in someone, you will still need to get to know her, woo her and court her."

"I understand what you're saying, but how will I get to that point if I treat her just like any other person?"

"Well, once you get past the initial get-to-know-you stage, things will change. Right now, we need to find a way for you to be comfortable having conversations with her."

His eyes widened in panic. "What do you mean *with her*? Who is *her*?"

"Whomever you choose."

"I—" His eyes darted around the room as though a woman would materialize out of thin air to jump out at him. His mouth opened then closed without a sound. Finally, he pulled himself together enough to frown. "Conversations? As in, more than one?"

She groaned. Her hands covered her eyes then came to rest near her temples. She stared at him, realizing that this was going to take forever. That should have been all right since the point of this exercise was to distract him and get him focused on someone else. However, she didn't think it would be wise to keep spending so much time with him. It was getting harder to ignore the way her heart fluttered every time he gave her one of his soulful looks or grinned or made her laugh.

No. She was fine. Perfectly fine. She might not know all that much about romance, having learned only by watching her parents or Amy, but she did know that pure physical or even emotional attraction did not a courtship make. Not that she was thinking in terms of a courtship concerning Rhett. Or a courtship with anyone really because she'd have the boardinghouse and that was all she'd ever wanted or needed. It was just that…

She shut down her wayward thoughts by focusing on the task at hand—which seemed monumental. "Rhett, we have so much work to do."

He stared right back at her for a long moment with

unusually inscrutable amber eyes. At first she was afraid she'd offended him. However, as he focused on his dinner, she couldn't shake the odd sense that he was satisfied with himself. Why shouldn't he be? He was getting help. All she was getting was a headache.

Chapter Seven

Rhett paused outside Gabe's door and glanced down the hall toward the stairs where Isabelle stood. She made a little shooing motion with her hands to urge him onward. With a sigh, he knocked on the door. Gabe opened it a moment later and nearly plowed Rhett over. Rhett hopped on his good foot until he was able to regain his balance. Meanwhile, Gabe blinked at him. "Oh, it's you. I thought Isabelle was stuck again."

"What?" Rhett glanced toward Isabelle for clarification only to find she'd abandoned him to his own devices.

"Have I missed dinner, then? What time is it? Where is my watch?" Gabe began digging through his pockets then gave up and patted his flat stomach, smearing paint across his disheveled shirt. "How long has it been since breakfast? Oh, well. It doesn't matter. I'll eat later."

Concern wrinkled Rhett's brow. What if Gabe didn't have enough money to buy dinner, the one meal not provided as part of the rent? "Why don't you eat now?"

Gabe shrugged. "Too busy. What did you say you wanted?"

"Well, I can't do much with my ankle the way it is. I thought that if you still wanted to do a portrait of me, we could arrange—"

Gabe's eyes lit up. "Ah, yes! The portrait. Come in."

Rhett expected to walk into a cluttered, chaotic room. Instead, it was exceptionally tidy. Light flooded the room from an uncovered window. The furniture was artfully arranged. A few canvases that seemed to hold finished works were neatly stacked on one side of the room while the unfinished ones were lined up against the adjoining wall. Another wall was filled with nothing but sketches. Gabe flipped through a large sketchbook then displaced a canvas to set it on the easel. "Come and stand over here so I can see you better."

"Oh, I didn't mean right now. I actually have an appointment to see a house I'm interested in renting…" He trailed off as he stepped close enough to see a rendering of his own face staring back at him from a piece of paper. Well, it was his face minus a nose. And the eyes were only faintly drawn in. "You've already started."

"Yes, step back a couple of paces. Thank you." Gabe began to draw. "I did a few preliminary sketches from memory. I needed a closer look at your nose. I also haven't decided on an expression I want for the final rendering. Or maybe I'll do a couple of different ones so you can have one for yourself."

"What are they for?"

"No frowning, please. They're for study. Truth be told, I'm more interested in doing at least one painting of you at the smithy once you're well enough to work. It would be for a new series featuring life in the West. I believe it would be of great interest to those back East."

Rhett leaned over slightly to rest on his crutches. He didn't want to sit down and give Gabe the idea that he'd be staying any longer than necessary. Then again, perhaps Rhett could get the answers he needed now and not have to worry about it later. "Is that where you're from?"

"Yes."

Sensing that was all he'd get out of the artist on that front, he switched tactics. "I've never known an artist before."

Gabe smiled but never broke concentration. "We're a strange species."

"How does it all work? You paint something, then what happens?"

"Hopefully, you sell it."

"But how do you find someone to buy it? In my business, you hang up a sign and let word get around about what you're doing, and then hope someone will show up with work for you."

Gabe's pencil hovered over the paper as he tilted his head to survey Rhett. "Actually, it's much the same for me. My work is my advertisement. I hope those who see it or buy it will tell others about me to generate more sales. I've been working on commission for a client who owns a gallery in Houston. However, more often than not, I try to sell my paintings on my own. When I paint a person into my work, I usually do more than one painting so that they can buy one if they wish."

"So if you did one of the smithy, I'd have a chance to purchase it? How much would it cost?"

Gabe quoted a price that was more than a little impressive, before asking Rhett not to talk for a few minutes. Rhett was glad for some time to collect his thoughts. It certainly didn't sound like Gabe was struggling. Nor did he seem to have much of an interest in anything outside his world of art. So much so that the man might walk right past a bracelet sitting on the floor without taking the time to notice it just as he'd nearly run into Rhett a few minutes ago. It was hard to believe that Gabe was capable of stealing the bracelet. Then again, Rhett was no detective. He could easily be wrong about Gabe—and Wes for that matter. Still, it would probably be best to move the investigation on to the other two boarders.

"I'm finished for now. Like I said earlier, my real interest lies in painting you at the smithy. When do you think you'll be back there?"

"I still have another week and a half on these." He lifted one of the crutches while balancing on his good leg."

Guilt flushed Gabe's face as he seemed to take stock of Rhett's crutches for the first time. "I'm sorry. I wasn't even thinking about that. I should have offered you a seat."

"That's all right," Rhett said even as he took the chair Gabe dragged over to him. He might as well rest for a few seconds before he made the somewhat difficult journey down the stairs. "To answer your question, I'll probably be back at the smithy week after next. I'll be pretty busy so I probably won't have time to do any posing."

"I just want to get a feel for the place and brainstorm some ideas at first. You won't even notice I'm there."

"I don't have a problem with you coming, then. You should have plenty of material." Rhett glanced at his watch and stood. "I'd better head out for that appointment."

Gabe followed him to the door. "A new residence, you said. I take it you aren't planning to stay here, then? Pity. It's a nice place."

"So you like it here?"

"Sure. The Bradleys are great. They treat their boarders like family. Not to mention they put up with my distracted, messy self."

"I heard there was some trouble a while back—what with Amy eloping and all."

Gabe grimaced. "Yes, indeed. Of course, I kept my nose out of it since it was none of my business. I'm surprised we didn't experience more fallout from that than we did."

"What do you mean?"

"Even I could tell the family seemed stunned and disillusioned. For a while there I was afraid they might shut down the whole operation and I'd have to look for new place to live. Happens all the time with boardinghouses, you know. They don't always give you back any rent you might have paid in advance, either."

"Have you lived in many boardinghouses, then?" Rhett knew that often boardinghouse thieves made their living by stealing from one boardinghouse after another.

"No, but I did my research before I came out here. It never pays to be ignorant when you're starting a new venture." Gabe glanced back into his room and Rhett could almost see him shifting gears. "Better get back to work. See you at supper."

"Sure." Rhett carefully made his way downstairs.

"There you are, Rhett!" Violet hurried over to him. She nodded her head to the parlor to show him that Wes and a few friends had taken up residence there, before she spoke quietly. "Isabelle told me you were doing a bit of investigating. Did you learn anything?"

"A little. I'd tell you more but I have an appointment to see a house across town. Unless… Do you and Isabelle want to join me? I wouldn't mind a female's opinion of it. If y'all are busy, we can talk later."

"No, we're not busy. Saturdays are a bit more relaxed for us. Besides, I've finished my chores. Let me check with Isabelle. I'll be right back."

Rhett made his way to a chair near the door of Mr. Bradley's study, knowing he'd need to conserve his energy for the trip to the potential new house. The door was ajar and, as Rhett sat down, he unexpectedly locked glances with the proprietor inside. The man stood from behind his desk and came to lean against the door frame. "Rhett, you're the man I wanted to see. I hear you won't be staying with us long, after all."

"I'm sorry, Mr. Bradley. I meant to tell you myself—"

"That's quite all right. I've been busy at the hotel this week, so I haven't been around the boardinghouse as much as I usually am. We actually sustained a bit of damage to the hotel roof from those wayward firecrackers. I had to make sure those repairs were handled."

Rhett frowned at the realization of how close he

and Isabelle had come to getting hurt up there. Or, rather, hurt worse. "I didn't know you were involved with the hotel."

"Yes, I've been something of a silent partner there for many years. However, I'm becoming less and less silent as time goes on, it seems."

Rhett nodded. So that was how Isabelle had known about the roof.

Mr. Bradley waved a dismissive hand. "That isn't what I wanted to talk you about, though. Have you decided where you'll stay once you leave here?"

"No, sir. I don't have a place yet."

"That's what I thought. You're still looking. That process might take you a while or it might not. In the meantime, I wanted to make the offer for you to stay on as a boarder on a week-to-week basis. That way you'd have somewhere to stay while you look for another place without having to make a long-term commitment. If you're interested, I can draw up the papers and have them ready for your perusal this evening."

"That would be great, Mr. Bradley."

"Excellent. This will give us a chance to convince you to stay after all." The man winked. "Ah, and here are my lovely girls. Where are you two headed?"

Violet grinned. "We're going with Rhett to look at a house."

Mr. Bradley frowned. "And point out all its flaws, I hope."

"I should have realized it would be a conflict of interest for y'all," Rhett said as he finally maneuvered to his feet. "Perhaps I should go alone."

"Nonsense," Isabelle said. "We'll be impartial. Besides, Pa is so convinced the boardinghouse will win you over that he provided his buggy so you won't have to walk. Isn't that so, Pa?"

"It's right outside. You're more than welcome to use it, though I don't know if there will be enough room with these two hitching a ride."

"Thank you, sir. I'm sure we can make it work."

"He's teasing. It's a four-seater, so there'll be plenty of space." Isabelle stepped backward to lead the way toward the front door. "Come on, y'all. Bye, Pa."

Rhett let them get a head start so he'd have room for his crutches then glanced at Mr. Bradley to offer a parting nod. The man was already watching him with penetrating green eyes. A smile more contemplative than warm appeared among his neatly trimmed gray beard and mustache. Mr. Bradley tipped his head toward his daughters. "Be careful."

"I, uh, will." Rhett waited for the man to close the door to his office before allowing his eyes to widen. He blinked then scratched his chin. Yep. He was pretty sure Mr. Bradley had just figured out exactly why he was looking for another place. Rhett had never been good at hiding his emotions. Still, he couldn't help wondering what had given him away. To his knowledge, he'd barely even looked at Isabelle during the entire exchange. He needed to do a better job of hiding his interest if he wanted to protect his blossoming friendship with Isabelle. She wasn't ready for the idea of a romance with him, and the last thing he wanted to do was scare her off.

Isabelle was ready to walk out the door with her coat, hat and reticule when she realized she and Violet were missing someone. Rhett seemed to have gotten stuck back by her father's office. At least, she assumed that was why he was staring at the floor with a thoughtful expression on his face. She grabbed Rhett's coat from the coatrack and waved the sleeve at him. "Hey, I thought you had someplace to be."

He blinked and glanced up with a sheepish smile. "Sorry. I was woolgathering."

His crutches sounded out a clacking rhythm on the wood floor until Violet took ahold of them so that he could slip an arm into his coat as he balanced on one foot. Isabelle helped him find the other sleeve then buttoned a few of the buttons for him. Violet handed him his crutches and placed his hat on his head. Isabelle set it at an angle that made even his grimace look dashing. Violet opened the door for him while Isabelle rushed ahead to open the garden gate.

She suspected she might be pushing it too far when she took hold of the reins as they all climbed into the buggy. She was right. After storing his crutches on the floor of the buggy, he took one look at her and said, "Absolutely not."

Her grip tightened on the slack leather. "But you're injured!"

"There's nothing wrong with my arms. Besides, when was the last time you drove a buggy? Oh, right. Never. And no. Watching your Pa drive does not count. Now, hand over the reins, Miss Adventure, and no one gets hurt."

She pressed her lips together, ruing the day he'd overheard her use that line on the livery owner. She'd refused to submit to the idea of being stuck in town when her father was out of town searching for Amy. Rhett had ended up driving her to Helen and Quinn's farm himself rather than letting her drive out on her own. He'd been none too cautious on the way, either—probably because she'd been complaining all the while. He seemed to read her mind for his voice gentled. "I promised your Pa I'd be careful with you two, and I will."

She sighed and released the reins. "Fine, but I'm sure I'd be a perfectly wonderful driver if I ever had the chance to learn."

"The problem is, you never ask to learn," Violet chimed in from the backseat. "You only ever ask to drive."

"I expect to be a natural."

Violet rolled her eyes. "I don't think that's how it works. We should get down to business, though. Rhett, what did you find out from Gabe?"

"He seems to be doing pretty well for himself." Rhett guided the horses into the traffic bustling on Main Street. "To be honest, I can't see him noticing the bracelet—let alone stealing it."

Violet nodded then sat back. "That leaves Peter and Hank."

It was still strange to think of either of them being thieves. Then again, Isabelle hadn't thought Hank would be capable of hiding contraband in his room. She should have taken the liquor out of his room and poured it down the drain. He wouldn't have been able to raise protest without exposing himself. Of course, leaving the bottles there meant her parents might eventually find them somehow. Would that discovery be enough to make her parents start packing?

Isabelle groaned. "I think maybe we've been going about all of this the wrong way."

Rhett's amber eyes clouded with concern as they sought hers. "What do you mean?"

"Even if we find the thief and the bracelet, we're simply buying time until the next crisis."

He turned his eyes back to the road but gave a nod of understanding. "The real problem is that your parents are ready to give up the boardinghouse at the slightest provocation."

Worry filled Violet's voice. "So what do we do? Give up? I don't want to move to Virginia."

Isabelle shook her head. "We're not giving up. I truly think we're making progress on the thief problem. We just need to do more to remind Ma and Pa of all the things they've enjoyed about running the boardinghouse."

Rhett turned off Main Street into a more residential part of town. "What do they enjoy?"

"Ministering through hospitality and service has always been a big draw for them. However, I think they already have a reminder of that in you, Rhett."

"Community," Violet suggested.

Isabelle nodded. "Yes, and that's something they've been shying away from recently because of what happened with Amy. They don't want our family as close to the boarders—at least, emotionally speaking. They can't do much about the lack of physical space in the house." She glanced at Rhett. An uneasy feeling filled her stomach as she realized how much personal family information to which they'd made him privy. She cleared her throat. "This is all confidential, of course."

"I'd never betray your confidence." He turned down another street lined with smaller houses on large lots.

"So y'all need something that will build community. Any ideas?"

"Actually, I do have one," Isabelle said then turned to look at her sister. "Remember how Ma and Pa used to love it when we did a talent show for them when we were little? What if we did one, but involved everyone in the boardinghouse?"

"I love that idea. To make it more interesting, perhaps we could have a twist of some kind so it wouldn't be too similar to the benefit the town is planning."

"Like what?"

"I'm not sure."

Rhett must have been searching for the right address for he slowed the buggy to a crawl. "How about we switch talents with each other?"

Isabelle's eyes widened. "You mean each person would have to perform someone else's talent for the show? That's brilliant. Don't you think so, Vi?"

"Stupendous!"

Rhett grinned. "Well, now that's settled, what are your first impressions of this house?"

It was the type of house folks in town had christened "Bachelor Boxes." Most of them had been built right after the railroad had swept through Peppin, and they were characterized by being small and sturdy with porches barely big enough for a chair and a spittoon. Most were made of wood. This was no exception, though the wood had weathered to a dull gray.

Rhett cleared his throat. "Well, the level of enthusiasm in this buggy plummeted, didn't it?"

"No, it really isn't bad." Isabelle bit her lip. "In fact, I think whitewashing it and painting the shutters a nice, bright color would make a world of difference."

Violet nodded. "Absolutely. It does look a bit small. However, I'm sure it would be fine for one person."

Rhett grunted. "I don't exactly plan to be alone forever."

Violet's blue eyes turned curious. "Are you planning to get married, Rhett?"

"Eventually. I doubt this house would help my case much." Rhett slid his searching gaze toward Isabelle as he maneuvered out of the buggy. "You really don't like it, do you?"

"We promised we wouldn't influence you, so I'm not saying another word. I can already see that we are coloring your opinion, so I think you should go in alone after all."

He set his crutches in place then gave them a slow nod. "All right. Don't go anywhere while I'm gone. No joyrides into the country."

She began to sputter a reply, but his wink turned it into nothing more than a huff. Violet's giggle was no help and probably only served to encourage him. They watched him walk up to the door and knock then waved at Deputy Bridger as he let Rhett into the house. Violet joined Isabelle in the front seat for warmth and Isabelle spread the blanket her father always kept in the backseat over their legs. "I hope I didn't ruin your fun if you wanted to go in, Vi."

"Honestly?" Violet sent her a guilty look. "I wasn't that interested in seeing the house. I wanted a chance to ride in the buggy. Pa uses it so rarely."

Isabelle laughed. "Well, I doubt Rhett will take this house if he's as serious about getting married as he seems."

"Who is he courting? Anyone I know?"

Isabelle shook her head. "He isn't courting anyone yet, but he wants to find someone soon."

Violet was quiet for a moment as though contemplating that before shrugging. "It doesn't hurt to be prepared, I suppose. I am a little surprised he got over Amy that quickly."

Isabelle eyed the Bachelor Box, thinking about the tone in Rhett's voice and the look in his eyes as he talked about that one girl he'd been certain he was going to marry. "What makes you think he's gotten over her? Even though he says he's looking for someone else, I don't buy it. Rhett may not have gotten to know Amy all that well, but she captivated him nonetheless. I doubt any woman is going to measure up to that ideal for Rhett or any of her suitors."

She could have added *especially not me,* but she didn't want her little sister to think she was feeling sorry for herself. She wasn't. She simply had a very clear picture of who she was and where she stood in the family. Amy had been the golden girl—beautiful, vivacious and a little too flirtatious for her own good. Violet was the dreamer—talented, creative and unnecessarily dramatic on occasion. Isabelle was the practical one—dutiful, responsible and boring. That wasn't to say she envied her sisters. Certainly not. She loved them for who they were. She simply wasn't all that satisfied with herself.

"Come now, Isabelle. Her powers of captivation weren't really that potent, were they?"

"It certainly seems like it at times."

Violet was quiet for a long moment as she tilted her head and narrowed her blue eyes. "How does a girl get that way? How does she make herself interesting and exciting and beautiful so that other people can't help noticing?"

Isabelle let out a hollow laugh. "I have no idea. Can you learn to be beautiful? I'm pretty sure it came naturally to Amy."

"Oh, she's pretty. There's no mistaking that, but I think she has the knack of knowing how to look her best without making it obvious that she's trying. She wears an inordinate amount of blue because it brings out her eyes and pastels because they set off her fair complexion. She styles her hair so that it's soft and romantic. Her clothes always fit her perfectly."

Isabelle couldn't help glancing down at the lilac dress that peaked out from beneath the coat she was wearing. It was a little too roomy in the chest area. It was also another one of Amy's castoffs. Didn't Isabelle have any of her own clothes? Why was she always dressed in Amy's? Frowning, she glanced at her sister. "Surely, it's more than appearance, though. Amy had such personality."

"Isabelle, everyone has a personality. Amy was comfortable and utterly unapologetic with hers." Violet snapped her fingers. "That's it. She was comfortable with herself, so people were comfortable being themselves around her."

Rhett wasn't. She blinked. What did that have to do with anything? Absolutely nothing. This wasn't a competition, so she needn't feel so smug about it, either.

Violet's eyes narrowed as she stared into the distance. "There was also a certain confidence about her—"

"All right, then." Isabelle softened her curt tone with a smile. Honestly, though, it felt as if she was suddenly in the buggy with John Merriweather rather than Violet. "I think we figured it out."

"Maybe. I'll have to give it some more thought."

Isabelle nodded and glanced at the door of the Bachelor Box wondering what was taking Rhett so long. "You do that."

"You know, our family hardly ever talks about Amy anymore. Don't you think that strange?"

"Not really. She eloped with a boarder who lied to our parents about who he was. That hurt them enough that they don't ever bring it up. On top of that, she lives in a different town, and she hardly ever writes."

Violet searched her eyes. "You're still angry at her."

Isabelle froze as realization wrapped around her. "I guess I am. I don't want to be."

"You really were as blindsided by the elopement as the rest of us, weren't you?"

"Of course I was. Yet, no one seemed to believe that after the elopement. Everyone assumed I would have known and that hurts even worse because I *should* have known. Amy and I were supposed to be close. We shared practically everything with each other. As far as I knew, she'd gotten over Silas and was interested in Rhett. Instead, she was pulling the wool over my eyes as much as she did everyone else's." Isabelle shook her head. "Worse than that, I ended up being her alibi without even realizing it."

"You did?" Violet frowned. "I didn't know that. No one ever told me exactly what happened that night. I only know that we found her letter explaining everything when you got home. How did she run away?"

"The two of us were supposed to be going to Ellie's shivaree together. She told me she suddenly developed a headache and turned back to go home. She ran off to get married instead, but our parents assumed she was with me, so they were none the wiser until I got back home later." Isabelle shifted in the seat so that she sat face-to-face with her sister. "She left, Vi. There was no warning, barely even a goodbye. Of course I'm angry. She broke my trust—our trust. On top of that, she left us in a mess. Now we might even lose the boardinghouse."

"I know," Violet whispered. "Out of everyone in our family I think this has probably been the hardest on you. In addition to our parents' suspicions, you've inherited Amy's chores and unwanted beaus. I see how you have every right to be upset, annoyed and frustrated. It's just—" Violet bit her lip. "I don't want all of this to change you."

"Change me?" She blinked in confusion. "Don't be silly. If I seem different, it's because everyone is treating me differently. I'm the same as I've always been."

Violet lifted a knowing brow. "Isabelle, no one is the same as they've always been. You, for one, are far more suspicious than you used to be."

"Yes, and I'm glad I am because I have very good reasons to be that way."

"I know." Violet gave her a sad little smile. "I only wish you didn't."

Isabelle squeezed her sister's hand, grateful for her show of support. "So do I, but don't worry about me. I'll be fine."

Violet was quiet for a long thoughtful moment before she sent Isabelle a sideways glance. "I know I'm probably getting on your nerves, but I have one more thing to say about Amy. No matter what she did, Amy is still our sister. She hasn't died or disappeared into thin air. I hate how everyone acts like she did because it makes them feel better."

Isabelle's words came out in a sigh. "You are absolutely right."

"I am?"

Isabelle nodded. "Yes. I might be angry and feel betrayed, but I've never stopped loving her. It just hurt less not to think about her. I guess that's selfish of me. If you want to write her, you should. I will, too… eventually."

"After you've forgiven her?"

"I guess so." Isabelle frowned at her sister. "Hey, when did you get so smart and grown-up?"

Violet gave a little shrug. "I *am* nearly sixteen. I haven't been a child for quite some time."

The clack of Rhett's crutches forestalled the teasing response she was preparing for her little sister. Isabelle turned to greet him with a smile. "How did it go?"

"All right. It's in good shape." He handed his crutches to Violet, who slid out to take her seat in the back, before he lifted himself onto the buggy. "There's definitely only room for one, though. I'll keep it in mind. Where to, ladies?"

Violet leaned forward and pointed. "Up there, to the left. Just beyond the clouds."

Rhett threw Isabelle an amused glance. She shrugged. "You heard the lady."

"That I did." He winked. "I'll do my best."

He kept them thoroughly entertained as they drove around, enjoying the day and the excursion. Later, as they finally climbed out of the buggy in front of her parents' house, Isabelle couldn't help reflecting on her conversation with Violet. Her sister was right. Isabelle was different. At least, she felt different. She felt…less—as though she'd put a guard up between herself and her emotions. That didn't have to be a bad thing, did it?

After all she'd been through, it was normal to want to protect oneself. However, it didn't seem to be working as well as it should. She had no problem feeling emotion when she was around Rhett. That was dangerous. It could also mean only one thing. It was time to find him a sweetheart. Past time, really. And she knew the perfect place to look.

Chapter Eight

Isabelle sure seemed distracted in church today. Rhett ought to know because he was finding it just as difficult to focus on the service as it seemed to be for her. Of course, it didn't help that he was sitting directly behind her. A few tiny curls had escaped her upswept bun. All service he'd been controlling the urge to blow on them to see if she'd jump.

He should be paying attention to Pastor Brightly's sermon rather than thinking like a schoolboy with a crush. He tried to do exactly that but the words seemed to bounce off his heart like a firefly trying to reach a lamp through a closed window. "There is no time limit on God's promises. When He gives His word, it stands forever."

Yeah, and sometimes they seem to take forever, too. Rhett grimaced at his rebellious thought right as Isabelle restarted the routine of craning her neck in different directions, providing a timely distraction. What *was* she looking at? What was more, why was it moving? First, she looked to the right. Then she looked slightly off center. Finally, to the left. It started all over again. This time he copied her. Right, center, left. Right, center... He froze. She wasn't watching something move. She was looking at different people. Women. Women who had one thing in common—they weren't married.

Ruth Milano was on the right. She'd recently brought several pots and pans to the smithy for mending. She was pretty enough with her raven hair and dark eyes. However, she seemed like the type of woman who wouldn't broker any nonsense from anyone, especially men. That pretty much disqualified him. Not that he wanted to be qualified.

Auburn-haired Lydia Kane sat a few pews up and slightly to the left. She was the town's seamstress. He'd heard she occasionally did a bit of tailoring on the side, which was why he'd gone to her for help with his pirate costume. She'd seemed nice, but there had been no spark between them.

Finally, on the far left, was Sophia Johansen. He knew her better than the others because he was good friends with her brother Chris. Sophia was sweet and cheerful, like a ray of sunshine. She was also the lone girl in her family, so if a man got any ideas about her, he'd have to contend with her parents and overprotective brothers. That made her off-limits.

In fact, all of them were off-limits. He didn't want to hurt any one of them by giving them the impression that he was interested in them. It wouldn't be fair to them. Not that he thought any of them would actually accept his suit. After all, no one had—ever. Not even Isabelle, which was why he wasn't technically pursuing her even if he was going out of his way to spend time with her and get to know her.

There also was the rather significant matter of the boardinghouse lease he'd signed yesterday by which he'd agreed to "refrain from even the most minor flirtation and/or excessive fraternization with any woman living within the Bradley Boardinghouse expressly and especially any female of the Bradley family under penalty of eviction." In other words, Rhett *really* needed to find another place to live. He was more than tempted to settle for the Bachelor Box he'd seen as a temporary solution in the hopes he'd find something more permanent later. However, even that wouldn't be available for several weeks. Then again, what was the rush? If he considered Isabelle's active search for a woman for him as any indication, she hadn't changed her mind about courting him. In fact, she seemed more determined than ever.

Once Pastor Brightly dismissed the congregation with a prayer, Rhett knew he needed to move fast if he wanted to avoid Isabelle's inevitable attempt at matchmaking. He almost made it to the church's foyer before he felt her stilling hand touch his arm. He barely held back a groan at how close he'd come to escaping, but he should have known the attempt would be a wasted effort. Outrunning a matchmaking woman was difficult on a good day. Being on crutches, he hadn't had a chance.

Isabelle smiled up at him. "Whoa. Slow down. Where are you going in such a hurry? I want to talk to you."

"Sorry. I was trying to get out of the flow of traffic." Glancing around to make sure he wasn't about to be trampled by an unobservant parishioner, Rhett caught Mr. Bradley eyeing Isabelle's rather lingering touch as he passed them. Rhett covered the panicked urge to remove Isabelle's hand by plastering on a polite smile. "If we're going to be talking, it would be easier for me if we sat down."

He followed her to the last row and waited for her to slide into the pew before settling beside her. "What's on your mind?"

"I found a few prospects for you." She spoke softly since several groups had decided to stay inside the sanctuary to converse rather than going out to brave the cold. "I thought we should discuss them now. That way I can introduce you to anyone you might not know."

"I suspected that's what you were doing all service—finding prospects for me."

"How did you know?"

He shrugged. "I sat directly behind you, so I could tell you were looking everywhere but the stage."

"Oh." She winced guiltily. "And now I'm realizing I didn't pay much attention to the sermon."

"I might as well confess... I didn't either."

"Were you thinking about prospects, too?"

"No, I was thinking about you." He felt his eyes widened in tandem with hers as he realized what had slipped out. "I mean, I was trying to figure out what you were looking at. That took me a while. Then I guess my mind started wandering..."

She nodded, which was good because he'd run out of excuses. "Well, from what I heard, it was a good sermon about...faith?" She shook her head. "This is horrible. It reminds me of when I was little and Amy would—" She bit her lip and glanced toward the church's frost-covered windows.

Wondering why she'd stopped, he prompted, "Amy would what?"

"She—she would always be able to tell when I wasn't paying attention in church. She'd tap my knee three times—sort of like rapping someone's knuckles, I suppose. She wouldn't do it hard, though, just enough to remind me to focus. Even at a young age, she took her faith very seriously. That inspired me to do the same." A gentle smile touched her lips as a faraway look entered her eyes. "She wouldn't let me get away with anything, though. It would annoy me to no end. If I got the least bit frustrated or anxious, she'd look at me and ask, 'Isabelle, have you been praying lately?' Usually, the answer was no. It would only annoy me more that she was right."

"Quinn and I do the same type of thing with each other on occasion. We all need to have someone in our lives who'll ask those tough questions."

"I don't. Have someone, I mean. Not anymore. Violet sometimes tries, but I want to help her and guide her like Amy did for me—not show her how weak I am."

He frowned and nudged her shoulder with his. "Hey, everyone is weak sometimes, Isabelle. It's important that Violet sees how to work through the times when our faith doesn't feel strong, too. But I understand what you mean about your role as the older sister. I think now that she's getting older y'all might find yourselves on more of an equal footing. In the meantime…" He cast about for a suitable solution.

She leaned back into the pew and sighed. "In the meantime, I still don't have anyone."

He was quiet for a long moment. Finally, he turned

toward her and leaned into the pew so that he was on the same plane she was. "So, Isabelle, have you been praying lately?"

She blinked then gave a little laugh even as her eyes glistened with unshed tears. She weaved her fingers through the curls at the back of her neck. "No. In fact, I can't remember the last time I actually did. I guess I should fix that. What about you?"

"It's been a while." He paused when a large hand landed on his shoulder then turned to find Sean standing in the aisle with an apologetic smile.

"I'm sorry to interrupt. Rhett, Lorelei is worried about the roast she left in the oven. We'd better head back to our place soon. Isabelle, you're welcome to join us for Sunday dinner. Rhett and I were going to talk about some business related to the fire and the benefit."

"I wish I could, but Ma is counting on me to help with supper."

Sean nodded. "Maybe next time, then. Rhett, I'll stall a little for you."

"Thanks, I'll be right there." He waited until Sean left before turning to Isabelle. "I'm sorry. I promised I'd have dinner with them."

Her shoulder lifted in a little shrug. "That's perfectly all right. I'll lay a little groundwork for you with those prospects I mentioned earlier, and we'll discuss them later. You'd better get going."

It was good advice. He'd be smart to heed it especially when it came to Isabelle. This whole conversation had started because she was trying to pair him up with another woman. Meanwhile, their friendship had him opening himself up and finding more reasons to like her. He was putting an awful lot of faith in his ability to woo her someday in the future. What else could he do? He'd run out of faith in everything else—at least when it came to love. There was nothing for him to do but press on. Even if he suspected that he was running full speed toward heartbreak.

Isabelle frowned as she stared at herself in the vanity mirror late that evening. Ignoring the brush, she raked her fingers through her hair until they interlocked among the strands, then pursed her lips to the side. Thoughts raced through her mind in a jumbled mix—most of them revolving around Rhett. She had to admit that it had been nice to have someone challenge her faith again. He'd done it in such a gentle way that she hadn't felt the least bit defensive. That seemed to be a pattern of his ever since New Year's Eve. He had a way of completely disarming her in the most unexpected ways whether through humor or warmth. It was disconcerting to say the least. She'd ended up revealing things to him that she hadn't even felt comfortable talking to Violet about. Stranger still, she'd felt totally at ease doing so.

They were getting too close, and that was making her nervous. After all, it was the exact opposite of what she'd been trying to accomplish by starting the courting lessons. She needed to find a woman for him and quick. She'd intended to do that at church this morning by introducing him to at least one of her friends. Instead, she hadn't even gotten as far as mentioning the names of his prospective matches.

She'd been rather relieved to look around the church and find that several ladies would do quite nicely for him. Of course, Sophia Johansen topped the list. Not only was she a sweet friend, but she had flaxen blond hair. No doubt there were a hundred other things more important than that—compatibility for one. Still, she couldn't help thinking that Rhett had a penchant for blondes. After all, Amy had been one. Isabelle supposed her own hair could be called blond, though it was dark enough that it looked brown in the right light.

She blinked. What did it matter what color her hair was? And why was she thinking about Amy so much recently? Perhaps it was a combination of Violet's earlier comments about her and being in church today. Church reminded her of Amy. Praying reminded her of Amy. Amy's beaus reminded her of Amy. Amy reminded her of Amy. This was ridiculous. She was getting worse than John Merriweather.

She automatically began to turn her thoughts elsewhere before stopping. *Why do I do that? Why do I avoid the very thought of my sister?*

The answer bloomed within her chest, a sharp stab of pain that only seemed to ache more as time went on. She didn't think about Amy because it hurt. It hurt badly. To numb that pain, maybe it was all right to avoid Amy's old beaus and ignore her parents' suspicious attitudes. However, she couldn't avoid or ignore God like she'd been doing for the past several weeks, if not months.

She needed to remember that her faith was as much its own entity from Amy as she was. She might not be willing to talk to Violet, unable to talk to her parents and nervous about talking to Rhett, but there wasn't anything holding her back from talking to God. She was just so out of practice that she wasn't entirely sure what to say to Him.

She was still trying to figure that out when she blew out the lantern, climbed into bed and stared into the darkness. She had to at least try to pray. If Rhett happened to ask her about it again, she wanted to be able to give a different answer. Closing her eyes, she forced out a whisper that felt clumsy and sounded tired. "Lord, I feel like there's a wall around my heart or maybe a callus or something. It keeps out everything and everyone—except for Rhett, which makes absolutely no sense. Can You reverse that, please? I don't mean— What I'm saying is… Oh, I don't know what I'm saying. Will You just help me feel something good for once? But not for Rhett…beyond friendship. That's all. Goodnight. I mean, amen."

Rolling her eyes at how ridiculous she sounded, she turned over and pulled the covers over her head. The ache in her chest remained, but she'd grown used to it, so it didn't keep her from drifting to sleep. She awoke to find the soft light of morning stealing through her room even as an odd sense of joy filled her heart. It didn't make a lick of sense. Nothing about her situation had changed. Yet, as she got dressed for the day, she found herself smiling anyway. This had to be an answer to the prayer she'd prayed last night. There was no other explanation for it.

With a new sense of confidence, she walked into the kitchen to help her mother and sister prepare breakfast. She was surprised find her father there, as well. He sat at the kitchen table with a cup of coffee reading the newest copy of his favorite Virginia newspaper, which his brother mailed to him regularly. The sight was a bit troubling since he usually made it a point to sit in the dining room and greet the borders as they trickled in for breakfast each morning. Resolving to stay positive, she walked over to kiss him on his bristly cheek. "Good morning, Pa. What brings you to the kitchen?"

He blinked in surprise at her affection, which made her feel incredibly guilty for not having shown it more often in the recent months. The guilt increased when he grinned in response. She suddenly realized the boardinghouse wasn't the only place that needed its feeling of community restored. Her father nodded toward his still-steaming cup of coffee. "I was just grabbing a cup of coffee before I head to the dining room."

"Oh." She must have sounded a bit too relieved for her mother looked up from scrambling eggs to give her a curious look. Isabelle smiled and wished her a good-morning before grabbing an apron off the hook. As she tied it on, she went over to greet her sister, who was pulling a pan of golden-topped biscuits from the oven. One look at her Violet's cloudy face had her asking lowly, "Is something wrong?"

Violet set the pan on the counter. She didn't bother to respond in a low tone, but sent an accusing look toward their father, whose face was blocked by the newspaper. "Pa is thinking about making a trip to Virginia. Is that right, Pa?"

Isabelle froze as her father's paper slowly lowered. He frowned at them. "That's right, Violet. I am."

"Why?" Isabelle frantically glanced at her mother, who continued cooking as though they were talking about nothing more important than the weather.

He turned the paper over to look at the back. "To look around."

"That's a long way to go merely to look around." Isabelle leaned back onto the counter as she waited for his response. When it didn't come, she pressed on. "What would you be looking for exactly?"

Her mother transferred the eggs onto a serving dish next to the bacon. "A house near one or both of our families."

"A boardinghouse?" she asked, for the sake of clarification.

Her father shook his head. "Just a house."

"But how would we live, then? Running a boardinghouse is all we know."

He folded the paper into crisp lines. "No. It's all *you* know. It isn't the only way I can support this family. Honestly, this matter is not up for discussion."

Isabelle controlled her rising temper with a sharp nod. "Fine. We won't discuss it. I simply ask that you wait before you take the trip."

"Wait for what?"

Wait for her to change his mind about moving, about the boardinghouse, about everything. She could hardly tell him that, so she cast about for something, anything to say to delay what was beginning to look like inevitability. Her gaze landed on Violet, who watched the exchange with tears building in her eyes. "Wait until Violet graduates this spring."

He shrugged. "She's almost done anyway. What does it matter where she finishes?"

"Maybe it doesn't matter to you," Violet said, clenching her fist. "But it matters to me!"

Beatrice set her spatula down with a clang. "Do not take that tone with your father, young lady."

"Why does my tone matter when it's obvious that you don't care what I think or feel or say anyway?" Violet grabbed her lunch pail and schoolbooks before brushing past all of them to leave without so much as a goodbye.

Silence reigned in the kitchen for what seemed an eternity until her father stood, taking his coffee with him. "Your mother and I know what's best for this family. It's high time you two realized that."

Isabelle wasn't likely to realize or agree to any such thing. He could visit Virginia all he liked. She wasn't ready to stop fighting for the boardinghouse yet. In fact, she was more determined than ever that she would find a way convince her parents to stay. She wouldn't give up yet. She couldn't.

A warm feeling surged through her, and she recognized it for what it was. Hope. Yes, she definitely had her feelings back. If God could give her that, then He'd find a way to keep her family from selling the boardinghouse and moving away. She was certain that He *could*, but how could she trust that He *would*?

She pushed her doubts away with the shake of her head. She shouldn't have trusted Amy. She knew better than to trust that any of Amy's suitors could have a genuine interest in her. She didn't trust her parents to know what was best concerning the boardinghouse since they were still overreacting to Amy's elopement. However, this was *God* she was talking about. Surely, He would see the situation clearly and not let her down. She could trust Him, so she *would* trust Him—and wear her knees out praying to make sure He knew exactly what she was trusting him with.

Chapter Nine

Rhett couldn't put it off any longer. The time had finally come and no amount of reasoning or procrastinating was going to change that. He had to go shopping. He'd prefer to do it next week when he'd be free of his crutches, but he'd plumb run out of clothes. Not that he'd had that many to begin with since all he'd had after the fire were the few things Helen and Quinn had bought him from the mercantile. Even the suit he'd worn on Sunday had been borrowed from Wes, who was the only man at the boardinghouse close to his size. However, just because the trip was necessary didn't mean he had to like it.

His thoughts must have shown on his face for he glanced over to find Isabelle watching him in amusement. He frowned at her. "Remind me why I asked you to come along again?"

"You needed a door opener and bag carrier." She pulled her navy coat closed against the cold wind that whipped down the street, then stopped in her tracks. "Don't you need clothes?"

He followed her gaze to see she'd stopped in front

of Sew Wonderful Tailoring. "The ready-made clothes at the mercantile will do fine."

"You'll still need a Sunday go-to-meeting suit."

"Yes, but I'd rather get my basics first."

"No use passing this place up. Come on." She tugged the door open, so he had little choice but to precede her inside.

Ruth Milano already had his measurements from the pirate costume she'd created for him, so it was only a matter of picking a style. They all looked pretty much the same to him, so it only took a few minutes to order what he wanted. Ruth made note of it before wishing them a good day. They'd barely made it out the door before Isabelle lifted her brows expectantly. "Well? What do you think about Ruth?"

He stopped to look at Isabelle. "Is that why you made me go in there? You wanted me to talk to Ruth?"

"I think she's a strong prospect for you. Plus, she's very pretty. Don't you think so?"

Now, how was he supposed to respond to that without boxing himself into a corner or insulting anyone? He swallowed and focused on placing the ends of his crutches on the wooden boards of the sidewalk. "Listen, Miss Meddlesome. I'm not interested in Ruth Milano."

"It isn't meddling. It's helping. If you aren't interested in her, then I believe my suspicions about you must be correct." The knowing tone in her voice stopped him in his tracks.

Panic tightened his chest. "What suspicions?"

She tilted her head and fluttered her lashes knowingly. "You prefer blondes."

"What?" He gave a laugh that was a little too hollow to sound anything but nervous. "What are you basing that on?"

"Amy and… Well, just Amy." She lifted her chin in pure challenge. "Look me in the eye, and deny it. I bet you can't."

He couldn't. It was true. He did prefer one blonde in particular. Although, *blond* was too simple of a way to describe her hair. It was richer than that, more like burnished gold. A strand of it came loose in the wind, taunting him to tuck it back into place. His hands tightened around the handles of his crutches. He lowered his chin and swept her face with his gaze before murmuring, "You're a nervy little thing, you know that?"

The gold from her hair seemed to spill into her green eyes as she laughed. She lifted one shoulder in a shrug in cadence with a flash of her eyebrows. "Hmm. By all means, let's proceed to the mercantile."

He frowned to let her know that he was onto her games. A graceful sweep of her hand urged him to continue down the sidewalk. He did so with caution. She opened the door of the mercantile for him, the jingle of the bell above the door announcing their entrance. Sophia Johansen popped up like a jack-in-the-box from behind the front counter to greet him. He blinked as light from the window illuminated her blond hair, turning it a shade close to white. Isabelle stood on her tiptoes, whispering as she passed, "She works every Monday afternoon, in case you were wondering."

He hadn't been. He watched Isabelle sashay forward to greet her friend with an over-the-counter hug. Their words drifted past him like water in a brook— loud enough to hear the babble, but too fast to catch anything. Or perhaps it was his mind that was moving too slow. Any minute now, Isabelle would expect him to come over and talk to Sophia. He should have thought this through before. He hadn't, so now he had no idea what to do.

Sophia glanced over at him and smiled. He suddenly realized that he felt no panic. Absolutely none. He hadn't felt any around Ruth, either. He had no reason to. He knew neither of them was going to be his future wife. He saw the women as he always did. Ruth was an acquaintance. Sophia was a friend—or, more accurately, the sister of his friend. His hopes on the courtship front concerned Isabelle. Consequently, as long as he was interested in her, he wouldn't panic with any other women. What was more, one of the growing plethora of reasons he was interested in Isabelle was because he *didn't* panic around her. That meant… he was cured.

The bell rang again, and he realized he was blocking the door. Rather than approach the women waiting on him, he set off down a random aisle to give himself time to gather his thoughts. What was he going to do? Isabelle hadn't seemed to notice he hadn't panicked around Ruth. However, if he acted the same way with Sophia and any other women she presented, she was sure to notice.

The meant the courting lessons would stop, and they'd spend less time together. Then again, they still had to catch the boardinghouse thief. They would also still be living in the same house. Perhaps he wouldn't lose that much time with her after all. Even better, he wouldn't have to submit himself to the humiliation of needing her help with his love life or lack thereof.

What if she figured out why he was cured, though? She wasn't ready for that. Now that it was a real possibility, he wasn't even sure *he* was ready for that.

He needed to focus on the problem at hand because, whether or not she figured out why he wasn't panicking, it would be impossible to hide that he wasn't. So what was he supposed to do right now? Put on a show and pretend to panic? He'd known Sophia longer than he had Isabelle. Surely, Sophia wouldn't buy that even if Isabelle did.

"Rhett, what are you doing back here?"

He jolted at the sound of Isabelle's voice then awkwardly turned to face her on his crutches. His brain still racing, he said the one thing that made sense. "I'm browsing."

"Corsets? You're browsing corsets?"

He blinked. Looking around for the first time, he found himself surrounded by lace and ribbons and all manner of women's underclothes frippery. He felt the color drain from his face then rise back with a vengeance. He didn't know where to look. He had even less of an idea of where to go. Eventually, he froze. He glued his gaze to Isabelle's face while emitting a tight whisper. "What kind of store is this? Why are these all out in the open? It's indecent."

She waved her hand over the curtain behind her. "It isn't out in the open. It's sectioned off. You went behind the curtain. Men are not allowed back here— there's a sign that says so. You walked right past it and Sophia didn't know what to do. I told her I'd take care of it."

He lowered his head in shame. He'd run for cover

without even realizing where he was going. "I don't know what to say."

"Oh, Rhett." Sympathy filled her voice. "I'm so sorry. I didn't know it was this bad. I mean, I saw you around Amy. This is even worse. You must really like Sophia."

His head snapped up. "What? No. That isn't why I came back here. I was distracted. I didn't realize where I was going."

She nodded slowly, her words even slower. "By panic. You were distracted by panic. You need to admit it or you won't be able to conquer it."

"I'm not panicked." His still-racing heart belied his words, but they were true at least in that he wasn't panicking for the reasons she thought. He shook his head, refocused. "As a matter of fact, I think we should call this whole thing off. I don't need help anymore."

She didn't believe a word. He could tell that right off. "Oh, *Rhett*."

Great! Now it was full-on pity. He leaned onto his crutch to keep it still and washed a hand over his face. "So help me, Isabelle. If you say that one more time... Look, I'll prove it wasn't panic."

He marched out from behind the curtain as best he could march on crutches. He headed straight for the front counter. Sophia's deep blue eyes widened in alarm. He suddenly realized that he was a pretty imposing figure even with his crutches. He was, without a doubt, scaring her. He grimaced. That only made it worse, which was evident by the way she backed away from the counter. He forced a smile to his lips instead. "I'm sorry, Sophia. I didn't mean to..."

Her gaze kept shooting to his right. He followed it

to see Mrs. Greene, one of the town's leading gossips, staring at the exchange with a forgotten jar of pickles in her hands. He closed his mouth in case the woman hadn't seen him wander in or out of the forbidden section. There was no need to enlighten her. He swallowed. "I, uh, didn't mean to…"

He shook his head. Nope. That was where he'd gotten stuck the last time. He needed a new approach. "I…"

Isabelle placed a hand on his arm, sending him a knowing look that made him aware of the fact that he'd sounded as though he'd been stuttering. "He was distracted."

"I can say it myself."

She gave a tight smile. "Rhett, really, this is not the time."

"Yes, it is the time." He turned back to Sophia. "I was distracted."

Eyes wide, Sophia nodded. "I understand, but gentleman are not allowed—"

"I know! I mean, I know." He sent a furtive glance back to Mrs. Greene. Her mouth was agape and the jar was perilously dangling between two fingers. "Careful, Mrs. Greene. Your pickles."

"I'm *what*?" A crash answered her as the stench of vinegar filled the air.

Isabelle jumped. Sophia rushed forward to help Mrs. Greene. Rhett covered his face with his hand. Freed from his hold, his crutch tumbled to the ground, taking a display of canned peaches along the way. Sophia tripped over a rolling can. He lunged, roping her to his side to save her from hitting the floor as she flailed backward, but her impact threw off his balance and his ankle gave way. Isabelle reached out to steady him. His weight was too much for her. All three of them landed on the floor in tangled mass of skirts, crutches, broken merchandise and women's screams.

Two of Sophia's older brothers and her father skidded in from the back room. August grabbed Sophia. Chris grabbed Isabelle. No one bothered to help Rhett, though he was the only one without the full use of his legs. He stayed sprawled out on the floor, lifting his head enough to check on Mrs. Greene, who'd covered her mouth with both of her hands. Mr. Johansen stood over Rhett with his hands on his hips. "What is the meaning of this?"

Rhett blinked, having never heard mild-mannered Mr. Johansen raise his voice let alone roar like that before. He closed his eyes hoping God would let the earth swallow him whole then and there. Nope. He wasn't that fortunate. He finally opened his eyes, met Mr. Johansen's gaze and shrugged. "I just want to buy some clothes."

An unmistakable sigh filled the silence. "*Oh*, Rhett!"

Isabelle felt all of nine years old rather than nineteen as she sat in her father's study watching him pace back and forth in front of her and Rhett. Thomas stopped to lean back against his desk and shook his head. "*Whispering* behind the curtains of the ladies' *intimates* department. Causing *complete* chaos in poor Mr. Johansen's store. The story is all over town."

"To be fair, sir, Mrs. Greene's pickles ought to take some of the blame. If they hadn't fallen, Sophia wouldn't have—"

"Do you think this is funny, Mr. Granger?"

Isabelle dared to peek at her partner in crime. A dangerous twinkle of mirth lingered in his gaze until it connected with hers. She had no doubt that her fear was apparent.

Her father hadn't mentioned taking that trip to Virginia since that tumultuous morning. She was starting to hope that her parents had forgotten about the idea just as they seemed to forget the bracelet. However, the stakes were still high. Even the slightest mistake or misunderstanding could give them the wrong kind of reminder, and this was a huge one. Rhett seemed to sense that, for he was suddenly all seriousness. "No, sir. I don't think it's funny."

Her father crossed his arms. "What even slightly respectable explanation can you two possibly offer?"

"I wanted to buy some clothes."

Isabelle closed her eyes. Why did Rhett keep saying that as if it should make everything all right? It didn't. It wouldn't. It couldn't.

"I fail to see how that explains anything."

"I went into the store looking for clothes. I didn't realize what the curtain was for. I found myself in the wrong section. In fact, I didn't even realize such a section existed in that store."

Isabelle ventured to speak, though her voice was small. "It's new. Sophia was trying it out for the first time this week."

Rhett gestured toward her as though that explained everything. "There you go. Isabelle, having anticipated my dilemma, was kind enough to try to rescue me. The whispering was merely us debating what I should do next."

Her father turned to her. "Is this true?"

"Yes." Every bit of it was true. Of course, Rhett had left out a few pertinent details. Since those details involved his own private affairs, which she happened to be privy to, she thought it best to leave his explanation as it was.

Rhett nodded. "It was all simply an unfortunate series of mishaps complicated by my own ineptitude and clumsiness. I take full responsibility for it. We both apologize for any embarrassment we may have caused you or the boardinghouse."

Thomas peered back and forth between them for a long moment over his spectacles. Finally, removing them completely, he rubbed the bridge of his nose. "I accept your apologies. However, it is not that simple. I wish it was. I wish we could brush it under the rug and forget it ever happened, but the story is all over town. There is nothing we can do to retract it. People will speculate. You must understand my position, how hard it is to run a boardinghouse that is above reproach. Especially considering that I have two very attractive, unmarried daughters with a house full of young men."

"Are you kicking me out, then?"

Isabelle tensed, ready to remind her father that Rhett had gone through a tragedy in losing his home and had not found a replacement for it yet. The incident at the store had been nothing more than a mishap. It could have happened to any man who'd taken a wrong turn in the store or missed the ladies-only sign above the new section. As much as she wanted to say all of that, she remained silent. She had a feeling that defending Rhett would probably make the situation worse.

"No. I'm not evicting you. However, I am asking you to be more aware of your surroundings. I also ask you to be mindful of the fact that while you are living under this roof, your behavior reflects upon the reputations of my daughters, my wife, myself and every other boarder in residence here."

Rhett nodded gravely. "I understand, Mr. Bradley, and I will keep that in mind."

"You may go, then," he said. Isabelle's relief came a moment too soon for as she rose, her father's gaze landed on her. "Stay a moment, Isabelle."

She sank back into the chair and waited until Rhett was gone before asking, "Yes, Pa?"

"Be careful around the boarders. I know you think you know them, but you don't. You can't. Not really. We have no idea what they might be hiding from us or what their true intentions or characters might be."

Thomas turned the chair Rhett had vacated toward her, then sat in it and looked into her eyes. "Isabelle, I want you to listen to me. The only ones who can possibly look out for you all the time are God and yourself. Be wise about situations. Don't take your safety or your reputation for granted. That is a reasonable request. Will you grant it to me?"

She stared back at him seeing his concern and worry for what they were—knowing they were legitimate. Hadn't she already seen the very things he was warning her about? Especially since there was the small matter of the thief, which she was keeping from her parents. While she was waiting on God to change their minds, the least she could do was try to honor her father's wishes. "All right, Pa."

"Thank you." He nodded to indicate that she could go. She found Rhett waiting for her by the parlor door with somber eyes and unease furrowing his brow. "I'm sorry, Isabelle. I didn't mean to cause trouble for you."

"Nonsense. Some of the blame really must go to Mrs. Greene's pickles." She waited until he smiled before continuing, "I'm just glad you didn't reinjure yourself."

The bell on the front desk rang, preempting whatever Rhett intended to say. She turned to find Chris Johansen shooting a grin at her over the mound of brown paper packages in his arms. "Delivery for Rhett Granger."

She rushed forward to greet him. "Let me help you with that."

"No need. I've got it. Just let me know where you want me to put it."

"I think Rhett's room would be best." She glanced at Rhett for confirmation. "I'll show Chris the way so you won't have to go up the stairs."

Rhett nodded and pulled his room key from his pocket to give to her. "Thanks, Isabelle. And thank you, Chris. I know the mercantile doesn't usually make deliveries, so I appreciate this, especially after what happened this afternoon."

"It's my pleasure. Don't worry about that. Everything is cleaned up and back in place, so my father is happy. I think he was more scared that someone might have gotten hurt rather than angry. It sounded like a battle was going on with all those loud crashes, thuds and bangs. Once the smoke cleared we all had a good laugh."

"That's good to hear." Rhett sent Isabelle a pointed look that clearly said *told you.*

She ignored it to smile at Chris. "I'll show you the way."

"Great." He began to follow her then paused at the foot of the stairs. "Rhett, before I forget again, I've been meaning to ask you something. I know you're doing a few solos for the benefit, but Quinn and I thought it might be fun if the three of us played a couple of songs as a group, as well. If you're willing, we thought it would be good to get in some practice this weekend. Can we count on you and your harmonica?"

"Always." He pulled it from his pocket as though he intended to start practicing right then and there. He might have, too, if he hadn't needed at least one hand to balance the crutches. Still, it put her in mind of the last time she'd seen him pull the instrument from his pocket—on the roof of the hotel beneath a canopy of stars as midnight crept ever closer. The faint melody of a waltz danced across her memory.

"Ready when you are, Isabelle."

She blinked, found herself standing halfway up the staircase while staring straight at Rhett. "Sorry. I was lost in thought. Right this way. I think you can put it all on his bed and let him sort through everything later."

"Sounds good." He waited as she unlocked the door. After depositing everything on Rhett's bed, his dark blue eyes sought hers. "Isabelle, about the practice I mentioned to Rhett… It's at Quinn's place, so Helen will be there. I was wondering if you might be interested in going, as well."

She couldn't help feeling a little disappointed. She'd started to hope that Chris had given up on the idea of a courtship between them since she hadn't seen or heard much from him after the chilly reception she'd given him for showing up as Mark Antony at the masquerade. Other than that small misstep, he'd been gentlemanlike in his attempts to court her. He hadn't called her Amy, and he hadn't tried to kiss her, so she tempered her frustration with a doubtful smile. "I don't know, Chris. I don't play any instruments—except the piano...rather badly, I'm afraid."

He laughed. "I promise no one will make you play anything. Unless you want to, of course."

"Embarrass myself in front of all you virtuosos? Not likely." She paused to come up with a graceful way to back out when a sudden thought made her pause. "Will Sophia be there?"

"I'm not sure. I haven't had a chance to mention it to her yet." Then, as if sensing how much was riding on his sister's attendance, he amended, "I could probably convince her if she knew both you and Helen would be there."

She locked the door to Rhett's room and led the way toward the stairs. "Well, I'll definitely go if Sophia goes. Otherwise, I might feel a little out of place if it's only me and the host's wife, you know?"

"I'll check with my sister and we can go from there," he said, but she could see the gears turning in his mind as he tried to figure out why she would feel out of place with Helen when everyone knew they were close friends. He couldn't know that she was trying to give Rhett a chance to get more comfortable around Sophia. Hopefully, Chris arrived at the conclusion that she regarded this as an outing among friends and not something particularly romantic—except for Rhett and Sophia, of course. Seeing how strong Rhett's reaction had been to Sophia earlier that afternoon, it wouldn't be long before Rhett forgot all about Amy. It would take even less time before he saw how wrong he'd been in even thinking about courting Isabelle. That meant Isabelle would have one less problem to deal with.

She swallowed back a sudden rise of irrational emotion. Who was she fooling? Rhett wasn't a problem. He was a friend. Any woman would be blessed to have him as more than that. She wasn't "any woman," though. She was Isabelle. Her future was tied up in this boardinghouse. She'd do well to remember that and disregard any wayward thoughts or emotions that might deceive her into thinking otherwise—no matter how tempting.

Chapter Ten

Rhett could hardly contain his jubilation when Doc Williams removed the brace from his ankle. He settled for sharing a grin with Isabelle, who leaned against the parlor wall next to her ma. He refocused on Doc in time to hear the instruction about how to strengthen the ankle through exercise without overdoing it. Rhett thanked the man and handed over an envelope with the fee for the services rendered. While Mrs. Bradley showed Doc to the door, Rhett took a few tentative steps toward Isabelle. Her arms lifted slightly as though ready to cross the room and steady him if need be. "How does it feel?" she asked.

"Honestly? A little shaky." He'd thought he'd immediately be able to resume his normal activities. He was still determined to do exactly that. However, if the speed at which he felt comfortable walking was any indication, he'd be doing everything a lot slower. When he finally made it to Isabelle's side of the room, he was frowning. "I was faster on the crutches. Not that I want to go back to them."

"Give yourself a little time. You'll speed up as soon

as you start regaining your strength." She shook her head as teasing filled her eyes. "So impatient."

He borrowed the dramatic tone Violet so often infused into her words. "Isabelle, do you have any *idea* how *long* it's been since I could walk normally?"

"Actually, I do since I was…" She seemed to run out of words. Making no effort to continue, she bit her lip as a blush swept across her cheeks.

He dipped his head slightly to capture her gaze before finishing the sentence for her. "You were with me when it happened. I remember that very distinctly."

"She was?" Mrs. Bradley asked as she returned from seeing Doc to the door. "I didn't know that."

Isabelle's eyes widened in panic. Thankfully, her back was facing her mother, so that and the blush escaped Mrs. Bradley's attention. He placed a stilling hand on Isabelle's arm to give her a chance to recover while he glanced over her shoulder to Mrs. Bradley. "She was very helpful. I'm grateful to her as well as you and the rest of your family for being so kind to me as I recovered."

The suspicion in Mrs. Bradley's gaze faded to compassion. "We're glad that we could help you through such a difficult time."

"Well, I truly do appreciate it." He glanced at Isabelle to make sure her color had returned to normal before stepping past her. "I'd like to try my ankle out on a short walk. Would y'all be willing to join me?"

"In this cold?" Mrs. Bradley gave a little shiver. "It's sweet of you to offer, but I'd rather head into my warm kitchen to get supper started. You're welcome to go if you want, Isabelle. Make sure y'all bundle up."

"We will. Come on, Rhett." Isabelle dashed out of

the room and was already buttoning her coat when Rhett finally caught up with her. She glanced down the empty hall toward the kitchen, whispering, "Did you see her come back into the room?"

"No," he said lowly as he shrugged into his gray coat.

Her gaze met his in surprise. "How were you so calm?"

"Why did you panic?"

Her eyes widened, and her hands moved in flustered circles as though to say it should be obvious. He hid a smile at her outright adorableness and deposited her bonnet into the hand that had landed palm up. "Use words."

She just sighed, handed him his hat and automatically opened the door for him. Realizing he'd have to break her of that habit, he gestured her through first. The late-afternoon sun battled against the cold wind that greeted them as they stepped onto the porch. He settled a hand beneath her elbow to help her down the stairs even though he had to have a little help from the banister to keep his balance while doing so. She matched her pace to his as they strolled down the path toward the main gate. "I'm starting to feel as though I may be fighting a losing battle with my parents on the boardinghouse. At any moment they could find out something or overhear something that would push them to sell."

"Let's focus on catching the thief and worry about the rest when we're done with that. I'll find a way to question Peter and Hank this week."

Isabelle nodded, though she didn't look very encouraged.

"Hey, Rhett, look at you!"

Rhett turned to find Violet waving at him from the sidewalk. It took him a moment to realize she was referencing his lack of crutches. Grinning, he waved a hand over his recovered leg to show off for her. "Almost as good as new."

"You must be over the moon." Violet opened the front gate and let herself into the yard. "Where are y'all headed?"

"Out for a walk," Isabelle said. "Do you want to come with us?"

"No, thank you. I've been dreaming about a steaming cup of hot cocoa all afternoon. Nothing is going to stand in my way. I have a note for you, though." Violet slid a square envelope out from between her books then tilted her head to study her sister. "It's from *Chris*."

"Oh?" The confusion in her voice was quickly replaced by complete understanding. "Oh!"

Violet frowned, hesitated long enough to send a quick look to Rhett before deciding to continue. "Have you given in, then? I mean, he seems like a nice man, and he's very attractive. I'm—"

Rhett's stomach dropped to his boots even as Isabelle rolled her eyes. "Violet, *please* stop talking, and give me the note."

He finally found his voice. "Is Chris courting you?"

"No." A flush of pink heightened the color in her cheeks as she kept her gaze glued to the envelope she was opening.

Violet looked anything but convinced. "Maybe not yet, but he sure seems to be making progress." She held up the hand not holding books and winced at Isabelle's glare. "I know. You want me to stop talking. How about I make my exit instead? Have a nice walk."

"Thanks," Rhett answered automatically as he watched Isabelle read the note.

She folded it and slid it back into the envelope before smiling at him. "This is good. Chris convinced Sophia to go to the musicians' practice session. He's going to pick us up here so we can all drive over together."

His mind struggled to catch up with this new development. He could only seem to focus on one thing. "Chris asked you to go with him to the practice?"

"Simply because it's at Quinn's house, so Helen will be there." She ignored the doubtful look he sent her and started walking again. "Why he asked me isn't important. The important part is that *Sophia* will be there."

He nearly groaned as he moved to the side closest to the street and extended his arm for her to take. "Sophia? Isabelle, I tried to tell you at the store that I don't think these courtship lessons are a good idea anymore."

"And that's *exactly* why we need to go through with them. You're right at the brink of beating this. I'm sure of it." She gave a determined little nod. "Besides, it's only fair that I help you since you've already helped me."

"What do you mean?" He crossed the street toward the courthouse's courtyard. "How have I helped you?"

"I prayed, Rhett. I prayed for the first time in a long time, and I got an answer."

He glanced at her in surprise. "You did? Already?"

"Yes." Her lips curved into a smile while her green

eyes deepened in gratitude. "I'm going to do a lot more praying thanks to your encouragement."

"That's good. I'm glad." He truly was. Yet, he couldn't ignore the dull ache that filled his chest at hearing that someone else's prayer had been answered so quickly when his never were. How often had he prayed for a wife? Yet, he was still unmarried, and the woman he was interested in would soon be courting someone else. Her reaction to Chris's note made that abundantly clear.

Rhett glanced unseeingly across the courtyard until his gaze settled on the smithy that was visible through the barren oak trees. Isabelle continued to talk but he couldn't focus on it or anything else other than what he'd learned during the past few minutes. It was only when her steps hesitated momentarily that he refocused.

"Oh, are we going to your shop?"

He glanced up surprised to find that was exactly where he'd been headed. Thankfully, he had the key with him, so he'd be able to manage a quick moment of desperately needed solitude. "Yes. If you don't mind, I need to check on something in the back room. It will just take a minute."

She agreed and patiently waited as he let them into smithy. He excused himself, made his way past the forge to the back room and closed the door behind him. Bracing his hands on the counter, he hung his head. He needed to stop fooling himself about Isabelle. His connection to her may have deepened on that roof at the masquerade. However, it hadn't affected her to the degree it had him or she wouldn't have refused his courtship. He'd thought that after spending time together, deepening their friendship, sharing confidences, she would at least be on her way to realizing there was the potential for so much more between them. Obviously, he'd been wrong.

Why else would she continue to push him toward Sophia with such determination and tenacity? Why else would she blush over receiving a note from Chris and agree to let the man escort her to the musicians' practice session? Rhett knew the reason. Though it hurt to admit it, he needed to stop denying it. Isabelle might accept him as a friend, but she'd never want him to be anything more than that.

The worst part of this was that she'd been telling him that exact same thing from the beginning. He'd simply chosen to ignore it. That made him wonder what else he'd chosen to ignore during the past few weeks and months. He knew without a doubt that his relationship with God was one of those things. Despite the encouragement he'd given Isabelle, Rhett couldn't remember the last time he'd prayed or even paid attention in church. That was all because he was too afraid to face the fact that God had already answered his prayer for love. He'd just answered in a way that Rhett hadn't wanted to hear—a resounding, irrefutable *no*.

Fighting against that knowledge, against what God willed for his life, would only cause more heartache. He should have done what he'd planned to do at the masquerade before he'd met up with Isabelle and stopped hoping for something he was obviously never supposed to have. It was time to make the most of the life he'd been given, move on, find fulfillment in something else.

He bowed his head. "Lord, I know I've been chas-

ing after a life not meant for me. I'm sorry. I promise
that this time I'm giving up—really and truly. Help
me focus my thoughts and dreams on something else.
Whatever that 'something else' is, let it be enough to
keep me from longing for something I'll never have.
Amen."

His resolve firmly in place, he went in search of Isabelle. He found her browsing the interior of the shop,
where customers weren't allowed to be. Her fingers
traced the shapes of some of his less threating-looking
tools until he could practically hear the curiosity filling her thoughts over how they were used. He resisted
the temptation to go over and explain it to her, to stand
close enough to smell the scent of lemon verbena she
wore, to see her eyes light up with the new knowledge
he could give her. It was enough to stand there and
watch for a moment.

This was the challenge. *She* was the challenge. It
would have been far easier to let go of the future he'd
hoped for if he hadn't let himself get so attached to
her. His hopes no longer centered on the mere idea
of a future Mrs. Granger. They centered on Isabelle.

He crossed his arms and shook his head. Well, he'd
have to uncenter them. It shouldn't be too hard. This
had started with a New Year's kiss, after all. The connection he felt to her was probably nothing more than
mere physical reaction. That should make it easier to
give her up.

She finally turned toward him, placing a hand on
the cold, smooth surface of the anvil without the least
bit of surprise, as though she'd sensed him there all
along. Tilting her head, she smiled. "All done here?"

Was Rhett truly done hoping, working, fighting

for a woman who said she didn't want him? He'd be a fool if he wasn't. Besides, he'd made a promise to God to do exactly that. How could he expect the Lord to help him find a sufficient future if he didn't truly let go of the one he'd been coveting? He swallowed hard, gave a quick nod and forced a hint of a smile to his lips. "All done."

Isabelle stole a sideways glance at the man seated beside her on the piano bench. Peter Engel was too busy watching her clumsy fingers trail across the keys to notice. They could barely hear the notes over the sound of the harmonica drifting in from the hall, but Peter was single-minded and focused. He'd taken the challenge of exchanging talents with as much seriousness as the other boarders had playful enthusiasm.

It was no mistake that Isabelle had been paired with him since she hadn't put his name or Hank's into the hat until she and Rhett were the last two people left to draw a partner from it. She'd assumed that would give them ample opportunity to discover any possible motive the two boarders might have for stealing the bracelet. Unfortunately, Isabelle had barely gotten one word out of Peter so far.

His fingers stumbled and struck an errant note. Before she could encourage him, he shook his head and muttered, "Again."

That was it. That was the one word.

He said it every time he messed up and automatically started over, every time he wanted her to repeat the song for him. She was starting to get concerned. It didn't help that her father's warning kept running through her head about how she couldn't truly know the boarders. Peter was more of an enigma than the others could even dream of being because he was so quiet and kept to himself. Even so, the town's telegrapher had always struck her as sweet, if a bit bashful, with a blush that could put his rusty hair to shame. He was hardly the kind of man she'd think would steal from her family. Then again, none of the boarders were. That was what made the whole situation so disheartening.

Due to her embarrassing lack of any other performance talent, she'd been obliged to teach him the one song she'd learned on the piano. He'd picked up the simple melody quite well. However, she had to admit his rendition of "Beautiful Dreamer" had somehow taken on a quality rather suspiciously like that of Morse code.

A quick glance at the Waterford crystal clock on the parlor mantel told her that she and Rhett would need to leave for the musicians' practice in a few minutes. She waited until Peter finished the song then stopped him before he could start over. "Peter, you've done very well. I have to go, but you can keep practicing if you want."

He stood as she slid from the bench. "I will. Thank you for teaching me."

"You're welcome. You never did tell me what talent you were going to teach me."

He suddenly grinned. "Magic."

"Magic?"

"You know…" He pulled a coin from behind her ear. "Illusion."

She automatically checked behind her ear as though another coin would suddenly appear. "How did you—"

"The hand is quicker than the eye."

She watched openmouthed as he pulled her cameo hair comb from his sleeve. "When did you—"

He winked then blushed at his own audacity before settling back at the piano.

She stared at the comb, realizing it would have been easy to remove from her simple hairstyle. Even so, she narrowed her eyes at his back. *Well, that was unsettling.*

The clock chimed the hour, prompting her to leave the parlor. She walked through the dining room into the kitchen to let her mother know that she and Rhett would be leaving soon. Beatrice was standing in the middle of the kitchen, holding a book and practicing a dramatic reading with a selection from what sounded to be *Wuthering Heights.* Isabelle paused in the doorway to watch, but Violet stopped the rehearsal, unimpressed if her shaking head was any indication. "Ma, you sound as though you're reading from a book."

Beatrice placed a hand on her hip. "I *am* reading from a book."

"Yes, but you mustn't sound like it. Think of how you feel about Pa and channel it into your words even though you're saying them about someone else." Violet rose from her seat at the kitchen table, a hand pressed to her chest. "'Nelly, I *am* Heathcliff!'" Despair infiltrated her voice, though a hint of a smile played at her lips. "'He's always, *always* in my mind…not as a pleasure, any more than I am always a pleasure to myself.'" Violet's voice softened to a whisper, a confession. "'But as my own being.'"

Silence filled the kitchen.

Violet's eyes refocused on their mother. "Do you see what I mean?"

"Yes, I do, and I'd like to know whom *you* were thinking of as you recited, young lady."

Violet placed her hands on her temples and sank back onto the chair. "Oh, Ma, honestly—"

Holding back laughter, Isabelle decided it was best not to interrupt them and slipped away without detection. She followed the sounds of raucous laughter to the main hallway. Since there were an odd number of people living in the boardinghouse, her father and Gabe Noland had been paired up and were being put through the paces of learning a Scottish dance from Wesley Brice. Rhett sat on the staircase with pure amusement on his face and his harmonica in hand. From what she'd heard in the parlor, it had been providing a surprisingly adequate substitute for bagpipes. His amber eyes snagged on hers. His smile widened to a grin, and he tilted his head to the empty spot on the step beside him.

The sound of her father's laughter caught her off guard and drew her attention. His voice was a tad breathless. "Wes, you're a slave driver. I am far too old for this nonsense."

Wes crossed his arms. "Nonsense. It has nothing to do with age. Gabe is just as horrible."

Gabe lifted his brows. "Oh, is that so? Well, remember you said that when you see my next portrait of you. There'll be two horns sticking out of your head and a tail coming from your—"

"Isabelle." Rhett stood to his feet, sending Gabe a censuring look. "Did you need something?"

Before she could say anything, Wes clapped his

hands together. "Ah, an audience! Come on, gentlemen. Once more for the lady then we'll call it a day."

"No." Thomas gave her a look that was a mix of desperation and warning. "Isabelle has no interest in seeing her father prance around like a leprechaun."

Wes slid his fingers through his hair. "Mr. Bradley, please. I've already told you that leprechauns are Irish lore, not Scottish."

"Did you?"

As Wes explained the difference between brownies and leprechauns, Rhett escorted Isabelle over to the stairs. "You'll be far safer over here with me. Their dancing can get a little wild, to say the least." He lowered his voice. "Your father has made comments about leprechauns five times. Wes hasn't figured out he's doing it to give himself time to rest."

She laughed. "Clever Papa."

He waited while she arranged her pale pink skirts then sat beside her. He nodded at the comb as she slipped it back into place. "What happened? Did it fall off?"

"No, Peter pulled it out of his sleeve."

Wes started clapping out the beat, so Rhett only had time to send Isabelle a confused glance before going into the introduction of a song. Hands on their hips, Gabe and Thomas bowed in unison. That was the last thing they did together. Once the actual dance started it became obvious that while her father had the steps down relatively well, he couldn't find the beat that went with them. Meanwhile, Gabe was right on the beat, but seemed to have no clue what his feet were supposed to do. They wildly hopped from side to side, bumping into each other more than once, and even managed a turn here and there. They ended the dance with another perfect bow then glanced at each other and burst out laughing.

Isabelle and Rhett gave them a standing ovation. Wes grinned proudly. "That was actually the best they've done it yet."

"Y'all were wonderful. If you do it like that, it will be the highlight of the show." Isabelle gave them all a quick wink then turned to Rhett. "We'd better go if you want to make it to your practice on time."

"You're right." He slid his harmonica into his shirt pocket. "Sorry, y'all."

Gabe rolled his eyes and wiped the sweat from his forehead. "Oh, please, don't apologize. You're doing us a favor."

Isabelle's father walked with them toward the door. "Where did y'all say you were going again?"

Isabelle barely held back an impatient sigh. She'd already told her father at least twice. He couldn't have forgotten, so why was he truly asking? "We're going to Quinn and Helen's so Rhett can rehearse for the benefit and I can visit with Helen."

"All right. Well, drive safely. Be back at a reasonable time. Watch the weather. It looks a little overcast."

"Yes, sir. We'll be careful," Rhett said before Isabelle could respond. Finally satisfied, Thomas nodded and went back to talk to the other boarders. Rhett leaned in to speak quietly as he helped her into her coat. "He's being a concerned father."

She paused to frown at him before tying on her bonnet. "He's being overprotective."

"It shows he cares."

"Or that he doesn't trust me." She waited until Rhett

finished putting on his coat to hand him his hat. "Either way, it makes me feel smothered."

He opened the door for her and tilted his head toward it. "Then how about a little bit of freedom?"

She laughed. "I'll take it."

"Right this way." He escorted her to the buggy he'd rented for the day.

"I wish you'd taken up Chris's offer for us to ride with him. Think of the extra time you might have had with Sophia."

"I'll see her plenty, I'm sure. I just like to be in control of when I leave music rehearsals." He spread the blanket over them and took the reins before giving her a sideways glance. "You still could have ridden with him."

She shook her head. That wouldn't have made any sense since Rhett was leaving from the same place she was. Not to mention it still would have defeated the purpose of getting Rhett and Sophia extra time together. There would be no use arguing the fact, so she changed the subject as he pointed the horses out of town. "How were your first few days back at the smithy?"

"Good. Busy after being closed for two weeks."

He wasn't kidding. They'd barely had a chance to talk over the past three days since he'd gone back to a normal work schedule. The few times they had, he'd seemed preoccupied. She drew more details out of him and still had plenty of time to bring him up to speed about what had happened with Peter before they pulled up to Quinn and Helen's cabin. Sophia and Chris must have arrived only a few minutes before them for they were still talking to Quinn and Helen in the yard. Isabelle gave Rhett a supportive smile as he helped her down from the buggy.

She lost track of him as they greeted the others then remembered to check on him in time to see Sophia wrap her arm around his waist in an enthusiastic hug. He laughed then hugged her back, saying something too low for Isabelle to hear. Rhett and Sophia took their time walking into the house. They seemed to have plenty to talk about. Obviously, Rhett would do fine without any help from Isabelle today—or perhaps ever again. That was exactly what she wanted, so why did it feel so wrong?

Chapter Eleven

Rhett barely held back a frustrated sigh as he realized that Isabelle had all but obliterated the distance he'd so carefully constructed between them. And she'd managed it in a matter of minutes. If this was some sort of test from God, he was failing miserably. Even when he wasn't with her, she was in his thoughts. What was he to do?

Get over it and move on, that was what.

Today ought to make it somewhat easier. Seeing Chris fawn over her on the way into the house hadn't exactly been pleasant. Rhett had done his best to focus on Sophia, who'd effusively thanked him for causing such a stir about the new section of ladies' intimates in the mercantile. Apparently, the story Mr. Bradley had been so appalled to hear circulating around town had drummed up quite a bit of business for Sophia's new pet project. The resulting sales had convinced her father to agree to keep the section, at least for the moment. Rhett had been glad to hear his blunder had profited someone.

Even so, it had been impossible for him to miss the

puzzled expression on Isabelle's face as he'd conversed freely with Sophia. He couldn't blame her for being confused. However, he had no intention of explaining why talking with women was no longer a problem. If he wasn't going to marry any of them, what was there to be nervous about?

It slowly filtered into his mind that the music around him had come to an unorganized halt. Glancing up, he was surprised to find Quinn's blue eyes focused on him. "Rhett, that was your cue to come in."

He grimaced. That made three times he'd messed up so far this practice. The first two had been because he'd been paying more attention to watching Isabelle sitting at the kitchen table chatting and laughing with her friends than he had the rehearsal. The women had disappeared into one of the cabin's back rooms, so he had no excuse this time. "Oh, sorry. Start over. I'll get it this time."

Chris lifted his fiddle into place and tapped out the beat with his foot, but Quinn waved a hand. "That's all right. I think we can all use a quick break. Plus, it isn't nearly as fun without an audience. Maybe I ought to ask the women to come back in. It might make it easier for us to concentrate. Don't you think?"

Rhett slowly narrowed his eyes at the subtle but knowing smirk Quinn sent him. "I think I'm going to get a cup of water. Can I get y'all anything while I'm up?"

Chris sank onto the settee. "I'll take some water, too."

"Nothing for me," Quinn said, absently plucking a few strings of his banjo.

Rhett kept half an ear tuned to the men's discussion

about the songs they'd chosen, but his gaze strayed toward the hall at the sound of Isabelle's giggle drifting in from the other room. He went back to the parlor and handed Chris a glass of water before settling back in the seat he'd vacated earlier. "Do either of you know what the order is going to be for the performances?"

Chris nodded. Setting his fiddle aside, he pulled a piece of paper from his pocket and handed it to Rhett. "I have the tentative schedule Ellie came up with."

"They have me playing solo first then our group is playing last." He glanced up at his friends. "I see both of you are appearing in other acts."

Chris smiled. "Yeah, my brothers and I will be playing several classical pieces."

"Helen and I will be singing with our oldest nephews and niece." Quinn glanced between them. "You two ready to get back to practice?"

Rhett took a big slug of his forgotten water and nodded. "Sure."

"All right. I'm going to get the ladies. I think we really do sound better when we have an audience to play off."

As Quinn stood, Chris leaned forward to rest his elbows on his knees. "Rhett, before the ladies come back, I want to ask you something. Would you mind switching companions for the ride home? I'd like to spend some time with Isabelle."

"Yeah, sure. That's fine." Amazingly, the words came out light and breezy, which was strange since the weight settling on his chest made it hard to breathe. "Here's the performance list back."

Chris grinned. "Thanks and thanks."

Rhett glanced up at Quinn to find his friend already

watching him. "Well, are you going to get the ladies or not? Because I'm ready to play."

"Hold your horses."

Rhett went over a difficult piece in the music until Quinn returned with the ladies in tow—each wearing a drastically different hairstyle than when they'd left. Rhett reigned in a chuckle and kept his mind on the music for the rest of the practice. After running through the entire set of songs they intended to play at the benefit, Helen rewarded them each with a hot cup of coffee and a piece of cake. As they all sat around the kitchen table, Rhett could see that Chris was getting impatient to leave and remembered Mr. Bradley's warning to get Isabelle home at a reasonable time. No doubt Chris would drive slowly to have as much time as possible with Isabelle. The two of them ought to get going.

He shot a meaningful glance toward Chris before pushing his plate away and leaning his chair back onto two of its legs. "Well, I guess we ought to head out pretty soon. Sophia, if it's all right with you, your brother said I could take you home."

Sophia didn't look the least bit surprised. Perhaps Chris had already told her his plan. He'd halfway hoped she'd put up a fuss, but the woman gave her customary bright smile. "That would be nice. Thank you."

Isabelle tilted her head, looking slightly offended. "Um, Rhett, your buggy only has room for two."

He probably should have let the man speak for himself, especially when the words came out sounding slightly accusatory. "Chris wants to take you home."

Isabelle's eyes widened slightly. "Oh?"

"Yes." Chris sounded a bit nervous. "We can leave whenever you're ready."

She stood. "Now is fine."

Suddenly, everyone was saying goodbye at once. Isabelle and Chris were out the door in a matter of moments. Rhett intended to stick around for a few minutes to give them a head start. Quinn made that easier by settling a heavy hand on Rhett's shoulder. "Hey, let's go out to the barn for a minute. There's something out there I've been meaning to give you."

"Sure. Excuse me for a minute, Sophia."

"Take your time. I was going to write out a recipe for Helen anyway."

Rhett followed his friend to the tack room of the barn. "What did you want to give me?"

"A piece of my mind." Quinn crossed his arms and sat on one of the stools near the worktable. "What could you be thinking?"

Shrugging, Rhett leaned one shoulder against the tack-room doorpost. "I'm thinking it's really cold out here. Get to the point, Quinn."

"You obviously care for Isabelle. Why did you let Chris run off with her, then act like the whole scheme was your idea in the first place?"

"What makes it obvious?" He needed to know so he could avoid doing it in front of others—like Isabelle's parents.

"You stared at her through the whole first half of practice then ignored her for the rest."

He narrowed his eyes. "Wait. So what gave me away? The staring or the ignoring?"

"Both." Quinn gave a quick shake of his head. "Don't get me sidetracked. The point is you're a fool for letting a woman you care about go off with some-one else. Especially when you know he intends to use the opportunity as an excuse to do his own courting."

"It isn't foolish if I know she doesn't feel the same way about me."

Quinn frowned. "You know that for a fact?"

"She told me so herself—or may as well have." He straightened from the door, ready to leave. "I appreci-ate your concern, Quinn, but I know what I'm doing."

Quinn stared at him. "What *are* you doing?"

"I'm letting her go."

"Why?"

"Besides the fact she doesn't want me?" At Quinn's nod, Rhett snagged a nearby stool to sit on and leaned his back against the wall. "I've always wanted the kind of relationship you have with Helen, the kind my par-ents and grandparents had. I wanted it so bad and for so long that when I thought I had the chance for that with Isabelle, I didn't take her *no* for an answer. I tried to deepen our friendship with the intention of transi-tioning it into a romance."

"What's wrong with that?"

"I wasn't respecting her decision." Rhett felt his jaw clench as he stared down at his boots. "I also happened to be running from God's will."

"Which is?"

"Not Isabelle. Or anyone, for that matter. I finally came to terms with that and gave up."

"Huh." Quinn frowned, scratched his jaw, then shook his head. "Something about that doesn't sound right. If I've learned anything about God, it's that He has good things in store for those who believe in Him."

Rhett shrugged. "That doesn't mean the good thing he has in store for me is Isabelle."

"Maybe not. However, the Bible does say that if we delight ourselves in the Lord, He'll give us the desires of our hearts. The desire of your heart is to find a wife, isn't it?"

He blew out a frustrated huff. "Why are you doing this? Why are you making it harder for me? I already gave up once. I don't want to go through that all over again."

Quinn held up his hands. "Look, all I'm saying is there is a difference between giving up on something and surrendering it to God."

"They seem like the same thing to me."

"Giving up means being overwhelmed, frustrated, tired, discouraged. Surrendering means letting it go, trusting God, believing that He'll work it out."

"But I don't." He was surprised by the anger filling his words. Once tapped, it seemed impossible for him not to let the thoughts he'd been thinking for years flow from his lips. "I don't believe He'll work it out. I think He's done all He intends to do. I think I need to accept that and move on because if I don't I'm going to live a discontented, upset, unfulfilled life."

Quinn crossed his arms. "It seems easier that way, doesn't it? Not to hope or trust or wait, but to simply give up. I don't think that way leads to fulfillment, Rhett. I think it leads to remorse because God *is* faithful. One day He'll bring the woman you've been waiting for into your life whether that's Isabelle or someone else."

"You can't know that for sure. No one can. You're right, though. I'm not putting myself through the waiting or hoping anymore. If God wanted it to happen, it would have already happened. Now, I've got to go, Quinn. Sophia is waiting on me."

"I'll be praying for you."

Rhett shook the hand Quinn offered, but it was all he could do to hold his tongue. *Don't bother. It doesn't do any good. Leastwise, not as far as my life is concerned.*

Isabelle was ticked—purely ticked—at both Rhett and Chris for setting up this little arrangement without so much as a by-your-leave. She recognized that it was a bit silly to be upset when she'd chided Rhett for not utilizing the time he'd been given with Sophia earlier. However, she hadn't realized that meant she'd be bumped out of the buggy to ride home alone with Chris. Where had Rhett gotten the gall or courage to come up with the idea let alone ask Sophia to ride with him?

She rolled her eyes at her own dull-wittedness. He'd gotten it from Isabelle, of course. She'd helped him get over his fear of women, though, for the life of her, she couldn't figure out how. All she'd done was give him a little encouragement. She hadn't had time to do anything else between her boardinghouse chores and their attempts to find the thief. Add the talent show and packing up Amy's room to that and she hardly knew whether she was coming or going most of the time.

She straightened in the buggy seat. Glancing around, she felt a moment of irrational panic at the realization that she had no idea where she was. Chris must be taking a roundabout way back to town. She wished she'd been paying more attention to where they were going.

She might have been able to deter him from making this trip any longer than it needed to be. She eyed an oak tree with barren gray branches that canopied the country road. It had a long brown gash down its trunk, a testament to the fierce lightning storms known to light up the Texas sky on occasion. It was distinctive enough that she'd noticed it before even in her distraction. "Chris, are we going in circles?"

His slow blink told her he hadn't been paying any more attention to their surroundings than she had. "Of course not."

"Are we lost?"

"Don't be ridiculous." He glanced around to get his bearings. "I know exactly where we are. I thought it would be nice to take a more scenic route back to town."

Right. She crossed her arms against the cold wind and leaned back into her corner of the buggy to survey him. His classically handsome features were taut with a nervousness that extended even to his white-knuckled grip on the reins. "Want to tell me what's troubling you?"

He glanced at her. She heard him swallow hard before he nodded. "Sure. There's a bit of a lookout point up ahead. Would you mind if we stopped for a minute?"

"I suppose not," she said even as she automatically took stock of everything she knew about Chris Johansen. They'd grown up running in the same crowd even though he'd been ahead of her in school. He'd never missed a Sunday service except for a time or two that he's been sick. The town and his father had him pegged to take over the family business one day.

Like Isabelle, he was known for being dutiful, responsible. However, he was the oldest child in his family and seemed to take that role very seriously. She felt quite safe with him even out in the middle of the woods, so she accepted his help down from the buggy and allowed him to lead her to sit on a fallen tree. He spread his coat over it so she wouldn't dirty hers, but she handed it right back to him. "That's sweet, Chris, but it's freezing out here."

"Sorry." He shot her an apologetic smile. "We won't stay long."

She patted a spot on the tree that was a respectable distance away from where she sat. "Sit down and tell me what's on your mind. You're making me nervous with all that pacing."

He put on his coat, then straddled the tree to sit facing her and ran his fingers through his hair. "Isabelle, we've known each other for quite some time now. Haven't we?"

She held back a smile at the realization that she'd heard this refrain before. "Yes, since I started school."

"Right. We get along well. We understand each other. I find you very attractive."

A sinking sensation filled her stomach. "Chris—"

He placed a stilling hand over hers. "Isabelle, let me get through it first." He waited until she bit her lip and nodded before he continued. "I would be truly honored if you would agree to become my wife." He released her hand along with a sigh. "All right, you can reject me now."

"Chris…" She shook her head, nearly groaning in commiseration. "*What* are you doing? Why would you ask me to marry you—especially when you clearly expect me to say no? We haven't even courted."

"I'm driving you home." He grimaced at her disbelieving look. "All right, we haven't courted. So what? Not every couple has to court to get married."

"You don't want to marry me."

"Yes, I do."

She rolled her eyes at his obstinacy. "Why?"

"I already told you."

"The real reason, please."

His shoulders lowered. She caught a glimpse of the Chris she'd known before all of this courtship silliness when tenderness filled his gaze. His hands caught her arms. "You do know that I care about you, don't you? As a friend, I mean. I'd so much rather marry you than a stranger."

"Well, thank you. I'm glad to hear that, but—"

He released her and shook his head. "No. You don't understand. If I don't marry you or someone else soon, my pa is going to send back to Norway for a mail-order bride. I don't want to marry a stranger. I want to marry someone I know, someone of my own choosing."

"Oh." She glanced out toward the woods stretching downhill from where they sat, searching for a response. "I truly am sorry to hear that, Chris. I just… I don't think you should settle for anything less than love. You need to choose someone else."

"There is no one else." The defeat in his voice was unmistakable and her heart broke for him until she realized what he'd said.

"What do you mean?"

"I mean, I've already asked everyone who could possibly say yes. They all turned me down."

"They *all*?" Tilting her head, she crossed her arms. "How many women did you ask before me, Chris?"

He winced as though remembering each and every rejection vividly. "Amy, Maddie, Ellie. I would have asked Helen, but Quinn got to her before I had a chance."

"So you finally decided I was worth a shot even though I was your last, *last* choice. Is that it?"

He grimaced. "Isabelle, I didn't mean it like that."

She shook her head and waved aside his words. "That's just typical. You know what? I don't want to know any more about this. Take me home, please."

She didn't bother to wait for him to agree. She jumped up from the log and climbed into the buggy on her own. She glanced over to see where Chris still stood wringing his hat in his hands. She lifted an expectant brow. He sighed, hit his hat against his leg, slid his fingers through his hair, then walked back over to the buggy. The trip back to town was tense with a silence only broken by a muttered apology when he helped her from the buggy in front of the boarding-house. Still fuming, she didn't bother to respond.

Rhett was seated on the steps of the porch waiting for her, still dressed in his hat and coat. He met her at the gate as Chris drove away. "What took y'all so long?"

"He proposed. That's what took so long."

Rhett's mouth dropped open and he seemed to pale slightly but she was too angry to care. "He what?"

She poked him in the chest. "You heard me, Rhett Granger, and it's all your fault."

"*My* fault?" He caught her hand to stop her continued poking. "How do you figure that?"

"You dumped me on him for the ride home. I mean, sure, I understand that you wanted to ride with Sophia. Still, you could have at least run it by me before you announced it to everyone. After all, you were my ride—"

He shook his head. "Wait. What did you say?"

She tried to tug her hand from his grasp, but his firm grip wouldn't give, so she settled for lifting her chin and flashing her eyes. "I said you *dumped* me on him."

"No." He frowned, leaning slightly closer with his amber gaze intent on hers. "What did you say to him?"

"Well, I refused, of course. That is not the point." Her wayward gaze slid to his lips. She forced it back to his only to find she'd lost her train of thought. "The point is…"

"You're angry." A maddening hint of a smile touched his mouth.

"Yes, I'm angry!"

"At me." The amusement in his eyes faded to seriousness and sincerity. "I'm sorry, Isabelle."

Realizing that at some point his hold on her hand had eased, she slid her fingers from his and poked him again. "Don't! Don't apologize because then I can't be angry, and I want to be angry at you and Chris and John Merriweather and maybe the whole world if I feel like it."

"That's a lot of people."

She let out a frustrated little growl and brushed past him intent on reaching the boardinghouse, though it hardly qualified as a refuge these days. She barely made it two steps before his hand caught her arm and gently but firmly turned her back to face him. Lifting her eyebrows, she glared at him, silently warning he'd better have a good reason for stopping her. He didn't look intimidated, only confused. "I get why you're mad at me, but what does that have to do with Chris or John?"

"Everything. It's all of you. Why am I never good enough to be anyone's first choice? Why do I always have to settle for being second best—or third or fourth or fifth or just plain last?"

She read the confusion in his eyes and knew he probably had no idea what she was talking about. That didn't stop the words from flowing. "Well, maybe I'm tired of it. Maybe I want more than that. Here's an idea. Maybe *I'm* not the problem at all. Did anyone think of that? Perhaps y'all are the ones who aren't good enough."

He understood her now. The flash of hurt in his eyes was proof of that. He glanced away, and when he met her gaze again it was gone. "I wouldn't be the least bit surprised if that was the case."

Suddenly exhausted, she lowered her head and battled the urge to rest her forehead on his strong chest for a minute. She had no right or reason to do that. What was more, she knew better. Hadn't she just railed against him and all his ilk? Didn't she mean every word she'd said? Of course she did—even the part where she'd admitted she wanted more than to be someone's second best or last choice.

She wanted the wild kind of love that had turned Amy's world upside down without all the hurting it had caused. She wanted the steadfast affection that had carried her parents through twenty-five years of marriage. She wanted the deep connection Helen had with Quinn that somehow managed to be gentle and fierce all at the same time. Unfortunately, she didn't seem capable of inspiring that in a man.

Even so, as impractical as it was, she'd rather be nothing than settle for being someone's afterthought. It seemed unlikely that she'd ever be anything more—perhaps not with anyone, but definitely not with her sister's former suitors. It was so easy to come to terms with that when it came to John and Chris even if it had been uncomfortable at times. Why was everything so much harder for her when it came to Rhett?

It didn't matter. The fact was that she couldn't trust any of her sister's former suitors to have genuine feelings for her. John had shown her that by being unable to distinguish her from her sister. Chris had shown her by proposing to her as a last resort. Rhett had, as well. He'd all but admitted that the reason he'd wanted more to come from their New Year's Eve kiss was that she was the only girl he'd been able to romance.

Judging from his behavior with Sophia, that was no longer the case. That was a good thing, too. Getting romantic thoughts about one of her sister's former suitors would be asking for heartache. She'd done perfectly fine without that in life so far. She had no intention of traveling down that road now.

Chapter Twelve

Rhett was frozen through after sitting on the porch for nigh on fifteen minutes waiting for Isabelle and Chris to show up, unwilling to go inside without her after promising her father he'd look after her. Isabelle would probably say he should have thought of that before letting her ride with Chris, but Rhett hadn't been thinking very well today. Otherwise, he wouldn't be tempted to pull the woman into his arms after she'd so successfully stomped all over his heart and put him in his place right beside the rest of Amy's former suitors.

It was frustrating to realize the main reason Isabelle had objected to him was because he'd taken a foolish fancy to a woman who'd barely given him a second glance. Still, her challenge was effective enough to make him question himself. Why *had* he been so drawn to Amy instead of Isabelle? He couldn't for the life of him figure it out.

Isabelle was every bit as beautiful as her sister, more feisty by half, playful, witty and everything he could want in a woman. Why hadn't he noticed all of that when Amy was still around? Perhaps it was because Isabelle never tried to put herself forward or draw undue attention to herself. In the three short weeks that he'd lived at the boardinghouse, he'd started to notice that made it easy for people to take her for granted. She always did exactly what she was supposed to do when she was supposed to do it. The second she stepped even slightly out of line, she was brought into her father's study for a talk.

A heavy sigh rocked her forward then back before the fan of her dark lashes lifted and her gold-green eyes met his. "Did you at least have a nice trip with Sophia? She didn't propose, did she?"

He laughed heartily at that and had to restrain himself from hugging her yet again. "No, she didn't propose."

"Such a shame." The crafty smile on her lips did nothing to soften her droll tone. "You seemed to do quite well with her."

Realizing his hand was still on her arm and his thumb had at some point begun brushing back and forth over the soft material of her coat, he released her. "Not as well as you might think. She informed me on the way home that she had no illusions that I was interested in her. She knew the driving arrangements had been made so that Chris could have a few minutes alone with you."

"She did? They were?" She shook her head and waved her words away as though they were unimportant. "Wait. Rhett, you missed the perfect opportunity to tell her that you *were* interested in her."

"Isabelle, I told you from the beginning that I'm not." He waited for her doubtful look and automatic protest. Instead, she looked confused. Encouraged that she at least appeared to be listening this time, he shrugged. "Honestly, I'm all right with being alone for a while. We don't need to bother with the lessons anymore."

She was quiet for a moment then lifted one shoulder in a shrug. "But you're doing so much better—"

The sound of the boardinghouse door closing made them both jump. Suddenly aware of how close they were standing, Rhett automatically took a step back. It was too little too late to forestall the knowing smirk on Hank Abernathy's face as the man glanced back and forth between them. "Don't mind me, folks. I'm heading to the café for some coffee. Rhett, I thought you might want to join me to talk about the talent-show act we're supposed to do together. However, I can see you two are busy…"

Isabelle's eyes widened. "Don't be silly. Y'all go right ahead. I need to help with supper anyway."

Rhett waited until he was sure Isabelle had made it into the house before settling his gaze on Hank. "I'm not sure I like your tone, Abernathy. Insinuations like that are liable to get a man thrown out."

"Hey, now. Don't get upset with me. I'm only trying to help." Hank slid his hands into his pockets and subtly tilted his head toward the house. "The old man's study door was open. I could see him staring out the window. I didn't know at what until I got to the foyer and saw the two of you in a tête-à-tête. I wouldn't be surprised if the little lady was getting an earful right now. Hope you didn't do anything unfit for standing on the front lawn of the boardinghouse."

"Of course not." Even so, Rhett's gaze casually

swept the front of the house in time to see the curtain close in the study window. Grimacing, Rhett fell into step with Hank as they left the boardinghouse behind. "I appreciate the warning, but Isabelle and I weren't doing anything wrong."

"You don't have to defend yourself to me. I wouldn't blame you if you were."

Rhett shot the man a measuring glance. "Come again?"

Hank shrugged. "Everyone knows boarders come to the Bradley's for the clean room and respectability, but stay for the cooking and the scenery."

"By the 'scenery' I assume you mean—"

"The women, of course."

Rhett frowned as they fell into step on the sidewalk. "In that case, I see why Mr. Bradley insists on that no-flirtation clause."

Hank lifted a skeptical brow. "Now, that's something I never understood. Why would you put something like that in a contract? It's pointless. No, it's downright counterproductive."

"What do you mean?"

"Think about it. There are only a few types of men who live in boardinghouses. There are the honorable ones who wouldn't have thought of looking twice at the proprietor's daughter out of their own sense of morality. Making them sign a contract is silly because they wouldn't have done it anyway, right?"

Rhett gave a slow nod. "Right."

"Then there are the scoundrels who care absolutely nothing about the rules and will do as they please regardless. The contract wouldn't affect their actions, either, because they wouldn't think twice about breaking their word." Hank paused in his diatribe long enough for them to enter Maddie's, find a table and order their coffee. "The few men it does affect are the ones in the middle. The ones who might have given the women a second glance and gone on their way. Now they have a contract saying they aren't allowed to look or touch or think a single untoward thought. What do you think that's going to make them want to do? It's like the forbidden fruit in the garden or the pie cooling on the windowsill. The fact that someone says you can't have it makes it more desirable."

"Putting aside the fact that women aren't 'fruit' or 'pie' or even an 'it,' I get your point." Rhett accepted his coffee from Maddie and waited until she left before lowering his voice. "What I'm wondering about right now is which category you fit in."

Hank narrowed his eyes for a moment then gave a slow smile. "I think for all of our perceived differences, Rhett, you and I both fit somewhere in the middle." Hank let that settle between them long enough to take a sip of coffee before continuing. "My real point in all of this is that you can't mandate respectability with a bunch of rules."

"I suppose you're right. True respectability is based on an internal sense of honor. It can't be forced."

"No, but it can be feigned. I think that's what scares the Bradleys."

"What do you mean it can be feigned? How?"

"How do people measure respectability? They can't see inside you to know if you're truly honorable or not. It's a perception based almost entirely on appearances. Feigning respectability is simply a matter of controlling appearances."

Rhett couldn't help thinking of the bottles of alcohol Isabelle had found in Hank's room. "Maybe so, but people can't hide their true nature forever. It shows through even when we think we've hidden it so well that no one can discover it. Sometimes all it takes a little searching, a little drawing out."

Hank had stilled, a frown on his face. Eventually, it eased to a smile, and he shrugged. "You're right, of course. I'm saying all of this for the sake of a good debate. Truthfully, I can't figure why anyone could go through all that trouble of trying to be something other than themselves."

"It depends on what they're trying to gain, I suppose, and their sense of honor." Rhett leaned forward. "I may be way off here, but it seems to me that you're the kind of man who doesn't like to be hemmed in by rules."

"Not ridiculous ones."

"Which you've already said some of the Bradleys' are, so why do you stay?" He forced a grin to make the question less threatening. "Is it truly for the women and the cooking?"

Hank laughed. "No. After seeing to the whims of others at the hotel all day, it's nice to go home in the evening and be taken care of myself."

"That's right. You're a clerk at the hotel. Isn't it a little awkward to live in the same house as your boss?"

"Not really. As long as I get paid and pay my rent I've got nothing to complain about." Hank frowned. "Except this talent show. I know this may surprise you, but I don't enjoy making a fool out of myself in front of others. I'm pretty sure that's exactly what's going to happen if I try to play the harmonica."

Rhett relaxed in his chair, glad the conversation was heading into a less controversial topic. "What's your talent?"

"Juggling."

Rhett winced. "I've never tried it, but it looks awfully complicated."

"It's easy once you get the hang of it."

Rhett laughed. "Yeah? So is playing the harmonica. How long did it take you to learn how to juggle?"

"About a week."

"The show is tomorrow."

"It sounds like we're in trouble, then."

"I know we're supposed to switch but how about this? You juggle while I play the harmonica."

"Fine with me as long as you smooth it over with Isabelle. Speaking of which, turnabout is fair play. I told you why I'm sticking around the boardinghouse. Why are you?"

The women. That was the answer and Hank knew it. However, it wasn't solely Isabelle that Rhett was sticking around for and not only for the reasons Hank assumed. Rhett was still there for Violet, too. He didn't feel comfortable leaving them on their own to try to catch the thief. They wouldn't have to try much longer. His conversation with Hank had given him an idea about how to put a stop the thief and how to do it quickly.

Realizing Hank was still waiting for an answer as to why Rhett was sticking around the boardinghouse, he simply said, "I'm not."

Then, waving Maddie over, he told her to tell her husband that he'd be willing to rent the Bachelor Box. Quinn's warnings aside, Rhett knew the best thing he could do was to let go of his feelings for Isabelle and move on with his life. That was exactly what he intended to do.

After supper on Sunday evening, Peter sat at the piano to start off the talent show with an accurate but rather staccato version of "Beautiful Dreamer." A hush fell over the gaslit room as each person in the seven-member audience watched Isabelle perform the three magic tricks Peter had taught her for the occasion. She'd found it nearly impossible to concentrate on getting each step right and talking at the same time, which was why they'd combined their acts into one. As it was, her gaze kept straying to her parents' smiling faces.

God was working on them and so were her prayers. How could that not be the case when they were so obviously enjoying this? Hopefully, it would remind them of all of the good times they'd had in this house. It might even help them see how easy it would be to make more memories like this. Then maybe they would be more open to the idea of preserving the business and passing it down to her.

For now, she'd be content if she could master the big finish Peter had planned for her. Offering the audience what she hoped was a distracting smile, she made the half dollar in her hand disappear. The appreciative gasp from the audience was gratifying, as was the applause when she pulled the coin out from behind Violet's ear. Isabelle curtseyed. Peter bowed. Isabelle sat down on a chair between her sister and Rhett, relieved to be done with the performance and happy to be a spectator for the rest of the show.

Beatrice took her place in front of the mantel and

began the recitation Violet had taught her. Though it wasn't as dramatic as the version Isabelle had seen in the kitchen, it came across as heartfelt and sincere. Isabelle barely heard a word of it. She was too busy staring at the empty spot on the mantel where the Waterford crystal clock should be. She closed her eyes and tried to remember the last time she'd seen it. It had been there yesterday when she'd left Peter practicing on the piano.

Her gaze slid down the row of chairs toward the man in question. She pulled in a deep breath and forced her eyes forward again. No. She mustn't jump to conclusions. It was entirely possible that there was a simple explanation for this. Someone might have moved the clock out of the way for the show. Yes, of course. Surely, that was it.

Isabelle didn't miss the hopeful looks Violet kept sending to their parents. She didn't want to involve her sister in the newest mystery until she knew for certain that the clock was missing. Rhett, on the other hand, wouldn't be too bothered by the news. He also still owed her a summary of his conversation with Hank yesterday. She needed to search the parlor for the clock after everyone went to bed. That would be a good time for a private conversation with Rhett, but she could hardly ask him to meet her later without it sounding clandestine or scandalous.

He was one of the last boarders to retire after the show. As he quit the room, she bumped into him when he tried to leave. Patting him on the chest, she apologized profusely before letting him depart. Peter peered at her on his way out the room, but didn't give her away. Perhaps what they said about there being honor among thieves was true. She yawned and glanced at her family. "I don't know about y'all, but I'm worn-out."

That was the cue they needed to turn in. Fifteen minutes later, the house was quiet. She was still dressed, so it was a simple matter to creep down the hall and unlatch the door separating the family wing from the rest of the house. She crossed to the parlor and grinned at the sight of Rhett standing in the middle of room in his bare feet, black pants and untucked gray shirt. He glanced about with his hands on his hips as if that would help him find anything.

Schooling her grin into nothing more than a slight smirk, she waved his harmonica back and forth as she whispered, "Looking for something?"

He froze, slowly turned on his heel to level her with his amber gaze. He kept his deep voice low, as well. "This is getting to be a habit of yours—stealing things from me."

"I always give them back." She stepped forward to place it in his open palm.

His hand closed around the harmonica and her fingers as he lifted an eyebrow. "Nope. I'm pretty sure I've caught the real thief in the boardinghouse."

Before Isabelle could respond, her sister's voice sounded softly from the doorway. "Well, la-di-da. Isn't this cozy?"

Isabelle rolled her eyes and pulled her hand from Rhett's grasp to beckon Violet into the room. "I was going to spare you, but you might as will hear this, as well. I came back to search for the Waterford clock. It seems to be missing."

"What clock?" Rhett asked over Violet's gasp.

"The one that used to sit here," Violet said, running a hand over the blank space on the mantel. "It was a wedding present to our parents."

Isabelle joined her sister, though her gaze swept the room again. Nothing else was out of place despite the festivities that had happened there earlier. "The last time I saw it was when I left Peter practicing in here yesterday."

Rhett shrugged. "Everyone in the house has had access to this room since then. Anyone could have taken it."

Violet grimaced. "What are we going to do?"

Isabelle jumped as a loud creak sounded from the staircase. She automatically grabbed her sister's arm and hid against the wall beside the entrance of the room. They'd be in full view of anyone who entered. Thankfully, Rhett moved into the hallway to intercept the person. He kept his voice low, but not so low that she couldn't hear him clearly. "Peter, what you doing down here?"

Peter matched his volume. "I thought I might find you. I wanted to let you know that there's no use searching for your harmonica. Isabelle took it when she bumped into you earlier tonight."

"She did?"

Relief filled Isabelle at the sound of Rhett playing dumb. It would do her no favors to have Peter report to her parents that she'd been sneaking around the boardinghouse at night to meet with Rhett. The fact that Violet was present might not make things much better in their eyes. They'd probably think Isabelle was being a bad example to her little sister. Truth be told, she probably was.

"Yeah. I guess it was a bad idea to teach her how to pick pockets. She was so interested, though. I guess we know why now. She probably intends to use it for some sort of mischief, so be warned."

"Thanks. I have to admit, you've made me curious. How do you know enough about pickpocketing to teach Isabelle?"

Isabelle could practically hear Peter shrugging. "Things haven't always been easy for me. I did what I needed to do, whether that meant performing magic shows on the corner or—"

"Stealing?"

"I always gave it back saying they'd dropped it on the street. Usually, I'd get a reward for 'finding' it with all of the money intact. It isn't something I'm proud of or something I like to talk about. You should come back upstairs. The Bradleys don't like boarders wandering the house at night."

"You go ahead. I'll be right up as soon as I turn out the lights."

The two men said good-night before Rhett reentered the parlor. He placed a finger over his lips to remind them to be quiet. Isabelle waited until she heard the stairs creak and a door close overhead before she let out the breath she'd been holding. "Peter barely said two words to me all week while we were working on our act. How do you get people to talk to you like that?"

Rhett shrugged. "I've found it helps to ask what you want to know point-blank. People might think you're nosy, but most of the time they answer. I also think he felt more comfortable with me because I'm a man. I take it you both heard the conversation, then?"

Violet nodded. "I know it's a point in his favor that he was honest about his past, but I still don't trust him. If he was willing to be underhanded when times were tough before, who's to say he wouldn't have a propensity to act that way again in a similar situation?"

"You're right." Isabelle gently elbowed her sister. "You're also a smart lady. How'd you know I was going to be out here?"

"You didn't look happy even though tonight was a success. I figured something was wrong and went to your room to find out what. You weren't there. You're a smart lady, too. Picking Rhett's pocket was genius. You'll have to show me how you did it."

"Ladies, please. You can compliment each other later. I have to get back upstairs before Peter comes looking again."

"Violet and I need to get back to our rooms before Ma and Pa miss us. But first, tell us what Hank said yesterday."

"There isn't much I'd care to repeat. Let's just say I don't trust him."

Isabelle exchanged a frown with her sister. "Well, that doesn't sound good."

Violet shook her head. "That means we have two real suspects—Peter and Hank. What do we do now?"

Rhett raked his fingers through the dark waves of his hair as he stared down at the banked fire in the fireplace. "I think we need to draw the thief out, use his own nature against him."

Isabelle nodded slowly. "Yes, but how?"

"So far all of the boarders have said they're going to the benefit on Sunday. Pick something you don't mind using as bait—jewelry, perhaps. Make a fuss over it by mentioning it during the week then let them see you leave it here before you go. They'll know they only have a limited amount of time to strike. Whoever leaves the benefit early to steal it is our man."

"That's a good plan," Violet said, "but we need to do more than that. We need to catch him in the act."

Isabelle lifted her chin. "I'll follow him."

Rhett shook his head, his voice stern. "Absolutely not. There's no way I'm going to let you confront this man alone. Before you offer to go with her, Violet—"

Violet froze with her mouth already open to do exactly that.

"Don't." He ignored Violet's glare to focus on Isabelle. "I'll be watching, too. If anyone leaves, I'll meet you at the front of the courthouse. We'll follow him to the boardinghouse and confront him together."

"How are you going to do that if you're supposed to be performing?"

"I only play in the first and the last acts. I have a feeling intermission will be the time our thief is going to strike. He'll be able to get in and out without being noticed. Violet, I'll get you a copy of the order of the show. We'll pick a set time. If you don't see us back by then, tell your father where we are." He cut off both their protests with a stern look. "I mean it. Something could have gone horribly wrong. We don't want you running into the middle of it."

"He's right, Violet."

"Fine, but what are y'all going to do if you catch him?"

Rhett's gaze landed on Isabelle's, letting her decide. That was good because she'd already thought that part through. "We're going to tell him that he needs to leave or we're going to notify my parents and the sheriff." At Rhett's uneasy look, she added, "The whole point is to keep my parents from finding out about the thefts, remember? Hopefully, the ultimatum will be enough to send him on his way."

"To steal from someone else."

"Maybe he'll recognize the second chance for what it is and stop thieving." Even as she said it, she knew it wasn't likely. What else could they do, though?

Rhett gave her a doubtful look, but nodded. "Are we clear on the plan?"

Violet nodded. "Crystal."

Isabelle grinned. "Let's finally catch that thief."

Chapter Thirteen

By the time the evening of the benefit arrived, everything was going according to plan. Isabelle and Violet had picked a pearl choker from Amy's jewelry box to use as bait. It was the perfect choice because they'd already mentioned mailing Amy's belongings to her. Isabelle made several comments about wearing real, honest-to-goodness pearls once before sending them on to their rightful owner. At the last moment she complained about how uncomfortable it was and left it in full view of the boarders on the front desk before leaving the boardinghouse.

Her parents followed behind as she walked toward the courthouse with Violet and the boarders. She couldn't help eyeing them. One of them was going to take the bait, but whom?

The group split up as soon as they reached the courthouse, much to Isabelle's chagrin. She held back long enough to track where Peter and Hank sat then went to sit with her family. Her father stopped her as she tried to pass him. Her mouth fell open as he slid the pearl choker into her hand. "You shouldn't leave things like this lying about. It encourages thievery."

She glanced over at Violet, who was talking with Beatrice, totally oblivious to the panic that filled Isabelle's thoughts. What should she do? She had to put the necklace back or everything would be ruined. There was no other option.

"Sorry, Pa." She smiled and forced words past her tight throat while slipping the choker into her reticule. "I'm going to look for my friends."

She did indeed look for her friends and spotted Helen and Ellie toward the front. However, instead of heading toward them, she aimed for the door. The judge chose that moment to ask everyone to stop moving and respectfully bow their heads. He gave a prayer of thanksgiving that the town hadn't been damaged further by the fire, then called Rhett to the stage.

Rhett was prepared to start playing his harmonica but Judge Hendricks stopped him. "Before Rhett plays, I want you all to know that this benefit came about because he selflessly requested that the money collected by the town to help him start over be put toward purchasing a fire wagon for Peppin. Rhett, this town appreciates the fine work you do at your smithy. However, I think we are more impressed by your humble and indomitable spirit. God bless you and continue to keep you safe."

This was all news to Isabelle. She joined in with the applause, smiling at how surprised and embarrassed Rhett seemed by all of the fuss being made over him. He cleared his throat. "I can't tell you how much the support and encouragement I have received from this town has meant to me. I may have been the only one who lost a house on New Year's Eve, but I wasn't the only one affected by the fire. This fire wagon is for all of us. If we all give what we can, I know we can come up with the funds we need to purchase it. I don't know what else to say besides thank you again, and the best way I know to do that is with a song."

As he started playing a few people began to move around enough to settle in. Isabelle took the opportunity to slip out the door. She hadn't had time to take off her coat, so she didn't stop or slow down for anything as she hurried across the street and down the block to the boardinghouse. She hopped up the porch steps and discovered the front door was locked. She groaned. How had they not realized that with everyone leaving the house her father would lock the door? She was stumped for a moment because she didn't have a key. She found the gate to the backyard was unlocked, but the back door wasn't.

Her gaze settled on the kitchen window. Her mother often opened it even in the winter to cool the kitchen down. There was a good chance it might be unlocked now. She tried it and breathed a sigh of relief when it easily slid open. It was a bit high, so she rolled the stump used to cut firewood beneath it. She removed her coat and spread it over the windowsill to keep the bricks from snagging the fabric of her dress. Hiking her skirt up past her knees, she boosted herself onto the ledge of the window then pivoted to slide her legs through the opening. She searched for footing in the sink. She found it among a pile of dirty dishes and cold, sudsy water. She jerked backward and nearly toppled headfirst onto the lawn. With a grimace, she rooted around the sink with her waterlogged boots until she knocked the drain cover out of place.

She waited for the water to swirl out before sliding through the window into the large sink. From there she moved to the counter then to the floor. She immediately emptied her shoes into the sink then groaned at the sight of the drenched top half of her coat. She pulled it from the window and tiptoed in her stockings over to a towel. Her feet were soon relatively dry, though she knew that would change as soon as she put her shoes back on.

Delaying that inevitable moment, she draped her coat over a chair as though that would help it to dry in the thirty seconds she would have before she'd need to return. She put the necklace back on the front desk where it belonged before unlocking the front door. She went back to the kitchen for her shoes and coat, but realized everything she'd disturbed in the kitchen needed to look precisely as she'd found it to keep her parents from being suspicious. She closed the window and began to pump water into the sink, deciding the block beneath the window could wait until later.

The front door opened and closed. She froze; her eyes widened. Heart pounding in her chest, her thoughts began to race. Talking about confronting someone on her own was one thing. Actually doing it was something else entirely.

Shouldn't she have some sort of weapon to defend herself in case, as Rhett said, something went horribly wrong? What did that even mean anyway? Suddenly, she was imagining all sorts of awful things. What had she gotten herself into? She wasn't sure, but apparently it would be up to her to get herself out of it.

Her hand strayed toward a steak knife. She pulled back, appalled by her hereto undiscovered violent tendencies. She reached for a cast-iron saucepan instead as footsteps sounded in the hallway. She crept toward the kitchen door with her weapon at the ready.

"Isabelle?"

She sagged in relief. "Rhett!"

"Where are you?"

"The kitchen."

He stepped inside and she wasn't sure who started it but somehow she was in his arms. Grasping his coat in one hand and the pot in the other, she growled, "You scared ten years off my life by coming in here like that, you scoundrel. I thought you were the thief."

"Sorry, Sleuth. I thought you had more sense than to come here by yourself. I almost had apoplexy when I saw you sneak out. Hey, the ribbon on your dress is torn in the back." He caught her arms and pulled back to survey her. "Look at you. You're a mess."

"I know, but this isn't my fault. Pa took the necklace with him. He gave it to me at the courthouse saying I shouldn't leave it lying about because it would encourage thievery. Stop laughing. It isn't funny at all. He left the door locked, too. I had to enter through the kitchen window. Ma left dishes soaking in the sink. I'm all wet, and you scared the life out of me."

"You already mentioned that." He pulled in a deep breath. "All right, let's both calm down. In fact, just sit down. I'll clean this up and we'll get out of here."

She hadn't noticed all of the puddles she'd left on the floor until he started mopping them up with a towel. Too nervous to sit still for long, she refilled the sink until Rhett took over that job for her. She crossed her arms and leaned against the counter to watch him finish up. "Is there any point in going back to the courthouse?"

"Yes. You've already been missing too long. We don't want anything to look suspicious."

She nodded and followed him out of the kitchen toward the front door. She had no intention of putting her shoes on any sooner than necessary, so she carried them with her and paused in the foyer to put them on. Her eyes strayed toward the front desk then widened as everything within her stilled. The necklace was gone.

The hair on the back of her neck lifted. She glanced at Rhett, who watched the empty street. Had he moved it? No. He'd have no reason to. That meant…

Panic filled her. She clutched Rhett's arm and pulled herself nearly flush against his chest once more. She hissed out a whisper. "Rhett, the necklace is gone. It's gone! Someone is in here."

Rhett stiffened. His gaze slid from Isabelle's to the front desk, where the necklace had been when he'd entered the house. He hadn't touched it and there was no way it could have fallen off or disappeared by itself. That meant Isabelle was right. Someone had come into the house and taken it. Where was the person now? Rhett had a clear view of the street all the way to the courtyard, so he would have been able to see if anyone had recently left the boardinghouse. No one was walking about since practically the whole town was crammed into the courthouse for the benefit.

Automatically easing himself between Isabelle and the rest of the house, he scanned the grand hallway. He could understand Isabelle being a bit spooked. There was something eerie about seeing a house normally so full of life completely empty of people and noise. Well, it wasn't completely empty. That was the problem.

It was safe to say that the family wing was locked up tight enough to keep out any wanderers. The same was probably true for Mr. Bradley's study. That still left the parlor and dining room, which they'd just passed, along with the entire second floor. He couldn't assume that the person was as oblivious to their presence as they had been to his. The thief could be trying to hide until they left or lying in wait for them to come after him.

He grimaced, suddenly realizing he'd left the gun he'd borrowed from Quinn at the courthouse in the mad dash to save Isabelle from herself. It would have been nice to have some other way than his fists to protect Isabelle if the thief didn't take kindly to being caught. It wasn't too late for them to turn back, to tell Mr. Bradley all that had been happening and let the man deal with it himself. But Rhett was pretty certain Isabelle wouldn't agree with that plan. Even so, he glanced down at her over his shoulder and pointed to the front door.

She flinched at the sound of the floorboard creaking overhead. He saw indecision in her eyes then she shook her head. She pointed upward before placing a hand on his back and pushed him forward slightly. He bit back the urge to tease her about being awfully brave for someone hiding behind someone else. Silence would be the key in catching the thief off guard. They didn't want him to bolt before they could confront him.

With that in mind, he moved soundlessly toward the stairs. She followed at his heels with one hand clutching the back of his shirt while the other held on to the shoes she'd never actually put back on. As one, they avoided the creaky step at the top. Muffled rustling issued from one of the rooms, but it was hard to tell which. Rhett took a step forward, eager to find out. Isabelle slid to his left, opened the door to the linen closet and frantically beckoned him inside while shaking her head. He blinked at her, looked down the hall, swayed forward then back in indecision. Finally, he threw up his hands at the entire situation and joined her in the closet.

His hand closed over hers on the doorknob as he pulled the door shut. He felt a soft blow to his side. Had Isabelle punched him? He supposed it was more of a kick and a damp one at that since she was still holding her shoes in that hand.

He glanced down to look at her just as she briefly rested her forehead on his arm right below his shoulder. Or was that a head-butt? He wasn't sure, but it was awfully nice until she glared up at him through the dim light filtering through a small, curtained window on the back wall. He stared right back at her as if she'd lost her mind, which she surely had. Why else would she pull him into a closet to beat him up after weeks of searching for the thief down the hall?

An instant later, a door opened and closed down the hall. Rhett tightened his hand around Isabelle's and the door handle, ready to open it and pounce. However, Isabelle released her grip, which caused his to slide away, as well. She then put a restraining hand on his wrist as heavy footsteps passed the linen closet and tromped down the stairs. It was only after the front door opened then closed that she released him.

"Rhett, you told Violet to send help if we didn't show up because it would mean that something must have gone horribly wrong. What did you anticipate? That we would be shot or stabbed or—"

He stared at her. "Is that why you pulled me into this closet?"

"I got scared." She removed her wet coat and draped it on one of the hooks on the wall. "He might have had a gun or a knife for all we know."

"Probably not."

She rolled her eyes. "Yeah, well, I panicked. I couldn't think clearly until I found myself locked in here with you while the thief got away with the choker."

"You should have let me confront him alone, then. I told you…" His eyes narrowed. "Wait. What do you mean *locked* in here with me?"

She lifted her chin toward the door. "The lock is faulty. That's why I still had my hand on the knob. I always keep it open at least a crack so that I can get out. If not, I have to bang on the wall to get Gabe to open it from the outside. But he's gone and no one else is here, so we're stuck."

"Please, tell me you're fooling." He turned the knob and tugged at the door. It wouldn't budge. He pulled harder. It stayed stuck. This went on for several minutes. He thought of trying to take it off the hinges, but those were on the outside. "Something is definitely not right with this door."

Isabelle sighed from where she sat on a waist-high laundry folding table along the back wall. "It's been broken for ages. I keep forgetting to remind Pa to fix it."

He leaned back against the door. Crossing his arms, he lifted his chin and stared down at her. "So is that why you punch-kicked me? Because I closed the door?"

"I'm sorry. It seemed like a pretty good reason at the time." She braced her elbows on the stack of towels behind her and leaned back. "Oh, and, Rhett?"

"What?"

Her green eyes held his intensely as she slowly shook her head. "We are in *so* much trouble."

He was well aware of that. He desperately needed to get back to the benefit. If he didn't show up in time to play the final act with Quinn and Chris, the whole town would be asking where he was. Having everyone find out he'd been locked in a closet with Isabelle would be even worse. That was hardly proper. In fact, it was nigh on scandalous.

He'd done quite well at avoiding her this past week. Truth be told, that had left him feeling more than a little miserable, but he'd get over it soon enough. Surely, he would. He'd noticed she hadn't tried to bridge the distance between them, either. That served to underscore what he should have known all along. Their relationship hadn't mattered nearly as much to her as it had to him.

He swallowed hard. "Remember when I told Violet if we didn't show up when we were supposed to, something must be horribly wrong? This kind of thing is what I actually meant—not the dime-novel ending you had in your head."

She tilted her head. "You mean the one where the thief turned out to be an evil, armed gunman who shot us both then escaped on a train with the family silver, no one the wiser save our bleeding bodies?"

"Whoa. That's only slightly horrifying. When you put it like that, this isn't so bad." He sat on the floor in front of the door. They were quiet for a moment as he tried to estimate how much time he had before he was supposed to be back on stage. If the thief had left at intermission, Rhett probably had a twenty-minute window before he'd be missed.

He eyed the window behind Isabelle, but it was far too small for either of them to fit through. Besides, they were on the second story. He sighed. "You do realize that after all of this, we still don't know who the thief is."

"Violet ought to know. She was supposed to watch for whoever left after we did." She grimaced. "It isn't going to matter much. She's probably going to have to... Did you hear that?"

He stood at the very idea of a possible rescue, cocking his head to listen. "It's a bit faint, but I think someone is moving around down there. Seems like it could be coming from your family's rooms. Maybe it's Violet."

With hope lighting her face, she slid from the table to join him at the door. Rhett saw what was coming but had no way to stop it as her momentum sent the table crashing to the floor. It must have caught Isabelle's skirt, for he heard fabric tear as she stumbled. Momentum pitched her forward into his chest. Driven back against the door, his arms automatically wrapped around her waist. The door gave way behind him. He staggered backward, struggling to keep an already off-balance Isabelle on her feet. He came to an abrupt stop when his back met the opposing wall of the hallway.

Thick, uncomfortable silence filled the hallway as Rhett took a moment to regain his wits and equilibrium. His gaze connected with the chilling glare of the man who'd freed them. Easing his arm from around Isabelle's waist, he gave a respectful nod. "Mr. Bradley."

Chapter Fourteen

Rhett felt Isabelle stiffen in his arms and glanced down at her in time to see her eyes widen then close tightly. Squaring her shoulders, she turned to face her father. "I can explain."

The man crossed his arms and lifted a skeptical brow. "Please, do."

Isabelle's troubled green eyes sought Rhett's. He gave her a supportive nod, aware that the story would probably sound better coming from her. She swallowed. "Well, Pa, we have a thief in the boardinghouse. Rhett, Violet and I have been trying to catch him. That's why I left the necklace on the counter. It was bait. I snuck out of the benefit to put it back where it needed to be. Rhett saw me leave and came to check on me. We almost caught the thief, but I got scared and jumped in the closet, taking Rhett with me. He closed the door not realizing it would lock. That's all there is to it."

"That's all there is to it?" her father repeated as though trying those words on for size while his gaze went back and forth between the two of them.

Rhett slid his hands into his pockets and found the comforting presence of his harmonica. It served as a reminder that Rhett needed to get back on that stage to avoid a scandal. However, he needed to deal with one crisis at a time. "Isabelle was sitting on the table in the closet. When she stood up, it fell, then she fell. I caught her just as you opened the door."

"I see." Mr. Bradley glanced into the closet then back at them. "And the thief? What has he stolen?"

"Ma's bracelet that I borrowed for the masquerade, the Waterford crystal clock that sat on mantel and—"

"Amy's pearl necklace?" He pulled it from his pocket.

Rhett stared, dumbfounded.

Isabelle gasped. "Pa, how did you get that—again?"

"Wes gave it to me."

Now Rhett was really confused. "You mean Wes is the thief?"

"No, I don't."

Isabelle shook her head. "Then why did he have the necklace?"

"Wes spilled something on his shirt at intermission simply to have an excuse to come back to the boardinghouse. He wanted to warn y'all that I was getting suspicious after we saw you both sneak out of the courthouse. Rhett, I'm of a mind to think he intended to wallop you pretty good if he'd found you in a compromising situation with my daughter." Her father finally smiled. "Nice boy, that Wes."

Isabelle gave an appalled little gasp. "Pa, really. How could you think we would do such a thing?"

Panic rattled his heart in his chest. Surely, Mr. Bradley wouldn't call him out on his feelings in front of Isabelle. Rhett didn't give him the chance. "That doesn't explain why he had the necklace."

"He gave it to me along with the keys I'd given him to get into the house. He said he couldn't find y'all in the house, but the necklace was proof that you'd been there so I might want to start my search there."

"What about the other things that are missing?"

Thomas shrugged. "The clock got broken after y'all left for Helen's place when Gabe and I tried to practice our Scottish dance in the parlor. We can't quite agree on which one of us is to blame for that."

Isabelle frowned. "If that's the case, then why didn't Violet know anything about it?"

"I'm not sure. I believe Violet might have been reading in her room by that point."

Rhett glanced at Isabelle. "What about the bracelet Isabelle wore on the night of the masquerade?"

"I found it lying on the floor by the desk. The clasp was broken, so I sent it off to be repaired."

Isabelle shook her head. "I still don't understand. Violet said you'd left for the hotel with her, and I know you didn't return until much later than she did."

"Actually, I did return briefly because I'd left my spectacles in my bedroom."

"I must have been in the kitchen with Ma because I never saw you. If you had the bracelet the whole time, why didn't you tell me?"

He gave his daughter a chiding look. "I was hoping that you'd come to me and admit that you'd lost it."

"Well, I would have if it had solely involved me, but Violet was the one who dropped it on the floor and left it there. I didn't want to get her in trouble. Then we thought someone had stolen it."

Mr. Bradley shrugged. "Unless you count me, the only thief in this house lives in your imaginations."

"Oh." The word eased from Isabelle's lips filled with a mixture of dismay, disbelief and relief.

Knowing this must be quite a blow, Rhett stepped toward her intending to put a hand on her back to comfort her. He stopped short at the realization that any physical contact between them would make things worse. His gaze connected with Mr. Bradley's censoring green eyes to see his fears confirmed. They'd been concerned about the thief being the final straw that would make her parents decide to sell the boardinghouse. Yet, that clearly wasn't the real threat to Isabelle's and Violet's hopes of remaining in Peppin.

All of this time, the only thing putting Isabelle's hopes of staying in town in jeopardy was Rhett's relationship with Isabelle. That was the only threat Mr. Bradley had ever seen, the only one he'd ever been concerned about. It was why he'd warned Rhett to be careful. It was why he'd watched them from his study window. It was why he'd gone after them when they'd disappeared from the benefit. Wes had seen that from the beginning, which was why he'd tried to warn Rhett to stay away. Rhett should have tried harder to do that. Instead, he'd ruined everything for Isabelle and Violet.

"This is my fault." The admission was out before he even made the conscious decision to say the words. He could see they garnered Mr. Bradley's interest. He knew he needed to continue for Isabelle's sake. "I know it looks bad, but we truly did think there was a thief and I truly did want to help Isabelle. That is part of why we spent so much time together. If our friendship broke the rules, it's my fault, not hers. Please, don't blame Isabelle."

"If our friendship broke the…" Isabelle turned from him to Mr. Bradley. "What rules could our friendship break? What is he talking about?"

"Isabelle, we will discuss this later." He ignored her protest to glare at Rhett, who did his best not to wince. "I believe if you leave now, you can return to the benefit in time to avoid a scandal. Isabelle and I will stay here to clean up the mess in the closet and to keep it from appearing as though you returned together. I trust that by Monday you will have found other accommodations."

"Yes, sir." He glanced at Isabelle, hating to leave after managing to make things worse for her. Her eyes were on her father and he could see the wheels turning in her head as she put everything together. He had a feeling she wouldn't like the result.

Isabelle waited until she heard the front door shut behind Rhett before asking her father, "What rules?"

He refused to meet her gaze, turning instead to enter the closet. "I think it's best that we wait to have this discussion when your ma and Violet are present."

"Pa, *please*." She followed him as far as the closet door and watched him set the table upright. "Tell me."

He sighed then turned to face her. He looked older than he had that morning. For the first time, she noticed the weary set to his broad shoulders, the lines around his eyes, the frown that covered his face more often than not these days. He dragged a hand over his mustache and beard before nodding. "Stay here."

She stepped out of the way so that he could brush

past her. He made quick work of the stairs and returned in a matter of moments with a small stack of papers in hand. He offered the bundle to her. She took it somewhat hesitantly when she realized it was a rental agreement since it was something her father had always insisted the women of the family leave in his capable hands. Frowning, she sent him a questioning glance before looking down at the page he'd placed on top. Her breath caught as her mind stumbled over the words Rhett must have been referring to a few minutes ago. Heat spilled across her cheeks. "I am mortified. How could you put this in there as if I'm some sort of wanton woman?"

"That clause has nothing to do with you."

Her mouth dropped open as she stared at him. "It has *everything* to do with me."

"I mean, it doesn't have anything to do with your behavior. Although…" He gestured to the mess of linens still spilled across the floor. "It would not hurt for you to use a bit more discretion. Even so, I'm not blaming you as much as I'm blaming myself and this confounded boardinghouse."

"Pa, I don't understand any of this. If this clause doesn't have to do with me or my behavior, then why is it in here?"

"What other defense did I have?" He slid his fingers through his dark, silver-frosted hair as he paced the hallway in front of the closet. "I've seen the way the boarders look at you—and even Violet on occasion."

She frowned, taken aback. "What do you mean?"

"They're men. They can't help noticing a beautiful girl." He shook his head when she tried to protest. "I know you think of the boarders as the brothers you've never had, but they don't see you the same way for a very good reason. They aren't your brothers. In essence, they are little more than strangers who usually stay a short amount of time before moving on. It causes me no end of worry because I never intended for my daughters to live among men like this.

"When your mother and I opened the boardinghouse years ago, nearly every tenant we had was a family or woman displaced by the war. Once the railroad swept into town, our tenants became increasingly male. I didn't worry about it much until Amy's elopement. That's when I began to realize how much of a fool I'd been. I'm done trusting men I don't truly know, can never truly know, to behave honorably while living in the same house as my daughters."

She stiffened. "So you've made the decision, then? You're going to sell the boardinghouse."

"Yes."

"But…" Her thoughts raced, making it impossible to finish that thought. How could her parents sell the boardinghouse when she'd been praying and believing and hoping that they wouldn't? Didn't any of that mean anything? Yet, her father's certainty made it sound as if he'd never had any doubts about doing exactly that. She couldn't help wonder if her attempts to sway him had been in vain the entire time. "How long have you known?"

"Your mother and I have been talking about the decision for several months."

"But you hadn't decided for sure until about five minutes ago when I fell through this door with Rhett. Isn't that so?"

He gave a small nod. "It gave me the confirmation

I needed. However, I would have arrived at the same decision sooner rather than later."

Oh, the decision to sell might have been made eventually. However, her actions had prompted him to decide earlier than he otherwise might have. In the interim, something might have happened to change his mind—something like her prayers and faith. Yet, wasn't God powerful enough to have worked within that period of time so that her father wouldn't have wanted to sell the boardinghouse despite finding her with Rhett? Of course He was. Did that mean He'd chosen not to? No. God wouldn't leave her high and dry like that. Would He?

Suddenly, she wasn't sure. One thing was certain. Her father had made his decision. He was going to try to sell the boardinghouse, and it was entirely her fault. What was more, her father had every right to be upset. She could have easily caused a scandal big enough to put Amy's to shame if the wrong person had found her locked in a closet with Rhett. Her reputation still might be ruined along with Rhett, her family, the other boarders and the boardinghouse itself if the story got out. Shotgun weddings had been prompted by lesser infractions. In other words, she'd made a grand mess of everything and she knew it.

Tears blurred her eyes as she gathered towels from the floor. "Will you tell Wes that Rhett and I weren't doing anything untoward?"

"Yes, I will." He knelt to grab a couple of bed-sheets. "He promised not to say anything about it to anyone, so I don't think you have to worry on that front."

She grimaced as she put a stack of towels back in

place. "Perhaps I ought to stay here. You could tell everyone that I left the benefit because I wasn't feeling well. I'm sure it wouldn't be hard to summon a headache at this point."

It was only when her father glanced up sharply that she realized she'd chosen her excuse poorly since Amy had pleaded a headache to remain behind on the night of the shivaree. "I think you'd better come back with me. The best way to avoid a scandal is to act like it never happened. Behave normally. If anyone asks, you can say you needed to get something from the house. It's close enough to the truth."

She glanced over at her still-damp boots. "Actually, it is true. I need to change shoes. Mine got soaked."

"I'd ask why and how you managed to get into the house I made sure to lock and any number of questions. However, I have a feeling that I don't want to know."

She finally managed a smile. "You don't."

They made quick work of straightening the linen closet before Isabelle put on a different pair of boots. Her father escorted her inside the courthouse just as Rhett, Quinn and Chris finished their last song. Judge Hendricks took the stage after a hearty round of applause. The hoopla increased when it was announced that the town had met its goal for the funds to purchase a fire wagon. Chris broke into a jig on his fiddle. A few other musicians joined him and a space in the center of the room was cleared as the benefit turned into an impromptu dance.

Her father nodded toward the dancers. "Go on. I'll see if I can find Wes."

"What about Violet? She knew we were trying to

catch the thief. Do you want me to tell her what happened?"

"No. I want her to hear it from me. She and your mother have spotted us, so if you want to escape you'd better go."

She had no desire to dance, but she relished the idea of another confrontation even less. Still, she hesitated. "Pa, I want to speak to Rhett. He's my friend. He's no longer a boarder, so—"

"Fine." The word was forced enough to let her know what it cost him to say it. "The last time I forbade a daughter to communicate with a man didn't turn out very well. Just…be careful."

On a whim, she kissed his cheek before skirting around the improvised dance floor toward the musicians. Rhett stood near the platform where they played, turning his silent harmonica end over end between his hands as he watched the celebration. He smiled when he saw her coming but the concern in his eyes asked her questions that would be difficult to answer circumspectly over the crowd and the music. She cut her gaze toward a door to the left and he was there to open it for her by the time she reached it.

Rhett caught her arm to lead her down a narrow hallway and up a spiral staircase that led to the courthouse's cupola. Each wall of the small, square room boasted an arched window that looked out over the town in one of the cardinal directions. Drawn by the streaks of gold and pink hinting the early stages of sunset, she eased toward the window that provided a breathtaking view of the tree-covered hills stretching beyond the east side of town. Rhett didn't seem the least bit distracted by the scenery. "What happened? What did your pa say?"

"We put the closet back in order and…" She turned to peer through the window that overlooked the boardinghouse and sighed.

"Pa said he is definitely going to sell the boardinghouse, but that doesn't mean that he will, right? Maybe he won't be able to find a buyer. Or maybe he'll change his mind at the last minute and not be able to go through with it. There's still a chance, isn't there? Perhaps if I—"

Comfort flowed through the warmth of Rhett's hand as he stepped up behind her to squeeze her upper arm gently. His touch stilled her rambling flow of words. Her shoulders lowered in dejection. "Oh, Rhett."

A gentle tug was all it took for him to turn her around into his embrace. "I'm sorry, sweetheart. I know how much the boardinghouse means to you."

He didn't. Not really. She hadn't told anyone that she planned on running the boardinghouse one day. She couldn't bring herself to say it now. She didn't want Rhett to laugh at her or tell her how impractical it was. It hardly mattered now, anyway. With her arms still around his neck from the hug, she pulled back enough to smile at him. "Thank you, Rhett. You've truly been a huge help this whole time."

He lifted a skeptical brow. "By getting you into more trouble?"

"You didn't get me into more trouble. You supported me and encouraged me and listened to me."

"Well, I'm glad I was of some use while I was recovering. Besides, it's…" He looked away and shrugged, which caused her hands slip down to his chest. "It's been a pleasure."

She became conscious of the fact that the hug was over and she should move away. However, in the next instant, Rhett's eyes captured hers. They'd darkened to a rich golden brown that was earnest, sincere and mesmerizing. She found herself swaying toward him, her gaze on his lips before she realized what she was about to do. She pulled back. Rhett must have guessed her intent for he'd already started to lower his head. He stopped, lingered with his forehead brushing against hers.

Realizing he would come no closer, she lifted her lashes enough for her eyes to trace the strong line of his jaw, his chin, his mouth. His arm tightened around her. His lips caressed her temple then her cheek. Finally, he kissed her lips.

She closed her eyes and gave in to the depths of emotions she could hardly fathom, dared not even name. She matched his intensity as he kissed her again. As one, they paused to catch their breath. Sanity filtered back into her mind as air filled her lungs along with a healthy dose of fear. He must have felt her stiffen, for his whisper was deep and entreating. "Isabelle?"

She couldn't meet his gaze as she pushed away from his chest. She hurried down the spiral staircase so fast that she was dizzy by the time she reached the bottom. It wasn't until she stepped back into the hubbub of the celebration that she was able to breathe again.

What was wrong with her? Why had she kissed him—*again*? There were so many reasons why she shouldn't have. He'd been in love with Amy. He was settling for her like John and Chris had before him.

The only difference between him and the others was she was better friends with him. Apparently, she was also attracted to him. That certainly wouldn't do. Since she couldn't seem to control her emotions when he was around, the best thing she could do for herself was to stay far away from him. From now on, that was exactly what she planned to do.

Chapter Fifteen

Rhett stared down the empty spiral staircase in Isabelle's wake. As passionate as their kisses had been, the look she'd given him afterward had been more than enough to bank the fire that sparked between them. At least, it should have been. He closed his eyes and took a deep breath in an effort to calm his still-racing heart. What had she done to him? It had been hard enough to get their New Year's Eve kiss out of his head, but this...

He shook his head in an effort to free himself from the fog their kisses had created before slowly descending the stairs. He wanted to give her plenty of time to put some distance between them since that had obviously been her intent in running away. Seeing the empty hallway, he realized he'd been hoping that he'd see her turning around to come back to him. That she'd tell him their kisses meant as much to her as they did to him. That *he* meant as much to her as she did to him.

He sank down to sit on the stairs and buried his fingers in his hair. Isabelle had to feel something beyond friendship to kiss him with that much depth of emotion. She wasn't supposed to, though. It didn't fit with his understanding of God's will for his life. It contradicted her assertion that there wouldn't be another kiss and that the first one was a onetime thing. It even called into question her refusal of his courtship. After all, no honorable man would kiss a woman like that without having a prior understanding with the young lady. And Rhett considered himself an honorable man. Yet the only understanding Isabelle's last glance seemed to seek was one of mutual distance.

The turmoil that inspired within him didn't make a lick of sense. He was supposed to give her up. That was what he'd decided God meant for him to do. That was what he was *trying* to do. Why was he so bad at it, then? Was he really so weak that he couldn't resist the attraction of the friendship they'd carved out, the connection they had with each other, her sense of humor, her beauty, her kiss…? He shook his head and smiled mirthlessly. At some point, wasn't God's will supposed to bring a sense of peace and purpose? So far, Rhett had merely experienced frustration, confusion and turmoil.

"What happened to you?"

Rhett started at the sound of Quinn's voice and glanced up to find his friend standing before him with a concerned frown. Rhett grimaced. "Isabelle happened."

"What'd she do?" Quinn asked with a grin that withered only slightly under Rhett's glare.

Rhett leaned forward to make sure the hallway was clear before answering, "She *kissed* me."

Quinn grunted. "The *nerve*—"

"Would you stop joking around? This is serious."

"I'm sorry." To his credit, Quinn only chuckled once more. "I'm going to assume you kissed her back. Then what happened?"

Defeat filled his voice as he braced his elbows on the stair behind him. "She ran away."

Quinn blinked. "Why'd she do that?"

"How should I know?"

"You could have followed her and asked her."

"Well, I didn't. Besides, if she'd wanted me to know she would have told me instead of running away, wouldn't she?"

Quinn shrugged and leaned against the doorway. "I don't know. Maybe. Maybe not."

"You're married. You're supposed to know more about women. Why don't you know?"

"Oh, *now* I'm an authority on women. You've never listened to me before."

"I'm listening now, so make it good."

Quinn rolled his eyes. "At least, tell me what the real problem is—because Isabelle kissing you doesn't sound like much of one to me."

"The *real* problem…" Rhett pulled in a deep breath and let it out slowly as he thought. "The real problem is… I…I love—" He clamped his mouth shut as the door down the hall opened to emit noisy townsfolk. Quinn grabbed his arm and hauled him out the back door. They stood in the undeveloped field behind the courthouse, staring at each other like two bulls in adjoining pastures. Rhett knew Quinn wasn't going to let him get out of finishing what he'd been about to say inside. An expectant lift of his friend's eyebrows told him as much. Rhett swallowed. "I love her."

Quinn nodded slowly as though silently willing him to continue.

"I want to marry her and have children with her and all of that, but I'm not sure that's what God wants for me. If He did, then why wasn't it easier to begin with? Why did she say no when I asked to court her the first time? But if He doesn't want me to be with her then why is everything so hard now that I've tried to give her up? None of it makes sense. I asked for a sign, you know? On New Year's Eve. At least, I tried to ask for a sign. I think I might have been interrupted."

"By the explosion?"

"No. I got hit by an arrow." He laughed at Quinn's befuddled expression. "It wasn't real. It was part of Ellie's Cupid costume. The point is—"

Quinn held up a hand. "Wait. You prayed for a sign then got hit with Cupid's arrow by the town matchmaker?"

Rhett's response was quiet, thoughtful. "Yeah, I did."

"Then what happened?"

He shrugged. "Nothing. I went outside and…ran into Isabelle. She stopped me from going home early, which probably saved my life."

Quinn tilted his head. "Sounds divinely orchestrated to me."

"Well, when you put it like that it does, but it didn't answer my prayer. I wanted a sign that I should give up." He frowned as he thought about his ease with Isabelle that evening, their kiss and everything that had followed. "Instead, maybe…" he said slowly, thinking aloud, "maybe God gave me a reason to hope." Rhett turned and began to pace. "I thought He was saying no when Isabelle said no." An image of the board-inghouse contract filled his mind, followed by Mr. Bradley's suspicious frown and Isabelle's chagrin at being caught locked in the closet. "What if the situation wasn't as cut-and-dried as yes or no? Maybe, all this time, He's been saying…wait. Am I crazy to even think this?"

"Actually, I think you might finally be gaining some sense."

Rhett shook his head. "But I keep coming back to the fact that Isabelle told me she didn't want to be courted by me."

"I reckon it's a lady's prerogative to change her mind. Since she's willing to kiss and be kissed, she might be well on her way to doing that."

Rhett stopped pacing to stare up at the evening sky and found himself praying without even making the conscious decision to do so. "I don't want to go off half-cocked this time, trying to force situations that shouldn't happen. I want to do this Your way. If You could give me one last sign, something to let me know this is what You want…"

He waited for peace or another explosion, but nothing happened. Finally, he heard a bit of rustling behind him, then something hit the back of his head. Rhett spun to face his friend. "Did you just throw something at me? I was praying. A little respect for the moment wouldn't have hurt."

Quinn shrugged. "You wanted a sign. I figured I might as well hit you over the head with it to see if it would do any good. It's by your boot, by the way, so don't step on it. I've been carrying it around for months waiting for the right time to give it to you."

Rhett sent Quinn a suspicious look before picking up the folded piece of paper. "Is this…?"

"The Bachelor List. You didn't bother to look for your match when I was looking for mine, did you?"

Until recently, Quinn had been illiterate, so he had needed Rhett's assistance to read the list so he could find out his match was Helen. Rhett had wanted no part of it then. Nothing had changed. Rhett frowned and tried to hand it back to Quinn. "Of course I didn't look for mine. I already know who I was matched with and Amy is long gone."

Quinn crossed his arms and stared at Rhett.

Rhett's mouth fell open. His eyes narrowed. Feeling his heart gain speed like a locomotive, he unfolded the sheet of paper. His eyes trailed down the paper until he found his name. A line connected it to another name, which had been written in Ellie's bold print and underlined for good measure. *Isabelle Bradley.*

Shock gave way to pure confusion. "I don't understand. There's no trace of Amy's name having ever been beside mine. Why would Ellie make me think my match was Amy if it was Isabelle all the time? Or did she change it after Amy eloped?"

"Ellie hasn't touched the list since her wedding day when she gave it to Amy. Near as Helen can figure, it was probably the confirmation Amy needed to run off with Silas. Their names are matched farther down the list. Amy gave it to Helen to return to Ellie but, as you know, Helen lost the list at Ellie's shivaree. That's where I found it. Now I'm giving it to you. You'll have to ask Ellie why she indicated that Amy was your match. She won't be too happy with me since she explicitly said not to give it to you."

"Oh, she did, did she?"

"Yeah." Quinn rubbed his jaw and gave a little wince. "She was also pretty annoyed when I told her the list ought to belong to the town's bachelors. She's probably going to ask for it back once she knows you have it. If you're still listening to my advice then I'd say to keep it. Pass it along to the next fellow who needs it."

"I'll do that." He nodded then stared down at the paper in his hand, feeling a little in awe.

Quinn must have followed his gaze, for there was a smile in his voice. "You know, it seems to me God's been answering your prayers before you can even get them out good."

"I think you're right about that. He gave me the sign I asked for. Now I've got to act on it."

"Go get your girl, then."

Rhett laughed. "Yeah, I don't think it's going to be that easy."

"Show her the list. It worked for me."

"That was back when you had custody of your nieces and nephews. You had four adorable children on hand who needed a mama, which, if I recall, helped your case quite a bit." Rhett shook his head and pocketed the list. "The mess I'm in is going to take some delicate handling to straighten out. Besides, I don't think Isabelle will be swayed by the list. Or by anything, really."

"Then what are you going to do?"

"Pray and do my best to sort through this without making anything worse."

Quinn nodded. "That sounds like a good plan."

It was also Rhett's only plan. He knew if he wanted

to do things the right way he'd have to start by asking Thomas Bradley for permission to court his daughter. That was a formidable prospect seeing as the man had recently kicked Rhett out of the boardinghouse. Time and distance would probably help in that respect. Mr. Bradley had given him until Monday to find a new place, but it might be better to move out immediately to provide the distance. As for time, Rhett didn't have much of it if the man was already looking for a buyer for the boardinghouse. Rhett supposed that's where prayer would come in.

There was also the little matter of convincing Isabelle to give him a chance, but a man could only handle so much at once. First things first, he'd have to convince Deputy Bridger to let him move into the house a bit early. Then, God willing, he'd set about winning Mr. Bradley's good opinion—and Isabelle's heart.

Isabelle managed to stay out of Rhett's path quite successfully that night by hiding away in the family wing of the house while he took what little belongings he'd accumulated to the Bachelor Box. She didn't emerge to say goodbye since she had no doubt that she would see him again at some point before her family left town. Peppin was too small to expect otherwise. When that happened, she'd… Well, she wasn't entirely sure what she'd do. She was far too tired to figure it out now.

She blew out the lamp with the intention of putting an end to a day that had been nothing short of disastrous when a soft rap sounded on her door. Violet's whisper soon followed. "Are you still awake?"

"Yes." Although they hadn't done it for years, Isabelle anticipated Violet's next move by scooting over to make room for her in the bed. Violet slid into bed beside her, and her head landed on Isabelle's shoulder. Normally, Amy would stretch her arm across both of them and they'd talk or laugh or cry or wait out a thunderstorm together. Instead, Isabelle rested her cheek on her sister's head. "I'm sorry, Vi. I tried."

"I know you did. It's all right. We all messed up together—you, me and Rhett. We were like the Three Musketeers riding into battle. We just didn't realize we were sitting backward on our horses or that our blades were made of rubber instead of steel."

There was a moment of silence before they burst out laughing. Eventually, Violet sighed. "I wish we didn't have to move all the way across the country. It seems a bit excessive, don't you think?"

"I guess Ma and Pa figure if they have to start over they might as well do it where they have family."

"But in the middle of my last term!" Violet propped herself up on her elbow. The moonlight flowing from the window across the room revealed her suddenly hopeful expression. "Hey, do we have to leave because our parents are? I mean, couldn't we get jobs and stay here together?"

Isabelle sat up to lean against the pillows lining the headboard. "Doing what and staying where?"

"Maybe we could stay here in the boardinghouse as tenants under the new owners."

"We wouldn't be able to count on that. The new owner might be an unmarried man. It would hardly be proper to stay here in that case." She hugged an extra pillow to her chest. "For that matter, it just isn't done for two respectable young ladies to leave the protection of their parents because they don't want to move towns."

"Helen left the protection of her parents when she lived here and taught school, before marrying Quinn."

"Helen had her parents' approval to set out on her own. That meant she knew she could fall back on her parents' financial support if things didn't work out. I assure you that Ma and Pa would not approve of this. To be honest, I don't think I approve of it, either. I'd be responsible for you, and I'm not sure I'd be able to find work that paid well enough to support myself, let alone anyone else."

"Why not? You're good at plenty of things."

Isabelle laughed. "I can cook and clean and organize parlor games. Maddie seems to have a corner on the cooking in this town. There doesn't seem to be much demand for maids. What else is there?"

"There's always marriage."

Isabelle rolled her eyes and sank down beneath the covers. "No, thank you."

"Well, if you don't want to be a cook or a maid or a wife, what do you want to do?"

"Sleep."

Violet peeled back the covers. "Isabelle, I'm being serious."

"And annoying."

"You must want to do something."

Isabelle stared up at her sister in the darkness. "Fine. I wanted to run the boardinghouse one day. Satisfied?"

Shocked was more like it from the way the girl's mouth fell open. "I had no idea. Do Ma and Pa know?"

"No."

"You should tell them."

"Why? They'd merely try to sell the boardinghouse even faster. A single woman who isn't a widow running a boardinghouse filled with men? It isn't seemly. Even I know that. I was hoping that by the time Ma and Pa moved on to something else I'd be so old that no one would care."

"Wait. You really meant what you said about not wanting to be a wife? I thought you were joking."

"Wanting to be a wife is very different from having the opportunity to do so with a man who doesn't hold your older sister as his ideal of the perfect woman."

"Huh." With that thoughtful statement, Violet slid down beside her to stare at the ceiling with her. "And the boardinghouse? You really enjoy working here enough to want to do it for the rest of your life?"

"Enjoy it?" Isabelle blinked. Was it strange that she'd never considered that before? It was work. Work that she knew she could do—work that would provide for her and give her a comfortable, stable life. What did it matter whether she enjoyed it?

"Isabelle, I enjoy living at the boardinghouse because something exciting is always happening. If it isn't, I can count on someone new coming through the door with a new story to tell." Violet turned her head and their eyes met, though they could barely see each other in the darkness. "What hold does this place have on you that would make you want to dedicate your life to something you can't even say you enjoy?"

Isabelle's mouth opened to speak, but she had no answer to give.

"I'll leave you to think about that."

"Thanks a lot."

"You're welcome." Violet gave her hand a quick squeeze. "Good night, big sister."

Isabelle sat up to watch her sister slip out of the room. Violet's question stayed with her, though. It taunted her as she drifted toward sleep, crowding out even the memory of Rhett's kiss, for which she was grateful. Still, it begged an answer while spawning other questions. Why did she want to run the boardinghouse?

The honest answer was, she didn't trust herself to be able to find a future outside of it. Violet had run down the list of possible occupations. None of them would do. Marriage was out of the question since no one seemed the least bit interested in her besides Amy's old suitors. Then again, she'd never paid attention to anyone besides Amy's former suitors and the boarders.

A shiver went down her spine at the memory of her father's insistence that the boarders looked at her with more than brotherly affection. As much as she'd been offended by her father's no-fraternization clause, she'd long since counted on the fact that she was safe with the boarders because they weren't allowed to think of her that way. Was that why she so rarely bothered to shoo them away at social functions? What had Gabe called them after the masquerade? Guard dogs?

What were they guarding her from? Other men. And there *were* other men in the town. Scads of them. Yet, for some reason, her thoughts and attention only ever seemed to focus on the boarders and Amy's suitors. Why? Was it because she didn't trust herself to be able to keep *any* man's genuine interest? Did that certainty lead her to spend her time with men she knew weren't interested in her, so she wouldn't have to be disappointed when they didn't fall in love with her?

She bolted upright as that single flash of insight illuminated so much more. *That* was why she'd focused her thoughts and attention on men she'd disqualified. With them, she didn't have to try to capture their attention by being the things she wasn't. She didn't have to be charming, flirtatious or beautiful. She didn't have to be Amy.

What was more, she'd defied the ones who'd tried to fashion her into that kind of woman by pushing them away. Rhett was the only one who kept coming back, but this wasn't about him. This was about Isabelle. It was about the fact that she'd spent so much time trying not to be Amy that she'd never once tried to be herself. Except, perhaps, on New Year's Eve and even then she'd been disguised.

She relit her lamp and sat down at her vanity to stare at herself. Who was she exactly? More important, who did she want to be?

She needed to be truthful with herself. While she might not want to *be* Amy, there were certain things about her sister that she'd always admired. What had Violet said a few weeks ago? *She was comfortable with herself, so people were comfortable being themselves around her. There was also a certain confidence about her...*

She knew from watching her sister that true confidence came from the inside. Isabelle did feel confident on the inside. She just wasn't entirely sure the outside always showed it. What if, in the meantime, there was something she could do externally to help with the process?

Like what, exactly?

She has the knack of knowing how to look her best… She styles her hair so that it's soft and romantic. Isabelle teased her hair so that it had a bit more volume on the top and blinked when it made her features appear more delicate. Her gaze slid to her wardrobe across the room. *She wears an inordinate amount of blue because it brings out her eyes and pastels because they set off her fair complexion… Her clothes always fit her perfectly.*

Opening her wardrobe, she stared at the dresses, skirts and blouses inside. Most of them were some shade of blue. If not blue, they were pastel. The majority of them looked rather worn. At what point had Amy's old clothes become almost the entirety of Isabelle's wardrobe and how had Isabelle never noticed until now?

Don't be silly. Practical people don't let good clothes go to waste. Hand-me-downs are the staple of every younger sibling's wardrobe…except Violet's apparently. She gets new clothes rather regularly. Of course, she isn't as close to Amy's age as I am, so they might not fit her. They don't fit me that well, either. That doesn't mean I shouldn't wear—

A knock sounded on her bedroom door, followed by her mother's whisper. "Isabelle, are you awake?"

"Come in, Ma."

Beatrice entered, her blue eyes filled with concern. "I wanted to check on you since I know it's been a trying day. How are you, dear?"

"I'm…trying not to think about it, I suppose." Willing the tears from her eyes, she turned to the wardrobe. "Actually, I was looking at my clothes."

"Really?"

The hope in her mother's voice made Isabelle glance back at her. "Yes, why do you sound so excited?"

"It's just that…" Beatrice sent her a cautious look before coming to stand beside her. "All of these are Amy's hand-me-downs."

"You knew that?"

"Of course. Didn't you?"

"Well, no." Isabelle sat down on her bed. "Why do I only wear Amy's hand-me-downs?"

Her mother shook her head. "I wish I knew. You know Amy and I always shared an interest in fashion."

"Yes, I know." Isabelle hadn't tried to infringe on that bond, either. She'd always been closer to her father, while Amy had always been closer to their mother. Violet was everyone's darling. Still, she wondered if she might have missed out on something by not trying to find her own thing to bond with their mother over.

"Well, I freely admit that she had wonderful taste when it came to clothes. However, she had a paler complexion and hair than you, so the colors are all wrong. She was also a bit more full-figured than you. Not much, mind you, but enough that her clothes don't quite fit you."

"Why didn't you say something?"

"I did once or twice. It seemed to offend you. You never were particularly interested in clothes or fashion. You thought it was too impractical, I suppose."

She did vaguely remember her mother offering to alter something for her. Even so, Isabelle frowned. "How long ago was it?"

"About two years, I think. Then after Amy eloped, you stopped asking for any new clothes at all except for the masquerade costume." Her mother stopped going through the clothes and sat beside her. "I thought perhaps it was your way of being close to Amy after she left."

Taken aback by the realization that her mother was right, Isabelle's eyebrows rose. "That's a little strange, isn't it?"

"No. You miss her. We all do. We merely have different ways of showing it." Beatrice took Isabelle's hand and smiled. "Just understand, you do not have to show it through your clothes."

They laughed together. Isabelle shook her head, realizing that she finally had something to connect with her mother on besides deciding what to cook for supper. "Will you help with my clothes and teach me how to do something better with my hair?"

"I'd love to. For now, though, I think we'd both better turn in." Beatrice patted her hand. She paused with a hand on the door. "Try not to worry about the move, Isabelle. Your father and I know what's best. Please trust us on this."

Isabelle smiled, but made no promises as her mother left the room. Trust. It always seemed to come back to trust. The only way she'd trust her parents was if they suddenly decided not to sell the boardinghouse. The only way she'd trust God…

Well, she hadn't entirely given up on His help. Yet, if He was going to rescue her, wouldn't He have already done it? Perhaps not. After all, the Bible was filled with stories of God showing up at the eleventh hour to save the day.

She glanced up at the ceiling. "This is my eleventh

hour, God. I'm letting You know in case You hadn't noticed."

She waited for some sort of sign that a rescue was imminent or some indication that her prayer had been heard. Her anxiety didn't ease one bit. She did the best she could to block it out and held on to what little was left of her hope, anyway.

Chapter Sixteen

Rhett's harmonica wailed out a lonely rendition of Chopin's Waltz no. 7 as he leaned his wooden chair against the wall near the fireplace in his Bachelor Box. *Cottage* was a more accurate term for the place. It was small for a house, but bigger than the room he'd had at Bradley Boardinghouse. Of course, the boardinghouse also had a huge dining room and parlor for the boarders to wander through—and Isabelle. It had Isabelle.

A note went sour as he sighed. He reapplied his attention to the melody, though only for a moment because he couldn't help wondering how much longer he had to submit himself to this self-imposed exile. Well, perhaps it wasn't entirely self-imposed since Isabelle hadn't exactly been seeking him out, either. He'd stolen a glimpse of her at church on Sunday, but she hadn't tried to approach him and he'd kept his distance from her, as well. That hadn't kept her from infiltrating his thoughts or wrecking his concentration in the three days since he'd moved out of the boardinghouse.

How much longer should he wait before approaching Mr. Bradley? Surely, the man had to have calmed down by now. Rhett wouldn't be able to hold out much longer.

He jolted at the thunderous knocking on his front door. His chair tipped backward perilously before the front legs landed back on the floor with a bone-jarring thud. He leaped across the room and flung the front door open. His heart dropped at the sight of the man standing on his porch. "Mr. Bradley? What's happened? Is Isabelle hurt, or—"

Mr. Bradley's eyes widened behind the rims of his spectacles. "No. No. It's nothing like that. Everything's fine. I didn't mean to pound your door down. I've been trying to get your attention for a few minutes, but I guess you couldn't hear me over the music."

Rhett offered a relieved smile. "That's all right. Come on in."

Mr. Bradley entered and removed his hat before glancing around. Rhett followed the man's gaze to take in the gleaming pine table and mismatched chairs that he'd set up at the far end of the room by the pump sink and cookstove. The middle of the room was a sitting area with a navy blue settee and a fawn-colored chair around a low-slung mahogany table. The back wall boasted a rather nice brick fireplace, where Rhett had placed a wooden chair. Meanwhile, the bedroom door was cracked slightly, allowing a glimpse of the sage-green quilt covering the bed.

It was comfortable and had everything he needed, yet Rhett knew it was no match for the homey yet elegantly styled boardinghouse. He shrugged when Mr. Bradley's gaze met his. "It came already furnished."

A twitch of amusement showed beneath the man's mustache. "Glad to hear it."

"You're welcome to sit. I'm afraid all I have to drink at the moment is water, but you're welcome to that, too."

"I'll take a seat, but I don't need any refreshments. I won't be here long." The man pulled an envelope from his coat pocket before sitting on the edge of the settee. "There's a problem with your account at the boardinghouse that we need to iron out."

Rhett frowned as he took the chair across from the settee. "A problem?"

"Yes." Mr. Bradley smiled. "You overpaid."

"Oh. Actually, I didn't. After everything that has happened, I thought it fair that I pay for the week you didn't charge me for immediately following the fire."

Mr. Bradley shook his head. "We had an agreement. I'll not go back on it. This money belongs to you."

Rhett hesitated a moment before finally deciding that starting an argument with the man was the last thing he wanted to do. He took the envelope. "Thank you, sir."

"I'm glad you found a place to stay. I knew you'd been searching for one, so I hoped you might have a lead on something that wouldn't take much arrangement. That's why I gave you until Monday. I don't take evictions lightly, you know, but after what I'd put in the lease, I had little recourse. I make no exceptions for anyone when it comes to protecting my daughters. I hope you understand that, while there was some frustration and perhaps desperation behind my actions, there was no ill will."

"I appreciate that." Rhett paused. Sensing this was the moment he'd been waiting for, he sent a silent prayer heavenward before continuing. "I was planning to go by the boardinghouse to speak with you, but since you're here, I'd like to take this opportunity to apologize again for any trouble I might have caused for you and your family. I am truly grateful for the hospitality you extended to me after the fire. I know it might not have appeared this way, but I have great respect for you, your daughters and your wife. I understand why you established the rules set forth in the contract, and I'm sorry I didn't do a better job of keeping them."

"I accept the apology, but there's no need to re-issue it. In fact, I should have accepted it when you first issued it outside the closet a few days ago. Please, don't try to explain that, either." Shaking his head, Mr. Bradley removed his spectacles and rubbed the bridge of his nose. "I've heard a detailed account of the circumstances of that incident and all that led up to it so many times from my daughters that I could recite it in my sleep. Isabelle has been quite adamant in stating that it was all an accident and nothing untoward happened in that closet, so I am satisfied."

Rhett felt a weight lift from his shoulders. "Thank you, sir."

"As for my rules… Well, according to my daughters, they were insulting and unnecessary. That wasn't my intention, and I can't say that I agree with them. There was no other way that I could see to serve notice to the boarders that I would not tolerate a repeat of what happened with Amy. That being said, the true solution is one I put off for far too long. It's past time my family had a fresh start."

Since the conversation was going well, Rhett decided to push a little deeper into the problem. "I hope you don't mind me asking, why does that fresh start need to be in Virginia?"

"I'll have a position waiting for me in the family business."

"I thought the family business was boarding-houses."

Mr. Bradley shook his head. "The boardinghouse is what I chose to get away from the family business in Virginia, which is fishing."

"Fishing?" Rhett tried to imagine the studious-looking gentleman before him hauling in fish and couldn't quite see it. "If you didn't like it, why are you going back?"

"I'd be taking an accounting position, so it wouldn't be quite the same as it was before."

Rhett raked his fingers though his hair. "What about the hotel? Aren't you involved there?"

Mr. Bradley grimaced. "Too involved, according to my partner. We've been clashing more often than not, lately. That's yet another reason for me to leave."

"Or a reason to stay." Rhett leaned forward in his chair. "This is just an idea, so please don't take umbrage. Why not use the money from the boarding-house sale to buy out your partner? You could do with the hotel as you wish and the ladies in your family wouldn't have to be so involved in the business."

Mr. Bradley shook his head slowly. "I've thought of that before and even hinted at as much to my partner. He didn't seem to like the idea."

"Perhaps he didn't see the merit of it the first time, but it wouldn't hurt to ask again. Especially if he knows he'll be getting the money right away."

"Perhaps." Mr. Bradley tilted his head as he surveyed Rhett through narrowed eyes. "First, you help the girls try to catch the nonexistent thief. Now this. Why are you so all-fired invested in my family staying here?"

This wasn't how Rhett had intended to approach the subject, but he could hardly shy away from it now that it had been brought up. He took his time in formulating the answer. "As I said, I respect you, Mrs. Bradley, Isabelle and Violet. I've been acquainted with Isabelle since I moved to town. However, it's been over the past couple of months and especially weeks that I've truly been able to get to know her. I have found her to be outstanding in every respect. She continually puts others above herself. She is fiercely loyal to those she loves. She is hardworking yet never puts herself forward in an effort to gain credit. I could go on, but the gist is that I would be incredibly honored if you would grant me permission to court her."

Unnerving, unmitigated silence filled the room for what seemed an eternity as Mr. Bradley stared at him. "Does Isabelle know that you're asking me this?"

"No, sir."

"And if I say no?"

Rhett cast about for an appropriate response then settled on the succinct truth. "I will be devastated."

"What is your intention in conducting this courtship, knowing that the amount of time Isabelle will remain in Peppin is limited?"

He pulled in a deep breath. "Should she agree to any of this, it's my hope to continue this courtship by correspondence or visits until we are ready for marriage."

"So, really, what you're asking is for my daughter's hand in marriage?"

Rhett's eyes widened. "Well, she hasn't agreed to anything yet, so I don't want to get that far ahead. However, you know my intentions, so I suppose the answer is yes."

Mr. Bradley was quiet again. His piercing eyes shifted from Rhett to stare into contemplative nothingness. He rubbed a hand over his chin and heaved what seemed to be a sigh before refocusing on Rhett. A hint of a smile appeared on the man's face. "Thank you."

Thrown off by the quiet response, Rhett could only ask, "For what?"

"Asking." The man's jaw worked as he battled his emotions. He finally gave in and removed his spectacles to rub at his eyes. "After going through what happened with Amy—" The man shook his head. "I cannot tell you—" he swallowed hard "—how much it means to me that you are honorable enough to do so."

Rhett felt a slow grin building on his lips. "Does that mean yes?"

"Yes." Mr. Bradley stood and extended a hand.

Rhett shook it heartily. "Thank you, sir."

Mr. Bradley clenched Rhett's hand tighter and lowered his voice to a tone of pure warning. "Of course, you realize that if you hurt her, I will hurt you."

"Duly noted." Rhett waited for the man to release him. "I'd appreciate it if you didn't mention our conversation to Isabelle. I'd like to approach the subject in my own way."

"Understood."

After they said their goodbyes, Rhett closed the door then leaned his head against it and whispered a relieved prayer. "Thank You, God!"

He'd been waiting for Mr. Bradley's approval to

move forward in his pursuit of Isabelle. Now that he had it, he wasn't entirely sure what to do with it. However, he knew Someone who did. The real test would come when he had to speak with Isabelle and ask her to allow them to become more than friends. But if God had sent Mr. Bradley to him, then He could send Isabelle, as well. Until then, Rhett would keep on waiting.

Isabelle stood outside the smithy with her heart beating wildly in her chest as she tried to gather the courage to walk inside. She wasn't sure what had possessed her to seek Rhett out after she'd spent nearly a week trying to avoid him. She just knew that it was time to see him. At the very least, she owed him an explanation for her behavior after the kiss. Her true aim, however, was to set their relationship back on the solid ground of friendship.

She'd also realized it wasn't wise to put off what was inevitable in a town as small as Peppin—seeing him for the first time after she'd left him standing alone in the cupola of the courthouse. She had no desire to have an audience for the conversation that was sure to follow. That was why she needed to gather her courage and step through that door.

She pulled in a deep, calming breath then did exactly that. Well, technically she only opened the door and put one foot inside. Even so, that was enough to make the air rush from her lungs. The place was empty. She'd purposefully come close to closing time so that she wouldn't disturb his work.

She stepped the rest of the way inside for a better look at the work area behind the front desk. The door hit the back of her heel as it tried to close. She stumbled forward, limping as it hit the doorframe and caused a bell to jangle loudly through the quiet shop. Rhett's deep voice called out from the storage room in the interior, "I'll be right there."

Her eyes widened. This was a bad idea. She should leave now while she had the chance. Her decision came a second too late for, as she took a step backward toward the door, he was already stepping out of the other room. She winced. There was no turning back now.

He took one look at her and stopped in his tracks. His eyes lit with something akin to awe, which didn't make a bit of sense considering the fact that she was still dressed in Amy's old clothes. It was a shame that her new wardrobe wasn't finished yet, because she could have used the boost of confidence the fashionable, well-fitted clothes might have provided. Doing her best to ignore the sense of anxiety building in her chest, she clasped her hands in front of her and offered a smile. "Hello, Rhett."

He spoke her name softly and with a reverence that took her breath away. His gaze stayed locked on hers as he tugged the leather apron from his waist and set it on the front counter. Then he frowned, his face filled with a mix of uncertainty and curiosity. "What are you doing here?"

"I thought we should talk."

He looked at her for a moment longer, then nodded. "Hold on a second."

He strode past her. Watching as he flipped the closed sign on the front door and pulled the shade down on the window, she was grateful for a moment to gather her thoughts. She needed to be firm with him. She had to make sure he understood that they were just friends despite all the evidence to the contrary. She'd let him know in no uncertain terms that there would be no more kisses.

He turned. Their eyes met. She swallowed. He held out his hand to her as he moved toward her. "Come here."

She countered his every step forward with one backward and shook her head. "See, that's what we need to talk about."

He rolled his eyes. "I'm not trying to kiss you."

"You aren't?"

"No."

"Then why—"

"Land sakes, woman. Would you stand still?"

She blinked, realizing they'd circled the waiting room locked in each other's gazes. She stopped abruptly. He didn't. His arms encircled her waist as he enveloped her in a hug. Arms akimbo, she stood frozen. This was definitely not part of the plan.

She closed her eyes. *Don't you dare hug him back. Don't even think about it. You are supposed to be putting up boundaries and... Oh, blast!*

She swayed into his chest and hugged him back. His powerful arms tightened around her waist. He straightened, which lifted her off her feet for an instant before he set her down and murmured, "I've missed you."

Her resistance melted completely at that. She rested her cheek against the soft waves of his coffee-brown hair and held on tighter. Her whispered words issued forth of their own volition. "I've missed you, too."

It was true. The boardinghouse hadn't felt the same without him. *She* hadn't been the same without his presence, laughter and teasing. It was truly unsettling how much she'd come to care for this man. More than that, it was dangerous. Out of all of Amy's former suitors, he was the one whose character she'd always admired—the one she'd found most attractive. For that reason, he posed the greatest threat to her heart. She'd tried to push him away so many times, but he kept coming back. Or she ended up going to him. It had to stop at some point. Apparently, this was not that point.

He lifted his head to look down at her. "It wasn't the time that bothered me so much as…"

"The distance," she finished for him. The distance she was supposed to be maintaining. She pushed away from his chest. She hadn't realized how close she'd been to the front counter until he picked her up and sat her on top of it. She found herself eye level with him. She tilted her head at the expectant look her gave her. "What?"

He braced one hand on the counter beside her. "You said you wanted to talk to me, so I'm listening."

"Oh." She grimaced, annoyed with herself for being so easily distracted. She let her gaze trace his features for a moment since she hadn't seen him in a while then focused on the top button of his green flannel shirt. "It was unfair of me to leave you in the cupola that way."

His hand nudged her chin upward so that her gaze found his again. "Why did you?"

She cast about for some explanation that would satisfy him while putting the boundaries between them back where they needed to be. It was a little hard to think with him staring at her like that and standing so close. "That kiss… It shouldn't have happened. It was—"

"A mistake?" He gave her an amused look and

shook his head. "Try again, sweetheart. That excuse didn't ring true the first time you used it."

She stared at him for a moment as her mind went blank. She hadn't intended to try the same tactic twice. She suddenly remembered the one that had worked so well with John, and tried again. "We should be friends."

"We *are* friends. That doesn't explain why you ran away."

He was absolutely right. No matter what boundaries she tried to put on their relationship for the future, it didn't explain why she'd behaved the way she had in the past. She spoke slowly, thoughtfully and with more than a little uncertainty. "I don't know. I suppose I was afraid."

"Of what?"

"Of you." The concern that leaped into his eyes made her smile. "I don't mean *you* specifically. I mean what I feel for you."

"What do you feel?"

That she couldn't answer—not even within herself. Her gaze shot toward the door as panic filled her. "Rhett, I should—"

"Hey, look at me." He waited until she focused on him before continuing. "It's all right. We don't have to analyze it. I certainly don't want you to feel like you have to run away from me again."

"But what about the kiss? Don't we have to talk about that?"

He shrugged. "It happened. It was pretty incredible, but we'll leave it at that and move on."

She searched his face, feeling relieved and hopeful at all once. "Really?"

"Really." He picked her up by the waist and eased her down until her feet touched the floor. "Let me lock this place up, and I'll walk you home."

She turned to watch him round the corner of the front counter and reach underneath it to retrieve a set of keys. "I thought you said you missed me."

"I did." He grabbed his apron from the counter with one hand and lifted the keys in the other. "Will you hold these for me while I get my coat?"

She took the keys then leaned against the counter. "Well, don't you want to talk to me?"

"Of course I do." He placed his hat on his head before reaching for his coat. "That's why I'm walking you home."

"Oh. But I don't want to go home yet."

He froze with one arm in his coat to give her a sideways look. "The last time you told me that, we ended up on the roof of the hotel with the sky exploding around us."

She laughed. "Well, this time, I was thinking something a little less adventurous."

"A walk around the courtyard perhaps?"

"No explosions necessary." She handed him the keys then glanced up to capture his gaze. "Thank you, Rhett."

He didn't ask for what. He just cupped her jaw, traced his thumb across her cheekbone and smiled. "You're welcome. I hope you don't mind if I spend as much time with you as possible before you leave for Virginia."

She probably should, but that didn't stop her from smiling. "I'd like that."

She was still hoping against hope that her parents

would decide to keep the boardinghouse—not because she wanted it for her future, but because it was her home. She'd also much rather spend that future right here in Peppin than across the country in Virginia. However, in case God didn't come through for her on this, she wanted to spend as much time with her friends here as she could. Rhett was one of those friends even if she couldn't let herself think of him as anything more. Considering how much she'd missed him this week, why shouldn't she enjoy his company while she could?

Perhaps because of those feelings she hadn't been able to name. She shook her head. She was a sensible girl. She knew how to keep her head about her and her heart firmly guarded.

Since he'd told her that he'd been hoping for more after their first kiss, she'd feared he'd have a similar speech prepared after their recent one. She was glad to find that wasn't the case because she was certain his reason for wanting more hadn't changed. He'd become interested in her because she was the only woman he could romance without panic. That didn't make her special. That made him desperate. He deserved someone special, and she was becoming increasingly convinced that she deserved to be more than someone's last resort.

Chapter Seventeen

He couldn't believe God had answered his prayer to send Isabelle to him one day after he'd prayed it. He was grateful, but to be honest this was getting downright scary. It seemed as if every time God moved, Rhett was forced to move as well—whether or not he was ready to do so.

He'd thought the true test of faith would come when Isabelle agreed to his courtship. After all, he had no experience courting a lady. He'd never made it far enough along the process to figure it out. He'd always assumed he'd know what to do when the time came. Well, that time might never come with Isabelle. At least, not formally.

He'd known he'd have to abandon that plan as soon as he'd seen her eyes shift to the door behind him in the smithy. She wasn't ready for the *C* word or the commitment that would come with it. However, she was ready to continue building the close friendship they had. More important, she'd admitted that she had feelings for him and that they scared her. It wasn't where he'd hoped to be at this point, but it was better than what he would have ended up with if he'd pushed too far too soon.

She'd agreed to spend time with him, and he meant to make the most of it—particularly since he had no idea how much time they would have together before her family pulled up stakes and moved across the country. The very thought of that had him reaching for her hand. Thankfully, they were crossing the street from the smithy to the courtyard, so he had an excuse—albeit a thin one. She didn't tug it away until they reached the oak-lined path that meandered toward the courthouse. Even so, she smiled at him. "Should I go first or should you?"

"You." He slid his hands into his pockets. "Tell me what I've missed at the boardinghouse."

She sighed, but didn't look nearly as distraught as she had been the night of the benefit. "Pa is still looking for a buyer. Of course, Violet and I hope he never finds one, but we've figured we've caused ourselves enough trouble and have decided to keep our mouths shut about it."

He chuckled. "I'm not supposed to comment on that, am I?"

"No. It would be far wiser of you to follow our example."

"What about the boarders? Do they know what's going on?"

She shook her head. "My parents say they won't make an official announcement until they've accepted an offer. I'm afraid it's going to come as an unpleasant shock to the men. After all, the boardinghouse is their home, too. This will be as big a change for them as it is for us."

"I'm sure it will." He frowned. "How are the boarders? I've seen Wes and Peter in passing, but we didn't have much of a chance to talk."

"They are the same as ever except that there's one less of them now."

"Who left?"

"Hank." She bit her lip. "He didn't exactly choose to leave. He sort of got evicted because I told Pa about the stash of liquor. I figured I'd caused enough trouble trying to hide things from Pa. He conducted a surprise inspection of the rooms and happened to look under the bed."

Rhett nodded. "Good for him. But that must make things a little awkward around the hotel since Hank works there."

"It shouldn't be too big of a problem. Pa is spending more time at the boardinghouse now. He's been making repairs. The linen closet door was the first on the list."

Rhett didn't know whether to laugh or grimace at that. "I'm sure."

"Violet is handling the prospect of the move with unexpected maturity. Although, I think she might be secretly trying to figure out some way for the two of us to stay here after our parents leave."

He looked at her with new interest. "Is that a possibility?"

"Since that would involve me supporting the both of use with my nonmarketable skills as a worker, I'd have to say no."

"I could always use a new apprentice."

Her laughing green eyes left his to peer through the trees toward the smithy. "Very funny."

He wasn't entirely sure he was joking, but he could think of a better way for her to stay in town. Since it involved putting his ring around the third finger of her left hand, he didn't mention it. Instead, he led her to a nearby bench and angled himself toward her as they sat down. "What about you? How are you handling all this?"

Sudden tears filled her eyes. She tried to blink them away but they sparkled in her lashes. "I'm not. I'm still praying that it won't happen. Perhaps this is God's way of growing my faith, and I'm supposed to keep trusting Him to save the boardinghouse. To be honest, I'm starting to lose faith that He will."

"I'd like more than anything to believe that He'll find some way to let you stay here." His mind automatically went to marriage again, but he shook his head. If Isabelle wasn't ready for that, then maybe God would find another way. "Let's not either of us give up on that."

"Or the boardinghouse."

He nodded. "Or the boardinghouse."

"Will you pray for me, then? For everything we've talked about and that I won't get discouraged?"

"Of course I will."

"Thank you." She glanced across the street in the direction of the boardinghouse, which was currently hidden by trees. "I'd better be getting back. Ma will be needing help with supper."

They retraced their path toward Main Street and were about to cross the street toward the boardinghouse when they ran into Wes, who was going in the same direction. After they exchanged greetings, the man gave Isabelle a knowing look. "Pretty interesting day, huh?"

Isabelle exchanged a confused glance with Rhett then asked, "Why's that?"

Wes glanced back and forth between them. "You don't know, do you? Amy's back."

"What?" Disbelief filled her voice. "Are you sure?"

"Of course I'm sure. I helped her and her husband get their luggage off the train nigh on thirty minutes ago. They sent it on to the hotel, but said they were going to visit the boardinghouse first thing."

Isabelle had paled considerably as Wes spoke. Rhett stepped toward her and placed a supportive hand on her back. "You go ahead, Wes. Isabelle and I will be inside in a moment."

Wes nodded at the rather obvious hint then hurried across the street into the boardinghouse. Rhett turned his attention back to Isabelle. "Are you all right?"

She nodded once then shook her head. Her gaze sought his and the panic there confused him. She grasped his free hand. "I can't go in there."

"Why not?"

"I haven't seen Amy since she left me the night she eloped."

"No one in town has except your pa, since he went looking for her after she'd eloped to make sure she was all right. Leastwise, that's what I heard."

"Yes, that's right. What I meant to say was…" She glanced over her shoulder at the boardinghouse then back to him before whispering, "I haven't forgiven her."

Rhett wasn't too sure about the particulars of Amy's elopement beyond what he'd heard from the town grapevine. It hadn't covered this. However, Rhett figured if Isabelle felt Amy had done something that needed to be forgiven, she was probably right. Chances were it wasn't any of his business unless she wanted to tell him. Right now, she looked too worried to explain. "Well, I reckon you're going to have plenty of opportunity to now."

She grimaced. "How long do you think she's going to stay?"

"I have no idea." He rubbed a circle on her back. "Why don't you take a deep breath and focus on doing this one step at a time? First things first, let's go inside."

"Don't you think I ought to forgive her first?"

"Do you think you can?" Her silence was all the answer he needed. He turned her toward the boardinghouse. "Let's go."

"Wait. I know this must be hard for you. You don't have to go in with me."

"Hard for me?" It took another moment and one significant glance from Isabelle for him to figure out what she meant. If he had any doubts that he was over whatever surface emotions he'd felt for Amy, they were put to rest in that moment. The only one he cared about in this situation was Isabelle. All he felt was concern for her. Realizing she was still watching to see how he'd react, he offered her a shrug. "I'll be fine. I doubt your sister will be bothered one way or the other if I go in. After all, it wasn't as though she and I ever courted."

Her eyes narrowed in suspicion. "I thought you loved her."

"Why?"

"The whole town said so."

"Well, the whole town was wrong." He frowned at her doubtful look. "I admit that I thought I felt something for her. However, after she eloped, I realized I wasn't the least bit heartbroken about it."

She blinked. "You weren't?"

He shook his head. "How could I be? I knew *of* her more than I actually knew her. The few times we did talk, I was too tongue-tied to say much of anything."

"That was because you liked her. Besides, you said yourself that you *knew* she was the woman you were supposed to marry."

"I said there was one woman who inspired that feeling of 'knowing' my grandfather talked about. I never said it was Amy."

She frowned. "Then who was it?"

She didn't want to know. He was certain of that. He glanced toward the boardinghouse. "Don't you think we ought to go inside?"

"So your feelings for Amy are resolved, then?"

"Well, there wasn't much to them to begin with, but of course they are. Land sakes! She's married to someone else. Even when she wasn't, she hardly gave me a second glance. Surely you wouldn't expect me to live on the memory of the few smiles or glances she bestowed on me when it's obvious they meant nothing to her?"

"And you knew all of this as soon as she left town?"

Rhett looked at her more closely. Was this what was holding her back from admitting her feelings for him? Her concern about the relationship he hadn't had with Amy? "Yes, I realized it as soon as I heard the news of her elopement."

Her eyes searched his. "But not before?"

"Well, I might have suspected it before then, but I didn't want to admit it."

"I see." She glanced past him to the boardinghouse. "Then it wouldn't bother you to go in?"

"No. Would you like me to?"

Her tone turned thoughtful. "Yes, I think I would."

Glad they'd been able to clear up that little misunderstanding and hoping it meant she'd be more accepting of her own feeling for him, he crossed the street with her.

Rhett's words had set Isabelle's mind awhirl almost as much as the news of Amy's arrival had. She'd been surprised by the odd sense of relief that had filled her after his admission that he had not been in love with Amy. However, whatever strange comfort those words had provided had been immediately undone by the fact that he hadn't realized the depth of his feelings— or lack thereof—until after Amy had left town. He'd thought his love was real, until it was put to the test. How could Isabelle trust that any romantic declarations he made to her wouldn't be based on feelings equally as shallow or passing, no matter how adamant he might seem about them at the time?

It was a good thing that they'd settled on a friendship of sorts for the time being. It also made the idea of moving out of town a bit more palatable. Not that she wanted to lose the boardinghouse, because she didn't. She wasn't ready to give up hope that her parents would change their minds. However, such a move might not be a horrible thing if it might provide a natural ending to her relationship with Rhett before her heart had time to get too involved.

Guilt immediately followed that thought. Rhett had been a good friend to her. Even now, he walked down the path to the boardinghouse beside her purely in an effort to provide moral support. Despite what he'd said, this situation couldn't be entirely comfortable for him, but it appeared that he cared more about helping her than protecting himself.

Violet met them on the porch with a wide-eyed look that reminded her that all might not be well inside the boardinghouse. Isabelle squeezed her arm. "I just heard. How are Ma and Pa handling it?"

"I don't know. They've been holed up in the study since Amy arrived." Violet glanced past her. "Is he supposed to be here?"

Isabelle followed Violet's gaze to Rhett. Suddenly remembering her parents had kicked him out less than a week ago, she found herself reaching for his hand. He wasn't the least bit concerned about that if the smile he offered them was any indication. "It's all right. I talked to your father yesterday. We reconciled our differences. I'm sure he wouldn't mind if I came in."

She blinked. "Oh. Well, that's good…and surprising."

Realizing Violet's curious gaze had fallen to their joined hands, Isabelle released Rhett's and forced herself to walk inside the boardinghouse. She should not feel this much dread at the prospect of seeing her sister. They'd been close for so long. Perhaps that was the very reason why Isabelle still felt angry and hurt nearly four months later.

She paused in the foyer to peek down the hall toward the closed door of the study and felt her nervousness increase. "I wonder why she came back."

Violet shrugged. "To reconcile, I guess. Also, I might have written to her about the fact that we were probably going to be moving soon."

Isabelle spun to face her little sister. "You knew she was coming, and you didn't tell me?"

"No. I didn't know. She didn't even respond to my letter. She simply showed up, so it's only a little bit my fault this time and you don't have to be so outraged about it."

"I'm sorry." She sighed then glanced at the clock on the wall behind the front desk. "What about supper? Has Ma started it yet?"

"No. She was right about to when Amy came."

"I'll do it." She glanced up at Rhett as he helped her out of her coat. "I don't suppose you know how to cook."

He nodded rather solemnly. "I can boil water with the best of them."

She grinned then glanced down at her light blue dress. It was another one of Amy's. Suddenly, she felt more than a little silly wearing her sister's clothes—as if she was a little girl playing dress up. "I wish I had my new clothes."

"They're here." Excitement sparkled in Violet's eyes. "Ma put them in your room. I can't wait to see them on you."

"Well, neither can I. Come on." Isabelle grabbed her sister's hand and rushed down the hall toward the family wing.

"Hey," Rhett called. "What am I supposed to do?"

"Meet me in the kitchen in five minutes." She laughed at the hesitant look on his face. "It's fine.

You're not a boarder anymore. It's no longer forbidden."

He gave her a little salute. That was the last she saw of him before Violet tugged her into the family wing then paused to let Isabelle enter the bedroom first. Isabelle's eyes widened at the sight of all the boxes piled on her bed. "I had no idea Ma and I had ordered so much."

"Ma wasn't the least bit surprised. She told Pa, 'I may have gone overboard, but it was long overdue.' Then she went to fix supper. That's when Amy showed up."

"Well, come here and help me open these boxes. I need to find a dress that looks nice but isn't too fancy for supper. Lock the door behind you. I don't want Amy to see me until I've changed."

Violet sent her a questioning glance but didn't press her. No doubt she didn't want to risk her position as Isabelle's helper. Isabelle pushed away a hatbox to open a thinner, square one. She found a new corset inside that she certainly didn't remember ordering. "I think Ma embellished the list of things I said I needed."

"Oh, look, I found one dress. The rest ought to be in similar boxes." A few moments later, Violet stared at the assortment of dresses laid out on the bed. "It's like opening a pirate's treasure chest—topaz, amethyst, emerald, ruby…"

"I think it looks more like a bowl of fruit—raspberry, cranberry, apricot…"

"That's because you have no imagination."

She rolled her eyes and grabbed the dress she'd deemed "raspberry." "Make yourself useful, but don't look until I tell you."

"You don't want me to leave?"

She shook her head even though her sister had already turned her back. "There's too much fancy equipment here. I might need your help."

A few minutes later, Isabelle was truly satisfied with her appearance for the first time in a very long time. The cut of the dress revealed that she actually did have a figure while the color of it brought out a blush in her cheeks. It also contrasted with the color of her eyes and made them seem more vibrant than usual. With a little help from Violet, she'd managed to re-create one of the upswept hairstyles her mother had been trying to teach her. It added a hint of sophistication to her look that hadn't been there before. A set of pearl drop earrings finished the ensemble, which Violet deemed divine.

The best part about it was that Isabelle looked like herself—not a shadow of Amy, but a woman who knew who she was and what she wanted. Well, perhaps she was still figuring out what she wanted besides keeping her home at the boardinghouse. However, being able to look in the mirror and see Isabelle Bradley staring back gave her the boost in confidence she'd known it would. She felt ready to face Amy or anyone for that matter.

Since the study door was still closed, she went into the kitchen instead. Rhett stood at the sink peeling potatoes as he talked with her mother, who was basting fried chicken on the counter near the stove. They both looked up when she entered. Rhett dropped the potato and, if the dazed expression on his face was any indication, had no idea how close he came to cutting himself with the knife. Beatrice took the knife from him and placed the potato in the sink before winking at Isabelle. "I think that means you look beautiful."

A flush spread across Rhett's face as Violet snickered. He sent her sister a warning glance before capturing Isabelle's gaze. "It definitely does."

It was her turn to blush. She murmured a thank-you before forcing her attention to her mother. "Where's Amy?"

"She and your brother-in-law are still in the study with your pa. You can go right in. I know she wants to see you."

Isabelle nodded and took a step back then paused to search her mother's gaze. "Is everything all right, though?"

Beatrice's eyes glistened with a hint of tears, but she smiled. "It will be, I'm sure."

Isabelle glanced at her sister to see if the girl would come along but Violet shook her head. "I already saw her briefly. We promised to talk after supper."

"All right." Isabelle glanced once more at Rhett, who gave her a supportive nod, before leaving the kitchen. She didn't allow her tread to slow until she paused to knock on the study door. Her father opened it and gave her a reassuring smile as she passed him. A couple rose from the chairs in front of the desk. Her gaze landed on Amy's blue eyes, which filled with tears, love and uncertainty. Suddenly aware of the tension filling the room, Isabelle took a deep breath and offered a tremulous smile. "Well, what took you so long to come back?"

The tension eased and Amy hesitated a second longer before embracing her. "I was afraid that you wouldn't forgive me. That none of y'all would. I shouldn't have let that stop me. I should have tried to make amends much sooner."

Isabelle wasn't sure she would have been ready to accept amends any sooner. She wasn't sure she was now. Even so, she hugged her sister back. For the second time today, the truth slid from her lips without her permission. "I missed you."

"I missed you, too." Amy stepped back to look at her. "You look absolutely beautiful."

"So do you." The sunlight shifting through the window set her sister's golden hair aglow. Her thick lashes, high cheekbones, slightly turned-up nose and china-doll mouth were as beautiful and familiar as ever. However, there was a new maturity in her bearing and understanding in her eyes that hadn't been there before. "I think marriage must agree with you."

"It does." Amy smiled then reached back to slide her hand through the crook of her husband's arm. "You remember Silas."

"Well, I remember Silas *Smithson*." That was the name he'd been using when he'd first come to town, working undercover to stop an outlaw gang from robbing a bank more than a year and a half ago. She'd been friends with him like she was with all of the boarders who'd come through Bradley Boardinghouse's door. "It's nice to meet Silas *Townsend*."

His brown eyes sparkled as he took her teasing for what it was. "Always a pleasure, Isabelle."

"Are you still working as a Ranger?"

He shook his head. "I've settled down as a sheriff in my hometown."

"That's good." She glanced back to Amy, who was

watching the exchange with a pleased smile. "How long are y'all staying?"

"A couple of days. We have a lot of catching up to do."

Isabelle nodded. "Helen will want to see you. So will Ellie, Sophia, Lorelei and probably the whole town for that matter."

Amy laughed. "I don't doubt it. Of course, I'll want to spend the most time with you and the rest of our family."

Isabelle nodded again for lack of anything better to do. She wasn't sure what she'd been expecting from their reunion—undoubtedly something a bit more dramatic. This was better. This was safe. It would be easy. They would spend some time together. Then Amy would go back to her husband's hometown. Isabelle would stay in Peppin—hopefully. They might not be as close as they'd once been, but they could still be friends and sisters. Isabelle could live with that. She just had to make it through the next couple of days first.

Chapter Eighteen

Rhett glanced around the dinner table wishing there was something he could do to make the conversation less stilted. It might help if Wes would stop glaring at Silas. It would also be nice if Peter would stop stealing glances at Isabelle. Rhett could always tell when Peter had snuck another glimpse, for the man turned bright red each and every time. He would've felt a little sympathy for the man, having experienced his own brand of shyness around women. However, this woman was Isabelle and that changed everything.

Mr. Bradley hadn't batted an eye at seeing him join the other boarders for dinner. Mrs. Bradley had been more than happy to put him to work in the kitchen. Violet had accepted his explanation about reconciling with her folks. She and Gabe were the only ones at the table who seemed unaffected by the situation. In fact, Gabe didn't seem to care about anything other than staring at the blank wall behind Rhett's head. He was obviously far more focused on whatever painting he was planning in his mind than the general conversation Silas was trying so hard to keep going.

Amy had seemed a little surprised to see him, but other than a polite greeting, they hadn't really spoken much. That didn't stop Isabelle from glancing back and forth between them every few seconds. Rhett knew that, because he couldn't keep his eyes off Isabelle for any longer than that. As supper ended, no one took up her suggestion of parlor games. It seemed all the boarders figured the Bradley family would want some time together for they thanked Mrs. Bradley for the meal and went up to their rooms.

Rhett pushed back from the table. "Thank you for inviting me to stay for dinner, Mr. and Mrs. Bradley."

Beatrice, as she'd told him to call her in the kitchen, rose and began to gather the dishes. "You're very welcome. It was the least I could do after I impressed you into helping prepare the meal."

"I have to say…" His wink encompassed Beatrice, Violet and Isabelle, who had watched him help. "The potatoes were the best part."

Beatrice laughed, while Isabelle shook her head and Violet rolled her eyes. Amy's questioning blue eyes met his from across the table. "But I thought you lived here now, since you had dinner with us and all."

"I used to live here until…" He glanced at Mr. Bradley, who lifted a brow. Holding back a chuckle, Rhett continued, "About a week ago."

"Oh." The confusion remaining in her voice told him that didn't explain his presence at dinner. It also made him realize that he probably should have offered to pay for his meal.

Mr. Bradley leaned forward. "Rhett is—"

"A guest," Rhett offered in case Mr. Bradley was about to identify him as Isabelle's suitor or something else that might get him in trouble. The man's confused look told him he'd done the right thing. "But I'd be happy to pay—"

Beatrice frowned at him. "Oh, don't be ridiculous. You're welcome here anytime."

That seemed to confuse Amy even more. He figured it was best to go while the getting was good. He stood. "Well, thanks again."

Isabelle touched his arm. "Hold on. I'll walk you out."

He pulled out her chair for her. Allowing her to precede him, he wished the rest of her family a goodnight. They all returned the same. However, it was Amy who caught his attention. She glanced from him to Isabelle then back to him before giving him a smile and an almost-imperceptible nod. Apparently, she'd guessed his true interest in the boardinghouse and was all for it. He suddenly remembered that she had seen the Bachelor List and knew who his match truly was. A warm glow filled him with the knowledge that he had all of the Bradleys' approval to pursue Isabelle. Well, Violet still seemed a little oblivious, but he had a feeling she'd approve.

Isabelle distracted him from his thought by sending him a sideways look as they walked toward the foyer. "Are you sure you can't stay any longer?"

"I thought you two talked and worked things out before supper?"

"Well…" She lifted one shoulder in a shrug. "We talked."

He gave that shoulder an encouraging squeeze. "The sooner y'all work through your problems, the easier this visit will be for the both of you."

She caught his hand before he could remove it and leveled him with beseeching green eyes. "Can't we take a walk or something?"

"Isabelle, we already took a walk earlier today, and don't try that 'didn't you miss me' speech. That isn't fair and you know it."

A guilty smile touched her lips before she grimaced and released him. "Fine, but won't you at least help me entertain them while they're here? We'll get a group together. You and me, Helen and Quinn, Lorelei and Sean, Ellie and Lawson…"

He lost track of whatever she said next, distracted by the fact that she'd paired them with all the married couples. Of course, that might be because most of their friends were married, but it was enough to give a fellow hope. He grabbed his coat from the coatrack and nodded once she finally took a breath. "That sounds fine."

"How are we going to get the word out on such short notice, though?"

"Wait. Get the word out about what?"

"Our party." She took his hat from the coatrack and frowned at him. "Weren't you listening?"

He frowned back. "You and I are giving a party?"

"My *family* will be giving a party tomorrow evening at seven o'clock. They simply don't know it yet. I need to figure out who we're inviting and how to get word to those people." She sat down at the front desk to pull out a pen and paper. Since she placed his hat on her lap, he had little choice but to lean on the front desk and watch her stall. It was actually a little impressive. She managed to plan out the whole party in a matter of minutes. "Can you think of anything I've missed?"

He fought back a smart reply, but she must have seen it in his eyes for she lifted a brow. He sighed. "How are you going to let people know about the party?"

"I can get Pa to go in his buggy. Or we could go in his buggy together."

He didn't have to think twice about agreeing to that. "I'll come by for you around ten, if that's all right."

"Perfect."

"Wonderful. Now, will you please release the hostage?"

She didn't even have the grace to look confused. She simply leaned over the desk to place his hat on his head. "Thank you, Rhett. You've been a big help."

"I'm sure." His gaze strayed to her lips. It sure would be nice of her to thank him with a kiss. However, he knew better than to suggest that no matter how tempting the idea was.

If she guessed the direction of his thoughts, she didn't show it. Nor did she lean back. Instead, her green eyes searched his. "You really weren't in love with my sister, were you?"

"No, I wasn't."

"But you thought you were." She finally leaned back and crossed her arms. "That being the case, how can you trust yourself to know in the future if your feelings are real and deep enough to last?"

He pushed his hat back to stare at her. Of all the questions she could have asked, he hadn't been expecting that. Yet the answer was a simple one.

"I reckon everything I was unsure of with Amy, I would be sure of with that person. I'd probably know the woman a sight better than I knew Amy and still want to find out even more about her. What I felt for Amy would pale in comparison to what I felt for her." He shrugged. "There would be a thousand little ways to tell, Isabelle."

The thoughtful look in her eyes warred with the hefty dose of skepticism in her frown. That was when he realized that everything he'd been doing to reassure her that his feelings for Amy had been small, insignificant and in the past had actually been undermining his future with Isabelle. "You don't trust me to know my own mind, do you, Isabelle?"

Her response was soft, but no less piercing. "Frankly? No."

This was a problem. This was a big problem. He waited for that sudden insight from God to show him what to do. He waited for the perfect words to rise within him. Nothing came.

Isabelle must have given up on hearing a response from him for she handed him a piece of paper. "I do trust you to handle this, though."

He glanced down to find it was the guest list. It was a start—though a small one at best. He nodded then put it in his pocket. "I'll see you tomorrow."

He headed home feeling more than a little discouraged. This day had not gone at all like he'd hoped. Isabelle wasn't even close to being ready to consider a formal courtship. That wasn't the end of the world. After all, she'd agreed to continue their friendship, which was romantic in nature whether she wanted to admit it or not. He'd thought the challenge would be in figuring out how to win Isabelle's heart by being her beau. Instead, he had to figure out some way to convince her that she could trust him and his feelings for her. Yet, he dared not mention the true depth of his feeling because it might make her bolt even though that very issue seemed to be her chief concern.

He shook his head. He didn't know what to do. God had given him sign after sign that this was the right path to go on. Yet, every step forward seemed more challenging than the last.

He glanced up at the darkening sky and felt a sense of peace descending along with the twilight. God had brought him this far. He had to have some plan to work everything out. Rhett didn't doubt that. He just couldn't see *how* it would happen…and that was the scariest part of all.

Wind rushed across Isabelle's cheeks as the rhythmic clomp of the horse's hooves against the road picked up speed and sent the buggy hastening down the street toward town. The feeling was exhilarating—especially since she was the one in control. Seeing that the road before her was flat, straight and free of obstacles, she made sure she maintained the proper amount of tension on the reins before stealing a quick glance at Rhett. "If I'm doing as good of a job as you said I was, why do you look so scared?"

"If your eyes are on the road as I said they should be, how do you know I look scared?"

She grinned. "Can you believe everyone we invited agreed to come to our party?"

"Yes, and I wouldn't be surprised if a few folks dropped by who haven't received an invitation. Amy and Silas's visit is the biggest news to hit this town since Sean commissioned the new fire engine." He eased slightly closer to her. "We need to make the final turn toward town. Better hand over the reins."

"Yes, sir."

He took control of the buggy then gave her a suspicious look. "You're such an obedient student. One might think you were angling for another lesson in the future."

"One would be right." She didn't press him on the issue, but made sure to pay close attention to how he handled the turn and the traffic they met in town. "Thank you for the lesson, Rhett."

"You're welcome." He pulled up to the curb in front of the livery and handed the reins to one of the livery boys before helping her down. "Just don't try to take any trips on your own for a while, yet."

"I won't."

A companionable silence settled between them. Rhett only broke it upon entering the boardinghouse to find it as quiet as they were. "Where is everyone?"

"My family said they were going over to the hotel to visit with Amy and Silas while we saw about inviting folks. They promised to swing by the mercantile to pick up a few things for the party tonight." Isabelle glanced at the stairs. "I suppose Gabe's probably in his room. The other boarders always come and go on Saturdays, so it's hard to say where they are."

Realizing it was getting close to dinnertime, Isabelle made them a simple meal of cold cuts, bread, cheese, fruit and a few cookies. They ate it picnic-style in the backyard while Rhett gave the boarding-house's fire pit a practice run in preparation for the evening's approaching activities. After they finished eating, Rhett leaned against the base of a nearby tree and played a few songs on his harmonica. Content to listen, Isabelle reclined on the picnic blanket with her hands pillowed beneath her head.

The music slowed then stopped altogether. "Hey, you never told me how your conversation went with Amy last night."

She frowned then winced, realizing that since her eyes were closed she might have been able to pretend she was sleeping to avoid the question. But if he'd seen her expression shift then he knew she was awake. "It didn't. She and Silas left shortly after you did."

He didn't go back to playing his harmonica. In the silence, she could feel his concern. For once, it aggravated her. "Listen, I'm not ready to talk to Amy because I don't have anything to say."

"The truth about how you feel would be a good start."

"The truth?" She opened her eyes to stare at the tree branches waving overhead. Searching her heart and mind, she settled on exactly that. "The truth is… I wish she hadn't come back."

"Isabelle."

She ignored his protest, not caring if he didn't like it. He'd asked for the truth and he was going to get every ugly bit of it. She burrowed farther into the blanket and closed her eyes as if that would help her block out the past twenty-four hours. "I'm sorry, but it's true. It was enough to know that she was happy. Seeing her here, it brings everything back. I look into Silas's eyes and all I can think about is how he carried on with my sister behind my parents' backs. Then I look into Amy's knowing she let him. I see the love between them and I wonder how I missed it the first time. How could they have possibly hidden it while he lived here? How did I not know they were still in touch after he left?"

She sat up to look at him. "Do you know how utterly stupid I feel not to have known what she was up to?"

She shook her head and stared unseeingly at the fire pit. "I trusted her so implicitly, so unquestioningly. Even if I had sensed anything was off, all she would have had to do was tell me that it wasn't, and I would have believed her. But she hid her feelings from me just like she hid her plans." She shrugged. "I've asked myself, so what? She didn't trust me the way I did her. It's hardly a crime to keep a few secrets. What business is it of mine?

"Then I remember that she made it my business by using me as her cover to get away safely. I remember the way my parents looked at me for weeks afterward— like I'd betrayed them by not somehow knowing it was going to happen or stopping Amy from leaving my side that night. They wouldn't let me out of the house for nearly a week after it happened unless someone went with me. When I stayed home, they'd watch me and the boarders for the slightest hint of impropriety. Yet, I'm supposed to welcome her here. I'm supposed to forgive her as easily as everyone else seems to when her actions are what set us on the path of losing the boardinghouse and changed everything for our family. Changed *me*."

Rhett knelt beside her on the blanket. "Stop—"

She shrugged off the hand he placed on her arm. "I changed because I had to face all the consequences of Amy's actions. I learned not to trust anyone or anything, if I can help it. Not myself or my family or you or the boarders. Maybe not even God."

She'd run out of words and resistance, so she didn't pull away when Rhett's hand covered hers. She loosened her fist to hold his hand back then glanced up to meet the compassion and caring in his gaze. Slowly, his amber eyes lifted from hers to focus beseechingly on something behind her. She froze. A sense of foreboding slid down her spine and prompted her to turn around.

Amy stood on the lawn a few yards away, her face ashen and stricken.

Isabelle's heart sank in her chest. Suddenly, she knew why she hadn't wanted to talk to her sister. It wasn't because Isabelle had nothing to say. It was because she hadn't wanted to hurt her sister with all the painful words she'd buried down deep. She hadn't wanted to push the breach between them open any further.

She stood, unsure what to do or say to repair the damage she'd caused. She took a step toward her sister. "Amy, I'm—"

"Don't you *dare* apologize to me."

The vehemence in Amy's voice drove Isabelle a step backward. Rhett's hands caught her waist to keep her upright as she stumbled over a buckle in the blanket. Unable to meet her sister's gaze, Isabelle lowered hers and battled against the tears that stung her eyes.

"*I* am the one who has wronged you."

Shocked, Isabelle glanced up to meet her sister's tear-filled blue eyes. Amy gave her a tremulous smile that quickly faded before shaking her head. "I wish that I could go back and change the way I did things. I wish I'd had the courage I should have had to tell the truth, to our parents and to you. You're right. I hid things from you. I used your good character as a means to cover my own failings. I betrayed the trust of our family. I didn't realize how difficult that would make things for you. I should have but I only saw myself and what I wanted. I don't ask you to forgive me, because I know I don't deserve it from you or the rest of the family. I just want you to know that I *am* sorry. I am *truly* sorry."

"I forgive you, Amy."

"You...you do?"

Isabelle nodded, making the choice to do so even as she left Rhett's gentle hold to embrace her sister. She waited for a weight to lift off her shoulders or the hurt inside her to ease. It didn't. However, as her sister hugged her back, she knew she'd done the right thing.

"Thank you. I didn't want to leave here without clearing things up with you. That's why I told Rhett to leave you be. I needed to hear what you had to say." Amy stepped back. "I hope we can move forward from here and regain some of what we lost over the past few months."

"I'd like that."

"Good." Amy smiled and let out a relieved sigh. "Ma was fixing dinner for us, so I was coming out here to find out if y'all wanted any. I can see y'all have already eaten, though. I'd better go back inside before there isn't anything left."

Isabelle caught her sister's hands before she could turn away. Leaning forward, she placed a kiss on her cheek. "I love you."

Tears fell down Amy's cheeks, which were beginning to regain their color. Amy tugged her into a quick embrace. "I love you, too. Now, please, excuse me. I have to go find a handkerchief."

They laughed together before Amy backed away with a little wave and hurried into the house. Isabelle pulled in a deep breath. Rhett stepped up beside her. "I tried to warn you that she was there even though she didn't want me to."

"I know you did."

"Feel better?"

She turned to him, allowing her confusion to show in her eyes. "Yes, but the hurt is still there. I thought it would leave once I forgave her."

"I reckon it might take a little while for our emotions to match up with our choices sometimes. It will get easier, though, as long as you keep choosing to forgive."

"Forgiving is the easy part. The real question is still, how will I ever trust her like I did before?"

"Maybe you can't, and that's all right." He smiled at her look of surprise. "What I'm trying to say is that people are fallible. It's unfair to expect them to be perfect. If you do, you will be disappointed."

"Then why trust at all?"

"Because what determines your character is not how someone fails you, but how you respond to it. You can choose to forgive, as you did, or to allow yourself to become bitter. Trust is a choice just like forgiveness and choosing to trust means doing so even knowing that your trust can be broken."

"Why would I want to do that?"

"You can't build a strong relationship with anyone without some measure of trust, Isabelle. You can't let one bad experience or even several bad experiences make you miss out on that."

His words settled into her spirit, but there was no point in continuing the conversation. He was right. Trust was the foundation for any number of things like love and confidence and mutual understanding. However, that meant she had to be willing to risk facing the type of pain she was only now beginning to recover from all over again. Looking into his eyes, for the first time in a long time her heart began to wonder if it might be worth it.

Chapter Nineteen

The Bradleys' get-together for Amy showed no signs of slowing down long after the sunset had faded to darkness. The lanterns Rhett had strung onto the old oak tree that canopied much of the yard provided plenty of light. The hot cider, sausages, biscuits and desserts kept everyone warm enough on the inside. Meanwhile, the fire pit and the blankets provided by the Bradleys kept their guests from feeling the cold wind that occasionally whistled through the slats of the fence.

Rhett left Isabelle's side to refill her cup of cider. In the kitchen, Beatrice poured the last of the steaming drink into the cup for him. Thomas frowned at his pocket watch. "Do you folks out there know it's nigh on eleven o'clock?"

Surprised, Rhett glanced out the kitchen window, where he could clearly see Amy and Isabelle sitting on one of the wider chairs together. Silas stood beside Amy. Violet sat on the blanket near her sisters' feet looking half-awake. At least ten other people huddled around the fire pit with them. The conversation and laughter was loud enough to carry through the closed window. Rhett leaned into the kitchen's doorpost. "I had no idea it was so late. Do you want me to start hinting that folks should go home?"

Beatrice began washing out the cider kettle. "It would probably be better coming from one of our girls. You might tell them for us, though."

"We'd be obliged if you would," Thomas said with one more look at his watch. "I don't mind the hour so much as the fact that church is in the morning. I'd hate for us to be the reason a good portion of the congregation doesn't show up."

Rhett agreed then took his spot in the chair next to Isabelle. As he handed her the cider, he whispered the message in her ear. She in turn whispered it to Amy. Amy turned to the gathering and said, "Well, folks, it's time to go home."

Her delivery was perfect in that it set everyone laughing good-naturedly, but also made the husbands begin to pull out their pocket watches. Meanwhile, Isabelle nudged Amy with her shoulder just hard enough to put her sister in danger of falling off their chair. "Amy! I said *hint*."

Amy laughed before announcing, "Don't forget about church tomorrow. Silas and I are leaving on the afternoon train, so that will be my last chance to see most of y'all."

Rhett helped clean up while folks lingered long enough to say goodbye. Violet yawned as she patted him on the shoulder to thank him for helping. He entered the kitchen with a stack of plates just as Thomas was shaking his head at Isabelle. "If Helen and Quinn parked by the hotel and Amy and Silas are staying there, what's the point of going with them since someone is going to have to bring you back here?"

Isabelle's gaze caught his. Rhett took his cue for what it was. "I can walk her back, sir." Thomas glanced between the two of them, the struggle apparent on his face. "I'll be watching from the front porch. If the two of you aren't back twenty minutes after you leave, I'm coming to find you and I'm bringing my shotgun."

Rhett turned to Isabelle. "Maybe you should stay home."

She sent him a look that said he should have known better. He did. Since she and Amy had reconciled, they'd seemed joined at the hip. Helen's presence was an added incentive. The three women had been thick as thieves when they'd all lived at the boardinghouse together. Or so he'd been told by each one of them at least twice. Rhett sighed. "I'll have her back on time, sir."

"See that you do."

With Mr. Bradley charting their progress from the front porch, Rhett was more than content to hang back and walk with Silas and Quinn. Isabelle, Helen and Amy walked arm in arm down the sidewalk in front of them. In tandem, the women swung their steps sideways as well as forward, which made them shift from one side of the sidewalk to the other like a hypnotist's watch. Quinn nodded toward them. "Now, that's a powder keg if I ever saw one."

Amy didn't even bother to turn around. "You do know we can hear you, don't you?"

Helen sent a bored look over her shoulder. "All I heard was a bear grumbling."

Quinn's smoldering glance at his wife's use of her

favorite nickname for him made Rhett entirely uncomfortable. Isabelle's voice provided a welcome distraction. "Well, I, for one, took it as a compliment."

Of course she would.

Isabelle broke rank and file to turn around and look at him. "What was that? I couldn't quite hear you?"

Silas glanced at him. "He didn't say anything."

"Oh, yes, he did."

Rhett caught her hand and looped it through his arm. "Reading a man's mind is a dangerous thing."

Amy reached for her husband's hand and grinned at them. "I'm glad I came back and got to see this."

"See what?" Isabelle asked.

"You two. You're adorable together. When Pa told me y'all were courting…"

Rhett didn't hear anything else. He was sure Isabelle didn't, either, because their eyes met. He made no effort to mirror the confusion in her expression, which made it turn to bewilderment. She glanced from him to the other two couples, then stared at the spot where her hand was tucked into the crook of his arm as though realizing for the first time that they had coupled off. Betrayal deepened the color of her eyes until they seemed nearly black. Tugging her hand from his arm, she turned and walked back toward the boardinghouse.

He followed her rapid steps. "Isabelle, wait."

She stopped but only because her gaze had landed on the distant figure of her father on the porch. With a huff of frustration, she grabbed his arm and pulled him across the empty street toward the courtyard. Relieved that she was taking him with her, he had the presence of mind to turn back to his confused friends and yell, "Someone tell Mr. Bradley we're not eloping."

"That is not necessary." Isabelle stopped at the corner in full view of her father, but too far away from her friends and the house for anyone to hear. Eyes flashing, she turned to him. "Explain to me why my family thinks we're courting."

"It's probably because I asked your father's permission to do so."

"Why would you do that?"

He stared into her eyes and couldn't stop the words that came out next any more than he could stop breathing. "I love you."

Her eyes widened and her mouth dropped open. Her question came out no louder than a whisper. "What?"

"It's true." Having said that much, Rhett knew he wouldn't be able to stop until he confessed to everything that might make or break their relationship, whether she was ready to hear it all or not. "I've been falling in love with you since you persuaded me to follow you onto the hotel roof. Ever since then, I've done everything I could to get to know you better and grow our friendship in the hopes that you'd one day change your mind about us. I even came up with the idea of 'spending time together' because I knew you weren't ready for the courtship I wanted. I don't know if that was wrong. I'm sorry if it was. I just couldn't stand the thought of you running away from me again."

Her silence gave him a moment to think. Finding one last thing that might shake her confidence in him, he placed his faith in God and revealed it to her. "Finally, you happen to be my Bachelor List match. I didn't know that until after our kiss in the courthouse when Quinn gave me the list. By then, I was already in love with you. It just gave me the confidence I needed to approach your father."

She looked a bit dazed. Whether that was in a good way or a bad way, he couldn't tell. He hadn't planned on taking this leap of faith tonight on a street corner between the boardinghouse, his smithy, their family and friends. Yet, it seemed oddly appropriate—as if this had been God's plan all along. Perhaps it had been, for even in the midst of all that was familiar and all that he'd held dear, the only thing he could truly hold on to was his faith in God and his love for the woman standing before him. Suddenly, he realized that he felt no fear or anxiety or hint of panic—simply the anticipation of knowing that God was going to do something incredible in his life and with Isabelle. Whether that happened today or ten years from now, in Virginia or right here on this street corner in Peppin, was entirely up to God and Rhett was content to wait.

Isabelle could scarcely breathe or think. Rhett's words created a warm glow inside of her that made it difficult to think clearly. It was hope. She tamped it down and forced herself to focus.

"How can you know that it's me you really want? What about Amy? You thought you wanted her until she left town. What about that other woman you were so certain you were going to marry one day? You never said what happened to her."

He shrugged. "I don't know, yet. I just poured my heart out to her but she hasn't told me how she feels."

She blinked. "You mean *I* was that woman?"

"Absolutely. As for Amy... Well, there is no doubt

in my mind that even if she had stayed, I would have wanted *you*. I would have *chosen* you. It was only a matter of time."

He truly meant those words. She could see it in his eyes and hear it in his voice. She simply wasn't sure she could trust them. "That's because you aren't nervous around me."

"I love you for who you are. Whatever I am or will be or can or cannot do has nothing to do with that fact."

"But—"

"Isabelle, you could come up with a thousands more reasons to doubt me. It won't change the fact that I love you or that I want to spend the rest of my life with you. At some point, you're going to have to choose to trust someone again. Start with me. I'm not perfect. I never will be. However, I will do everything I can to be worthy of that trust, because I know how much it means to you."

Her eyes filled with tears. She glanced over his shoulder at the boardinghouse—at the dream she'd thought she'd wanted, the dream she'd prayed so hard for God to rescue. She hadn't been able to understand why He had taken it away. Perhaps He'd been planning something altogether different all along. Something that didn't involve her living the rest of her life insulated in the familiarity of the boardinghouse because she was afraid to trust anyone.

She decided then and there that Rhett was right. She couldn't go through the rest of her life refusing to trust and cheating herself out of meaningful relationships with her family, her friends…or with God. Her breath caught in her throat at the realization that God hadn't failed her. Her story was still being written. She might not be sure of *how* God would work things out. She just had to trust that He would even if she didn't understand His plans, even with situations left unresolved and especially when she couldn't see how life could possibly turn out as she'd hoped it would.

Realizing that Rhett was still waiting for her response, she met his gaze and nodded. "All right. I choose to trust you. I choose to trust God. I choose to let go of all the fear I've been holding on to. I release all of the hurt I've collected. I let it all go."

He stepped a bit closer. "Does that leave room for other things, then? Like my love for you."

"I suppose it must."

"What about your feelings for me? You said you had some the other day in the smithy. Do you... Can you tell me what they are now?"

She closed her eyes and focused on the feelings welling up inside her. She'd denied, ignored and refused to acknowledge their existence for so long. Apparently, that hadn't stopped them from growing or deepening because they swept over her now with overwhelming power. She opened her eyes to stare at the man before her. She couldn't have stopped the smile that spread across her face if she'd tried—and she didn't try. Not one bit.

Hope lit his amber eyes. She stepped toward him then stopped. She glanced over his shoulder at the boardinghouse, where Beatrice and Violet had joined her father to watch from the porch. Lifting her chin, she grabbed Rhett's hand as she tugged him down the street toward the hotel. She waved off Amy, Silas, Quinn and Helen when they tried to ask questions before giving them a firm look that said very clearly from them to stay put. Rhett didn't ask any questions until they reached the base of the hotel's fire escape. Even then, his only protest was a groan as he followed her up the stairs. She stepped onto the roof. She walked right over to the edge, tipped back her head and yelled, "I love Rhett Granger! I don't care who knows it."

A cheer traveled up from the sidewalk. Rhett caught her arm, spun her into his embrace and claimed her with a kiss. Breathless and smiling, she pulled back slightly to look into his eyes to make sure he understood. "Rhett Granger, I love you with all that I am and I will shout it from the rooftops. You are the best friend I've ever had. The best man I've ever known. The only man I want to give my heart to. I don't merely choose to trust you, Rhett. I choose *you*, and I will love for as long as you want me."

"I guess that means forever, then." He frowned. "I don't know about you, but I think this moment is missing something."

"What's that? Music? Dancing? Fireworks?"

"Fireworks. Definitely fireworks."

She laughed as he lowered his head and let him make a few of their own.

* * * * *

Dear Reader,

Welcome home to Peppin! Like any small town, the lives of the people who live here are always intertwining. Rhett Granger surprised me by popping up fully formed as a character in *The Runaway Bride*, where he spoke only one line. He has appeared in every book I've written about Peppin since then. His role increased in importance with each book until he finally demanded his own story and his own chance to find love. I hope he's satisfied, but have no doubt that he and Isabelle will be appearing in some capacity in one of my future works.

As happy as I was to finally have the chance to tell their story, I must admit there were times when I despaired of ever being able to finish it. I faced many challenges during the few months in which I wrote it. All in all, it was definitely one of the most physically demanding, time-consuming, emotionally draining and mentally exhausting seasons of my life.

The fact that this book somehow got completed in the midst of all that is a testament to the support of my family and friends, the patience and understanding of my editor and God's grace. The deeper I got into this story, the more I found myself identifying with Rhett and Isabelle. Their struggle to trust God when you can't see how or if things will ever work out became my own. That made it even more difficult to write about. How do you show someone how to work through a problem when you don't have the answer yourself?

You keep seeking, keep working and keep praying until you find it in God. That is exactly what I did with Isabelle and Rhett's story. I learned that God's rescue may not always come in the way we expect or be what we think we want. However, it *will* come. If things don't seem to work out on our timetable, it isn't because God has failed. It's because He has a better plan. We have to trust that He is battling and managing the unseen on our behalf, whether or not His efforts are visible to us. Our role is to rest in the finished work He is establishing in our lives day by day.

I encourage you, dear reader, to always believe, always hope and always trust.

Love,

Noelle Marchand

REQUEST YOUR FREE BOOKS!

2 FREE INSPIRATIONAL NOVELS
PLUS 2 *FREE* MYSTERY GIFTS

Love Inspired ® HISTORICAL

YES! Please send me 2 FREE Love Inspired® Historical novels and my 2 FREE
mystery gifts (gifts are worth about $10). After receiving them, if I don't wish to receive
any more books, I can return the shipping statement marked "cancel." If I don't cancel,
I will receive 4 brand-new novels every month and be billed just $4.99 per book in the
U.S. or $5.49 per book in Canada. That's a saving of at least 17% off the cover price.
It's quite a bargain! Shipping and handling is just 50¢ per book in the U.S. and 75¢ per
book in Canada.* I understand that accepting the 2 free books and gifts places me under
no obligation to buy anything. I can always return a shipment and cancel at any time.
Even if I never buy another book, the two free books and gifts are mine to keep forever.

102/302 IDN GH6Z

Name	(PLEASE PRINT)
Address	Apt. #
City	State/Prov.	Zip/Postal Code

Signature (if under 18, a parent or guardian must sign)

Mail to the **Reader Service:**
IN U.S.A.: P.O. Box 1867, Buffalo, NY 14240-1867
IN CANADA: P.O. Box 609, Fort Erie, Ontario L2A 5X3

Want to try two free books from another series?
Call 1-800-873-8635 or visit www.ReaderService.com.

* Terms and prices subject to change without notice. Prices do not include applicable
taxes. Sales tax applicable in N.Y. Canadian residents will be charged applicable taxes.
Offer not valid in Quebec. This offer is limited to one order per household. Not valid
for current subscribers to Love Inspired Historical books. All orders subject to credit
approval. Credit or debit balances in a customer's account(s) may be offset by any other
outstanding balance owed by or to the customer. Please allow 4 to 6 weeks for delivery.
Offer available while quantities last.

Your Privacy—The Reader Service is committed to protecting your privacy. Our
Privacy Policy is available online at www.ReaderService.com or upon request from
the Reader Service.

We make a portion of our mailing list available to reputable third parties that offer
products we believe may interest you. If you prefer that we not exchange your name with
third parties, or if you wish to clarify or modify your communication preferences, please
visit us at www.ReaderService.com/consumerchoice or write to us at Reader Service
Preference Service, P.O. Box 9062, Buffalo, NY 14240-9062. Include your complete
name and address.

LIH15

SPECIAL EXCERPT FROM

Love Inspired HISTORICAL

*Still healing from emotional—and physical—wounds
left by her late husband, widow Meg Thomerson turns
to Ace Allen for help running her business. Promising to
remain at her side while she recovers, can he also mend
her bruised heart?*

Read on for a sneak preview of
WOLF CREEK WIDOW,
*available in September 2015 from
Love Inspired Historical!*

"Look at me, Meg," he said in that deep voice. "Who do you see?"

"What?" She frowned, unsure of what he was doing and wondering at the sorrow reflected in his eyes.

"Who do you see standing here?"

What did he want from her? she wondered in confusion. "I see you," she said at last. "Ace Allen."

"If you never believe anything else about me, you can believe that I would never deliberately harm a hair on your head."

His statement was much the same as what he'd said the day before in the woods. It seemed Ace was determined that she knew he was no threat to her.

"Elton used to stand in the doorway like that a lot. For just a moment when I looked up I saw him, not you. I…I'm s-sorry."

"I'm not Elton, Meg."

His voice held an urgency she didn't understand. "I know that."

"Do you?" he persisted. "Look at me. Do I look like Elton?"

"No," she murmured. Elton hadn't been nearly as tall, and unlike Ace he'd been almost too good-looking to be masculine. She'd once heard him called pretty. No one would ever think of Ace Allen as pretty. Striking, surely. Magnificent, maybe. Pretty, never.

"No, and I don't act like him. Can you see that? Do you believe it?"

Still confused, but knowing somehow that her answer was of utmost importance, she whispered, "Yes."

He nodded, and the torment in his eyes faded. "You have nothing to be sorry for, Meg Thomerson. That's something else you can be certain of, so never think it again." With that, he turned and left her alone with her thoughts and a lot of questions.

Don't miss
WOLF CREEK WIDOW by Penny Richards,
available September 2015 wherever
Love Inspired® Historical books and ebooks are sold.

Love the Love Inspired
book you just read?

Your opinion matters.

Review this book on your favorite
book site, review site, blog or your own
social media properties and share your
opinion with other readers!